A SAVAGE PLACE

A SAVAGE PLACE

A NOVEL BY

FRANK G. SLAUGHTER

DOUBLEDAY & COMPANY, INC.
GARDEN CITY, NEW YORK

All of the characters in this book are fictitious, and any resemblance to actual persons, living or dead, is purely coincidental.

"Let Me Live Out My Years" from *The Quest* by John Neihardt. Copyright 1916 by The Macmillan Company, renewed 1944 by John G. Neihardt. Reprinted by permission of the publisher.

A SAVAGE PLACE

But O! The deep romantic chasm which slanted
Down the green hill athwart a cedarn cover!
A savage place! as holy and enchanted
As e'er beneath a waning moon was haunted
By woman wailing for her demon-lover!

SAMUEL TAYLOR COLERIDGE

ONE

"And how does it feel to be home again, Doctor? Is New Salem a foreign land, after nearly ten years away? Or do you have all the emotions of a native's return?"

"Ask me tomorrow," said Mike Constant. "I may have better answers."

Aaron Zeagler leaned back in his executive's chair—a massive posture-throne of red leather—and glanced again at the file folder on his desk. Deliberately, he let his eyes sweep the huge office before they returned to the man in the visitor's chair. Again, he was both startled and reassured by what he saw. He had expected the new staff surgeon for New Salem Memorial Hospital to be a rough diamond—resentful of his origins, prepared to defend his medical honors with an excess of pride. He had not anticipated Dr. Michael Constant's assurance, his caution at all commitment, his ability to fill the visitor's armchair as though he had belonged there always. . . . *Myself at thirty,* thought the man behind the desk. *The same gift of humor behind an almost-solemn mask. The same hard-jawed need to defeat the enemy on his own terms.*

"When I first arrived on Dutchman's Hill," Zeagler said, "I had yet to make contact with the town below the Heights. New Salem was a name to me, and nothing more. I was too busy establishing a new factory to wonder if I would be accepted."

"How long ago was that, sir?"

"Three years exactly. I won't deny that Zeagler Electronics has brought great changes to New Salem Heights—though we have yet to penetrate New Salem itself. Don't judge the invasion too harshly until you've checked the new against the old. You might start at my office window."

Mike Constant moved to the pane of thermal glass that formed the eastern wall of the office. Watching his visitor cross the carpet, Zeagler reached for the first forbidden cigar since lunch. The move was automatic, the gesture of a man who needed a pause for thought; until Dr. Constant relaxed his guard, he could judge him only by externals.

The surgeon's best friend, thought Zeagler, would not have called him handsome. The strength in his rugged countenance—it suggested a latter-day Lincoln—and a sense of dedication that went deeper than words were compensation enough. The wide-set gray eyes that looked down on the latest unit of the Zeagler factory chain had seen their share of the world's cruelty. They had endured its indifference, and kept their vision clear. Sure now that Michael Constant would respond to the challenge awaiting him here, Zeagler moved to join him at the window.

To a stranger's eye, the scene below would have suggested another—and perhaps better—planet. The architect who had designed the plant had known that today's factory-in-the-field should blend rather than dominate: he had found no way to play down these rows of chrome and glass rectangles, untouched by grime or smoke and humming with a vitality of their own. Surrounding them were acres of parking lots, ranked with gleaming cars whose price tags proclaimed the prosperity of their owners. A mile beyond the factory site was Zeagler's company town, as knowingly landscaped as the plant it served, complete with supermarket, drive-in, and community center. One knew without asking that those neat colonials and ranch houses were designed for the best in family living, that most of the television masts would be balanced by stereo outlets, that its deep freezers would be filled with new vegetables, fresh dairy products, and prime sirloins.

On a hill to the west—an eminence that dominated New Salem Heights—was the wide-winged hospital where Dr. Constant would soon begin his duties. The panorama, Zeagler reflected, was almost too perfect to be real. Only the computers downstairs could furnish proof that its well-being had been earned.

"Do you remember the Heights before I built here?"

"Most of these fields were pasture land," said Mike Constant. "The Van Ryns kept Guernseys on the flats. Their milking sheds stood on Dutchman's Hill."

"I never saw the hill in its pastoral state," said Zeagler. "When I put my factory in operation, the Van Ryns had long since sold the land for inheritance taxes. As you see, we spared no expense to justify our purchase."

"What do you use for power? The Bear Creek dam?"

Aaron Zeagler smiled tolerantly. "New Salem's water table ceased to function long ago. Mostly, we rely on the Niagara grid."

"I'd heard you were experimenting with atomic energy."

"We've gone beyond experiments, Dr. Constant. I'm fitting reactors into my work patterns, as fast as Washington will allow. When the pattern's really functioning, New Salem will be an ideal halfway point for shipping. It's already an ideal climate for industrial growth—if I can continue to find room here."

The industrialist made a quick, almost explosive gesture, like a man dismissing a bad dream. Feeling the warning drumbeat at his temples, he forced a slower tempo on an eager brain. He had not missed the younger man's glance at his too-red cheeks, the tremor in his fingers after he had discarded the cigar.

"Lack of breathing space can be fatal, Doctor," he said, in more measured tones. "I need the whole town's support to gain it."

"Just what does this factory produce?"

"Electronic equipment, of all kinds. Computer parts, precision instruments for defense—most of these, of course, are classified. In my downstate plants, I manufacture submarine equipment. My factories abroad are devoted to the automobile of tomorrow. Here in New Salem Heights, I'm devoting my newest unit to lasers. You've heard of them, I take it? A device that amplifies light energy by bouncing it inside a ruby rod?"

Mike Constant nodded. "In Berkeley, some friends of mine were working with lasers—in deep-space communication."

"We're prepared to do business with other planets, as needed." A gleam of appreciation showed in Zeagler's eyes, as he took his place behind the desk. "As you see, I've given my executives and their technicians ample living space. The hospital I built on Indian Hill serves the whole community. So will my schools and my welfare center, if New Salem will accept them. In its present form, Zeagler Electronics gives work to twenty thousand men and six thousand women. With proper factory space, I could employ twice that number. Enlightened self-interest would suggest that New Salem meet me halfway—" Again, the man behind the desk broke off abruptly, lest he say too much too soon.

"I take it you have enemies here?"

"A man in my position has enemies everywhere. In New Salem it's the tyranny of the past. The Van Ryn family, and those who still worship in its shadow."

"I assumed your troubles with the Van Ryns were behind you. Didn't your daughter marry Paul Van Ryn?"

"Six years ago. The marriage brought me to New Salem in the first place. I meant to give my son-in-law a real chance here—make him my successor, if he showed himself capable." Zeagler smiled, as he noted the shrug of dismissal from the visitor's chair. "You attended Cornell together, I believe?"

"We did, sir—until Paul left the campus."

"In that event, you'll know my hopes are without foundation. Even if my son-in-law had been made of stronger stuff, he'd have needed his mother's approval to give me a foothold in New Salem."

"Is Madame Van Ryn living?"

"If you can call it living, Doctor. She continues to rule that Gothic pile on Bearclaw Point, with the family's dead foundry across the way."

"It still makes her the Duchess of Rynhook."

"That's her local title," said Zeagler. "I suppose it's a term of affection—if one doesn't question her right to hold it. To my mind, it lost its point in the nineteen-sixties."

"Not if she can give Paul orders, and see that they're obeyed."

The industrialist nodded morosely. "Part of those orders keep him under her roof. When he married my Anna, I offered them land on Mohawk Knoll—and a house of their own, designed as he wished."

"Including a studio?"

"You know he paints?"

"It's the one thing Paul cares for—"

"Except women?"

"I'm glad you said that, sir—and not I."

"There's no need to dwell on that facet of his personality. He preferred the tower suite in his mother's mansion, when they returned from their honeymoon. So Anna knocked out the roof, and put in a skylight. They've lived there ever since." Zeagler broke off, as he felt a fresh rush of blood to his temples. "How much of this do you know? How much have you guessed?"

"I've been away a long time, I'm afraid."

"Your record's before me. A master of science at Cornell—Korea—a medical degree at Stanford—brilliant residences in two West Coast hospitals. You're still a native of this region. Isn't it true that you can take a boy from New Salem, but can never take New Salem from the boy?"

"I won't dispute the folklore." When Mike Constant smiled, his rugged face seemed years younger. "As you see, I'm back again. It's quite true I was sent for. I can't imply you did the sending, but—"

"Naturally I put pressure on the doctors who lease my hospital," said Zeagler. "I could hardly do otherwise, when Dr. Artemus Coxe recommended you."

"Dr. Art is an old friend—"

"The final decision was theirs—and it was based on your record. But I rejoiced in their verdict. From the moment your name was mentioned, I've counted on you to help me cure this *town,* as well as its citizens."

"That's asking a lot of a surgeon who expects to be fully occupied with his duties."

"New Salem Memorial is a nerve center, Dr. Constant. Now that the old County Hospital has closed, it's the only institution of its kind in the area—not counting Dr. Coxe's place in the Old Town. You'll soon be treating valley patients, at all levels. When you do, you'll appreciate the problems I'm facing here. I trust you'll have ideas for their solution, which we can discuss together. Old ties you'll renew to your profit and mine—"

"My family has died out long ago. Aside from Dr. Art, I'm not sure I could name a single friend."

"For the sake of argument, let's assume we could make this town over—give it a new place in the sun. Would you join hands with me?"

"As a doctor, I could hardly say no."

"Perhaps you think me a visionary, because I make instruments to contact another planet. The human mind is a much more elusive target. If I could lure a citizens' committee to this office—and make them listen—no problem would exist. Unfortunately, the minds I must reach in New Salem seem closed to argument."

"Just how could I help you, sir?"

"First of all, I want you to call on the Van Ryns. My daughter, my son-in-law, and his mother."

"The Duchess will send for me, when she hears I've come back. One doesn't visit Rynhook unasked."

"Surely you know Paul well enough to drop in."

"We were never boon companions, Mr. Zeagler."

"Not even at Cornell?"

"We had football in common—and nothing else."

"I hardly expect the Van Ryns to *welcome* you, when they realize your connection with me. At least we can draw a battle line, and plan our strategy. As I've explained—and you doubtless know—my son-in-law is controlled by his mother, who is ruled in turn by her private furies. My daughter refuses to intervene. You will understand why when you meet her."

"What should I ask for, when I see the Duchess?"

"The sale of her land, so I can build a new factory."

"I'm almost sure she'll refuse."

"Of course she'll refuse. My offer will be on the record—and you'll be my ambassador. If need be, my observer in enemy country."

"Spying's a bit out of my line, Mr. Zeagler."

"Your mission is hardly that sinister, Doctor. After all, a man of your profession has a certain entree." The industrialist studied Mike with veiled eyes. "Do you recall a New Salem family named West?"

It was the last important question of the interview. The flush on the visitor's cheek told Zeagler he had been wise to defer it.

"Next to the Van Ryns, the Wests are the town's oldest settlers. They served as factors for the estate, in the days of the patroons. Their Gate House still stands at Rynhook."

"Then you know the surviving members?"

"Sandra West is a nurse, I believe. She's been living in New York." Mike Constant, Zeagler noted, had been careful to answer his question indirectly. "I believe she came back a month ago, to care for her brother Jason."

"I once knew Jason West. An actor of the old school—"

"You've described him exactly, sir."

"Anna tried out in one of his shows, when she still had ambitions in that field. Now, I'm told he's fighting a cardiac condition—not too successfully. Will you call on them as well?"

"Only if I'm asked."

"Situated as they are, between town and castle, I hoped they'd give you added information." Zeagler rose from the desk, with the quick, warm smile he could summon at will. The visitor ignored the obvious hint that the interview was over.

"What would you say, if I turned your job down?" he asked.

"Your appointment at New Salem Memorial, Doctor—or the investigation I've just outlined?"

"At the moment, I'm thinking of declining both."

"I'm sure you'd regret that impulse," said Zeagler. "It isn't often that a returning prodigal can play God in his own back yard."

"I hardly qualify for *that* title, sir."

"I beg to differ. In the biblical sense, you're a true prodigal. A wanderer in far places who has turned home to find his roots."

"Even though no father is waiting with a fatted calf?"

"Even so, Doctor. I'll extend the parable, if I may. The Wests also deserve the name: the once-great actor who has come home to die—the sister who has left a career in New York to care for him. So, God knows, does my son-in-law—"

"We can agree there, sir." Mike Constant rose at last from the visitor's chair—and Zeagler grasped his hand. He was reassured by the firm pressure of the surgeon's fingers. *I've made you curious,* he thought. *I've given you a new sense of power. You'll fight on my side from now on—and you'll fight hard.*

Aloud, he said only, "Nothing we've discussed today is binding. You have a contract with New Salem Memorial Hospital. Your first duty is to the group who employ you. I've only tried to give that employment an added dimension."

Mike smiled. "You spoke of playing God just now, sir. Haven't you cast yourself in the role of Jehovah—with me as your chief angel?"

"I've been accused of that tendency, by friends and enemies alike," said Zeagler, with an answering smile. "You'll admit that the universe I've created around this factory is self-sustaining?"

"So it appears."

"I enjoy watching people earn money for me, Doctor. And I enjoy the knowledge that I've helped *them* to a better life—with more creative leisure than any working man in history. Could the Van Ryn patroons say as much?"

"I'm afraid not. Of course they flourished at a time when the divine right of bosses was unquestioned."

The industrialist shrugged. "I deal with the living—as you do. Not with Tory ghosts. Form your own conclusions. I'm sure you'll agree my way is best for New Salem."

"I'll give you an answer tomorrow, if you like."

"Tomorrow I must be in Rome," said Zeagler, with the air of a man who held a shrinking globe in his palm. "Next week, I go to Tel Aviv to open my first factory in Israel. Use the time between to decide if we're to be allies. Pick up the threads of your old life here—and see how much they're tangled with today. Would you care to tour the plant before you go?"

"I walked through before our appointment, sir. Most of it seems stranger than Mars."

"I'm sure I'd be as badly confused by your operating room. It's the tragedy of our day that men like ourselves must stay locked in their specialties. Even so, I think you'll find we speak the same language."

Ten minutes later, following the hogback curves that led to the Overlook (a tor above the Hudson that commanded the best view of New Salem), Mike could still feel a slight ringing in his ears, a natural aftermath to his exposure to a dynamo in human form. It was a feeling not too different from intoxication. He was careful not to yield to it while he concerned himself with the immediate problem of the jalopy he was driving.

For the last hundred yards, he was sure the ancient car would never make it to the top. During most of his trip across the continent, the motor had wheezed like an asthma victim: the ailment showed no sign of improvement in this final test. It would have been safer to approach his hometown by the river road—but the need to enjoy a familiar vista had been compelling. . . . When the jalopy gained the crest of the tor, he coasted to a stop in the parking area, happy to find that he was alone there. For a moment more, he sat beneath the wheel—listening to the sounds of the cooling motor as he reviewed the talk in Zeagler's office.

The industrialist, Mike reflected, was a near-perfect example of his kind. Like most men who have succeeded brilliantly in a chosen field, he had a tendency to oversimplify when he looked beyond his daily round—to overreach, in his impatience to join ends and means. His driving energy had exacted its toll. Mike had easily diagnosed the cause of those sudden breaks in his monologues as deliberate attempts to throttle down. The pattern of a marked hypertension was plain to a doctor's eye.

Zeagler's assurance that they spoke the same language, he knew, was justified. Both were the descendants of immigrants, and both had fought hard for their success. In Mike Constant's case, the tools had been a scalpel, a surgeon's instinct for healing that had always been as natural as drawing breath. In Zeagler's, it had been sheer mechanical know-how, the inventor's knack for thinking in terms of the future.

His career was proof that the American success story had lost none of its magic. It included the giant strides of legend: the rise from the ghetto, the barn-factory on Chicago's South Side, the youthful marriage that had produced his one offspring. Within two decades, the Chicago plant had exploded into an empire. After the death of his first wife, a second marriage had allied Zeagler with one of America's oldest families, making his place secure. . . . It was small wonder that he had bridled at the strictures he had met in New Salem. It was even more natural that he should bewail his daughter's marriage to Paul Van Ryn.

Mike let his thoughts veer to Paul, knowing in advance that none of the images revealed would be pleasant. First, there was the Paul of New Salem High—the boy whose still-wealthy father, a man of democratic principles, had refused to send to prep school. Even then, he had combined Byronic looks with an ability to score touchdowns; even then, he was an artist who painted wild canvases no one could understand, a Casanova in a cut-down roadster who picked his girls at will.

The image blended with the campus demigod at Cornell who had spurned all molds, and abandoned the gridiron for an easel in junior year. Paul had gone on to art study in Florence—the pilgrimage ending abruptly with his father's death and the collapse of the Van Ryn Foundry. Returning to survey the wreckage, he had learned that his mother's trust fund had saved Rynhook, for the time being. A determined effort on his part might have saved the foundry as well. Paul had shrugged off the opportunity, permitted the creditors to swarm over the buildings on Bearclaw Point, and returned to his art.

Mike—who had been drafted that same year for service in Korea—knew little of his classmate's moves thereafter. He had heard the story of Paul's marriage to Anna Zeagler secondhand—including her father's magnificent job offer, if Paul could persuade the Duchess of Rynhook to sell the foundry land. Mike had not been surprised when Paul had declined the offer; it had been quite like him to make a wealthy marriage, and spurn its perquisites thereafter. It had been even more in character that he should respect his mother's obstinate refusal to budge from Rynhook.

Marcella Van Ryn had been a towering presence in Mike's youth—a figure glimpsed through a kitchen door when he delivered orders from his father's grocery on Lower Street, a jeweled hand offering a quarter tip. When his football scholarship to Cornell had been announced in the New Salem *Reporter,* he recalled his summons to the great double parlor of the mansion: the booming voice that had commanded him to do his best, the appraisal of the Duchess' piercing eyes—and her order that he report to her when his education was completed. New Salem, said its first lady, had done much for him—and the town could always use a good doctor. It was his duty to bring home the fruits of his training. . . .

Like the Van Ryns, the West family had always been part of New Salem. Unlike them, they had been just below the salt, in that no-man's land between estate and foundry, where the factor's Gate House stood. Jason West had ridden a spectacular talent to the pinnacle of show business. Jason's sister Sandra—two years younger than Mike—had danced as madly as any teen-ager at the high school proms; she had fought the hardest, even in those years, for the honor of a ride in Paul Van Ryn's roadster. At Cornell, she had seemed only half aware of Mike's existence. Paul had remained her chief concern—until her transfer to the St. Luke's School of Nursing in New York. Even then, Paul had cut classes to follow her for week-end dates; it was campus gossip that they were lovers, that the liaison had ended only with his departure for abroad.

While Paul was in Florence, Mike had returned briefly to New Salem, to work through the summer with Dr. Artemus Coxe. Sandra had taken a leave of absence from her training, to put the Gate House in order after her parents' death; she had remained there, to nurse an ailing brother, for whom the bottle had proved too frail a crutch.

Jason West's breakdown had lasted through September—the month Mike was scheduled to depart for service in Korea, on the commission he had earned at Cornell. The night before his departure, he had found the courage to ask Sandra for their first date. He would never know if the image of a departing warrior had softened the girl's heart—or if Jason's crotchets had made her welcome an evening's escape.

She had called for him in her brother's car, a Duesenberg roadster complete with exterior exhausts and a built-in bar. They had driven to the Overlook—then, as now, an after-dark trysting spot. . . . Merely by closing his eyes, he could bring back the moment once again, complete with misty moon and the enigma of a girl who had never seemed more desirable—and never more remote.

"Aren't you going to ask me why we're here?" she asked.

"No, Sandra. I hoped it was for the usual reason."

Sandra took a cigarette from her purse, and waited for his offer of a match. "It wasn't, Mike—but I do want to hear about you. If you insist, I'll even tell *you* about *me*. Do you still plan to be a surgeon?"

"It's what I've wanted from the start. Dr. Art says I should give it all I have."

"I'm sure you will, Mike."

"After Korea, I've set my sights on a California medical school. Probably Stanford. I should have enough G.I. money for tuition."

"I'd wish you luck—if you weren't the kind of person who makes his own."

"How soon will you go back to New York?"

"In another week, I hope. My temperamental brother is beginning to get bored with his illness. They'll welcome him in Hollywood, if he stops breaking contracts."

"Will you ever return to New Salem?"

"Will you, Mike?"

"I've no idea, as of now."

Sandra drew deep on her cigarette. (He could still remember how she had held the burning end between them.)

"You've the sort of new blood this town needs," she said at last. "For New Salem's sake, I hope you decide to practice here someday."

"That decision's a long way off. With luck, I'll intern in San Francisco. If I'm good enough, I'll get a residency on the Coast. With the Army, it adds up to over ten years."

"You're going to be a fine surgeon, Mike. When your training's finished, you'll have your choice of worlds."

"So will you—in New York."

"My case isn't so simple. I'm still not sure what I have to offer."

"I can answer that now, if you'll let me."

"I'd rather you didn't, Mike."

"Why—when you know I've been in love with you, since the ninth grade?"

"It wouldn't be fair. One-sided love can be a destructive thing. I'm an authority on the subject."

"Because *you're* in love with Paul Van Ryn?"

"It's hardly a secret in New Salem."

"I'm glad you aren't under the illusion he loves you."

"He's a strange person, Mike. How well do you know him?"

"We were classmates at Ithaca—but we hardly spoke, off the football field. I suppose he felt I was below his notice. That's his privilege, as a future squire of Rynhook."

"Will you believe me, when I tell you he lives only for his painting?"

"It's one way of excusing his manners."

"He means to be a great artist someday. It's why he borrowed from his mother to go to Florence."

"For my money, he's strictly bad news. Especially where a girl like you is concerned. For your sake, I hope he *stays* abroad."

"You can't dismiss him as another playboy, Mike. Paul's far more than that. Granted, he'll never be what New Salem would call a worker—"

"His father's dying. They say he's half-mad because of the way the foundry's gone downhill. What will Paul do when the chips are down?"

"Go on with his art."

"Even if the family loses everything?"

"I've told you he lives only for his painting."

"How could *you* be happy with such a man?"

"Love and happiness don't always come in the same package. When Paul returns from Italy, I'm ready to share any future he offers me."

"When you see his faults so clearly?"

"The heart doesn't always take orders from the mind, Mike." Behind the flickering glow of her cigarette, he sensed that Sandra was crying quietly. It was shattering to admit he had no way to comfort her—that she had brought him here only to unburden her spirit.

"I'm glad you realize that loving someone like Paul is no bargain."

"It could also be the wish projection of a schoolgirl who refuses to grow up. Paul hasn't written me in months. Perhaps he's forgotten me entirely. That, of course, would be my salvation."

"Get out of New Salem fast," he urged. "I'll help you, if you'll tell me how."

"Don't pity me, please. I couldn't bear it."

"Because the son of a Greek grocer should know his place—and doesn't?"

"No Mike. Because I like you too much to hurt you. After all, you aren't the first man to fall in love with someone who doesn't deserve you. When you've done your tour of duty and gone into medicine, I'll seem like good riddance."

"If you don't mind, I'd prefer to go on hoping."

"For what? That I'll get over Paul—and see what I missed in you?"

"A man needs something when he goes off to a war. Even if it's only a dream that won't come true."

"Thank you for that much, at least." She bent across the wheel and kissed him softly. It was not a coquette's kiss, or a kiss of passion. His heart was leaden as she started the car, now that the good-by gesture was behind her—the blessing that women have used down the ages to send men to war.

It had been a disturbing dialogue. A decade later, recalling each word as clearly as though Sandra West were beside him, he knew he was still clinging to the same hope he had taken to Korea.

He was interning at San Francisco General when he had read of Paul's marriage to Anna Zeagler. Wondering how Sandra had reacted to the event, he had been sorely tempted to bridge the distance that divided them. . . . A year later, he had seen Jason West in a revival of *Liliom.* It had shocked Mike deeply to see how liquor and illness had reduced Sandra's brother to a shadow.

Only a few months ago, he had read that the actor had returned to New Salem for another prolonged rest. The news that Sandra had interrupted a nursing career once again to see Jason West through a new breakdown, and the offer of a post at New Salem Memorial Hospital, had arrived almost simultaneously. It was as though a predestined pattern had enmeshed their lives, and he had not thought of refusing. . . .

The son of Spiros Constantinos had kept a fierce pride in his ancestry. A descendant of Homer's warriors, he had told himself, could yield to no man; he had even been vaguely troubled when his father had shortened their name, a few years after their arrival in New Salem. It was only an accident of birth—he insisted—that Paul Van Ryn should live in a mansion on Bearclaw Point, while Mikhail Constant, and his widowed father, could barely afford two rooms in one of the tenements that housed the foundry workers.

During those first years, Spiros Constant (who had hoped for a farm in upstate New York) had earned a living of sorts by peddling vegetables from a fruit cart. Eventually, he had established his own store on Lower Street, the name New Salem gave to the cobbled lane that skirted the wrong side of Bear Creek. Mike had delivered his father's groceries after school. Between terms, he had earned what he could on a paper route, as a picker in the fruit orchards, as a floor boy in the Van Ryn Foundry.

Every dollar he could save had gone into a fund for medical school. It was the goal he had chosen after his first visit with Dr. Artemus Coxe, whose ten-bed cottage hospital had always been an institution in the Old Town.

In high school, Mike's prowess as a halfback had won him honors, and his first real friendships. From his freshman year, he could hardly complain that his origins had been a bar to his acceptance—though it was true that certain doors had remained closed. . . . The larger world of Cornell had welcomed him without question, as an honor student and an athlete. His luck, in the past decade, had been excellent. In Korea, his outfit had reached Pusan just too late for combat duty. He had sat out the long truce, and returned in time to enroll for the next term at Stanford.

The G.I. Bill had financed his education there; summer work in the experimental surgery lab had paid for the vintage Ford he had used to drive to New Salem. The trunk held his entire possessions —a Val-A-Pak and a small traveling library. An attaché case contained his Army papers, his notes on case histories during his years as a resident, and his coveted diploma from the American Board of Surgery.

Medicine had been his life, from his first class in anatomy. The years between had been so stimulating he had seldom paused to wonder if he was happy. Only at odd moments did he admit that his miragelike memory of Sandra West was his only substitute for love, that the things of the spirit continued to elude him, in the rare pauses his work allowed. The memory picture—and the need to show a few stiff-necked nabobs that he had succeeded in his chosen field—had been enough to lure him back to New Salem.

When Mike Constant left his car at last, a few steps brought him to the edge of the tor. Here, the sheer face of the cliff dropped to the valley, almost three hundred feet below: from that height, the town lay open for his inspection, clear-cut as a museum diorama. A glance was enough to convince him that he had never been away.

In Mike's youth, New Salem had been a small-factory community —too large for a village, too small for a city—whose future seemed rock-ribbed as the cliff on which he stood. Its compact business district, clustered on the riverbank, had been typical of a score of Hudson Valley enclaves that had prospered in the last century, next door to the industry that nourished them. Its lawns had been immaculate, its brick-and-clapboard houses tidy; its streets, arched with elm and maple, had belonged less to New York State than to New England. Upper Street and Yacht Club Road had featured a few sedate mansions. The Bear Creek tenements that housed the Van Ryn Foundry workers had been no more sinister than the saloons on Railroad Avenue that solaced those same workers on payday.

This afternoon, the familiar landmarks in the so-called Old Town were in place: a glance told the visitor that almost no new houses had been added to the residential streets surrounding it. To the east—where the Hudson widened into the Leyden Zee—the same boats seemed to ride at anchor along the yacht club ways. It was here that Bear Creek emptied into the river, after its long meander through the township. On its far shore, Bearclaw Point supported the towered mass of Rynhook, the fortress-home that had been a Van Ryn command post for almost two centuries.

The foundry—the Old Town's focal point and its *raison d'être*—filled a triangular area between creek and river. Even at this distance, Mike saw that it was now only a cluster of sooty, red-brick rookeries—blind-windowed, deep in weeds, an enterprise that had died before its time. To his surprise, the tenements that faced it were still inhabited. Smoke curled from more than one chimney; the children at play on the stoops suggested that the foundry's labor force had found ways to subsist in its shadow.

A closer inspection, Mike realized, would have shown further effects of industrial blight in the Old Town itself. Here on the Overlook, it was easy to pretend that ten years had passed like a waking dream. His ear was still tuned for the familiar clanging of the foundry's ingot cranes. A deep breath, he felt sure, would bring back the acrid odor of the forges—a sour miasma that filled this end of New Salem when the wind was right. . . .

In those days, the foundry had been a dark colossus whose rule was unquestioned. Most of those neat, elm-shaded houses had been mortgaged to the Van Ryns. The cars the homeowners drove, the future of their children and the contentment of their wives depended on iron prices—and full shifts in those sooty buildings across Bear Creek. Even the cemetery was on a hillside donated by the last of the patroons—when New Salem had been called Nieu Leyden, and Peter Stuyvesant had governed down-river. A town wit had once noted that—since patroon lumber was used for the newborn's cradle, as well as the casket in which he was buried—every soul in New Salem was owned by the barons of Rynhook.

From the tor, the town and factory Aaron Zeagler had built in New Salem Heights were hidden by a fold of the hills—well beyond the placid waters of the dam that had once served the foundry. The industrialist had asked Mike to ponder the contrast between old and new: the community at his feet, frozen in time like an Egyptian beetle in amber, was an object lesson he could ignore no longer. . . . Its epitome, he told himself, was that grim castle on the point —and the granite Gate House that stood at its boundary line, where the Van Ryn estate ended and its lifeless factories began.

Mike was still fighting a nameless malaise—one his stubborn mind had refused to define too precisely—when he returned to his car and slipped beneath the wheel. His hand was on the starter when he heard the roar of another motor on the steep road below—and a brick-red Porsche roadster shot into view, breasting the last slope of the tor like a rocket before it braked in a scream of drums and tires. It had passed Mike's ancient Ford on the blind side, near enough to spatter a mudguard with gravel—but the man at the wheel, and the girl beside him, were too intent on their own concerns to note his presence.

When the sound of the motor died, Mike could hear their voices raised in furious debate. He was too distant to catch the words, but he had already recognized Sandra West and Paul Van Ryn.

There was no easy category for Sandra. In Mike's ten years away, she had changed to a woman, without losing the beauty of the girl he had loved—her hair dark red and curling, her skin translucent as only a true redhead's can be. . . . Paul, he saw, had scarcely changed: it was incredible—and faintly disturbing—that a man well over thirty could seem so insolently boyish, so cameo-handsome, so positive his word was law. For the first time, Mike found himself studying his classmate with the eyes of a doctor. To those eyes, Paul Van Ryn's profile was too finely boned to make the good looks valid. Somewhere behind that careless assurance, Mike knew, was a basic weakness he could not define.

The reaction, he admitted swiftly, was colored by his own deep dislike—but he had seen the type too often, as a soldier and as an intern, to trust it for a moment. And he remembered, quite vividly, how Paul had fouled his opponents in football, when he was sure the referee's view was blocked.

Aware that he was still unobserved, Mike wondered if he could coast downhill without starting his motor. He was reaching for the hand brake when his attention was riveted by a commotion in the other car, a brief, panting struggle that ended abruptly when Sandra opened the door on her side. While he watched, she wrenched free of Paul. Before he could follow her, she had rushed headlong to the rim of the tor.

"Wait!"

The cry had burst from Mike's lips without thought; as he uttered it, he realized the folly of his intervention. Like a man locked in nightmare, he saw Paul swivel in the bucket seat of the Porsche. Sandra still hung at the very edge of the tor. What happened thereafter was not too clear—a rain of falling pebbles, as the girl's heels loosened an already precarious foothold. Then, like an awkward swan diver, she vanished into space.

Mike would never remember how he reached the edge. His first look downward assured him a dim memory was accurate, that a narrow shelf protruded from the cliff's face, perhaps ten feet below. The ledge had broken Sandra's plunge, trapping her body in the branches of a stunted tree that grew there, leaving her wedged—not too securely—between the trunk and the stone cornice. She had been knocked out by the fall; an odd angle of the left forearm suggested it had been broken, and blood oozed from a scalp wound.

The ledge, where she lay, sloped upward to a spot on the far side of the tor, where the roots of a live oak twined in the loose stone. As a boy, Mike had walked down that treacherous slope on a dare; he could remember swinging giddily into space, on the branches of the same tree that had just spared Sandra's life. With luck, he could still make the descent. There was no other way to save the girl—and no time to spare in her rescue. Should she gain consciousness, the slightest move would finish the plunge she had begun, sending her to certain destruction three hundred feet below.

"Is she dead?"

With a start, Mike turned toward the voice; intent on the task ahead, he had half forgotten the man in the sports car. He saw that Paul Van Ryn still hung inert above the wheel, his body rigid as a cataleptic's. The eyes that met Mike's held no hint of recognition.

"A shrub broke her fall," he said tersely.

"Can you bring her up?"

"I think so—but you'll have to help."

Paul made no move to leave the bucket seat as his glazed eyes continued their sightless staring.

"What can *I* do?"

"We'll need a sling. Is there a rope in your car?"

"Of course not."

"Then we must improvise." As he spoke, Mike loosened his belt and stepped out of his trousers. The man in the Porsche still hesitated, his brow knitted in a puzzled frown. Then, as he understood Mike's purpose, he moved at last to the rim of the tor, his tapered slacks folded on one arm.

"Are you sure you know what you're doing?"

Mike had already gone halfway along the edge, to check the terrain below the live oak. Later, he would recall the cool insolence of that question. There was no time to notice details as he took the slacks, buckled the belts together, and knotted the cuffs of the trouser legs to his own.

"This will do as a sling. We'll need it to bring her up."

"I can see that, but—"

"When I start back, you can use it as a hoist."

"Are you going down the cliff?" Paul's voice was still cool—and strangely remote. Though he had grasped Mike's plan, he still seemed unwilling to accept it.

"I've told you it's the only way. Do your part, and we can save her."

Gripping the tree roots, Mike lowered himself over the edge. For a dizzy second, he hung suspended in space before his feet found the ledge, which seemed far narrower than he remembered. Still clinging to the roots, he flattened his body against the tor, and began to inch his way toward the girl. Once he had cleared the live oak, he found there was barely room to approach her, on hands and knees. . . . He glanced quickly upward—and noted that Paul had not budged from the shade of the live oak.

"Follow me along the cliff! We'll need that sling in another moment!"

Paul shrugged, and began a parallel move, until he stood above the spot where the crumpled body lay. At this point, the ledge was a trifle wider, and Mike risked rising to his feet. He saw that Sandra's injuries were probably not serious—though there was no mistaking the broken forearm. Her rhythmic breathing fitted the picture of a minor concussion, from which she would soon recover. Dazed by the fall, she could still defeat his purpose if she regained full consciousness—particularly if that plunge into space had been deliberate. He could not imagine a worse spot to cope with a would-be suicide.

Steadying himself with one hand on the shrub—and praying it would bear the added weight—he worked his arm beneath the girl's body. Then, without pausing to look up, he extended his free arm toward the cliff's edge—and the help he expected from Paul Van Ryn.

"Let the sling down," he directed. "I can't move without it."

There was no action from above. He repeated the order sharply, without daring to take his eyes from his burden.

"*Let the sling down!* There's no time to lose."

Paul complied slowly. As Mike felt the impromptu hoist touch his shoulder, he risked a glance upward—and saw that the other man's face was still a glazed mask. Clinging to a knob of rock his groping fingers had found beneath Sandra's body, he slipped his arm through the cloth loop.

"Anchor your heels, and walk toward the tree," he said. "Move a step at a time—and lean back. *Far* back. If you don't, we'll go together."

Paul nodded, and rocked back on his heels. With the shift of weight, Mike was able to rise from his knees and stand erect with his burden. Step by step, they moved toward the live oak. Halfway to their objective, realizing he could no longer support the girl in his cramped position, he shouted to Paul to stop, and shifted her across his shoulder, in a semblance of a fireman's carry.

"Keep moving! We're almost there."

Above him, he could hear the other man gasp, and guessed that he was tiring. There was a sudden rain of stones, while Paul's feet fought for purchase. The tangle of tree roots was now only a long step distant; Mike was fumbling there for a secure handhold when he felt an abrupt slackening of the loop. Even before his eyes met Paul's, he guessed the slackening had been deliberate—that Paul's mind was toying with an impulse to finish what Sandra West had begun. While that impulse lasted, he knew that his life—and the girl's—were not worth a farthing's purchase.

"Hoist away, damn it!"

There was another panting breath from the leaves above, a vigorous tug that tumbled Mike and Sandra into the nest of roots. Here, it was a simple matter to throw his weight forward, a move that pitched Sandra into the grass above. With his burden removed, Mike's own body felt light as air, and his head spun with giddiness. He waited a moment for the vertigo to subside, then scrambled to the top.

Paul had carried Sandra to the space between the two cars. When Mike approached, he was staring down at her incuriously. Most of his attention was devoted to unbuckling the belts that joined the two pairs of trousers.

"That was quick thinking," he said—and his voice was as cool as his manner. "I'm glad it ended well."

Mike stared at him briefly before he knelt beside the injured girl. He could not believe that Paul had failed to recognize him; it was even stranger to detect no sign of tension. Apparently, in a quick convulsion of the ego, the other man had already shrugged off the incident. The fact that Mike had risked death to wipe out the aftermath of his quarrel had been accepted as his right.

"Her arm is broken, and she has a scalp wound. There may be other injuries. We must get her to a hospital at once."

"You talk like a doctor," said Paul—and again, his eyes met Mike's in a flat stare that refused all communion.

"I *am* a doctor."

"In that case, I suggest you carry on. There's a back seat in your car. *You* take her."

It was an outright order, and Mike ignored its impact while they bore the still-unconscious girl to the back seat of his Ford. Paul did not pause a moment longer. Moving toward the Porsche, he slid under the wheel and gunned the motor. Mike was still staring—and still unwilling to accept the evidence of his eyes—when Paul threw in the clutch and left the Overlook in a spurt of gravel.

TWO

Mike Constant stood beside his jalopy, listening to the diminishing roar of the sports car on the road below. A moan from the back seat recalled him to his duties. Now that he was adjusting to the shock of Paul's abrupt departure, he was glad to be alone with the girl whose life he had just saved.

Sandra was already showing signs of returning consciousness when he shifted to low gear for his descent to the valley. He had noted the new highway connecting New Salem with the Heights—and the side road that led to the crest of Indian Hill, where the hospital stood. Ten minutes later, he was driving through the gates.

A closer view confirmed first impressions—though he was still too concerned with his patient to take in details. The wide-winged building seemed well planned, in an ultramodern fashion; the spacious grounds were a fitting setting for its severely functional lines. Devotees of such architecture would have called it a handsome edifice, though it was not to Mike's own taste. At that moment, in the glare of afternoon, he found it curiously lifeless, a model of medical efficiency awaiting a set of puppets to explain and animate it.

Turning into the bluestone drive marked AMBULANCE ENTRANCE, he shrugged off the bizarre notion. To his surprise, there was no orderly in attendance at the admitting booth—and the double doors to the hospital proper were closed and locked from within. Repeated pressure on the bell brought no response. He had raised his fist to knock when the portal opened grudgingly, revealing a girl in the uniform and bib of a famous nursing school. She was handsome in a Junoesque way, and fighting mad at the noise.

Mike cut short her protest. "I have an emergency case in my car. If this *is* a hospital—"

"Certainly it's a hospital. But we don't take emergencies."

"What are you saying?"

"We accept no emergency cases, unless a surgeon is attending. Try Dr. Coxe, on Lower Street."

The rejection was both crisp and assured; its cold finality left Mike stunned. At another time, he would have realized that his dirt-stained clothing and his battered car might have suggested he was a migrant farmhand. For the present, his only concern was the fact that an emergency case had been refused by a hospital. Tempted to state his identity and force Sandra's admission, he found himself restraining the impulse—even as he had held his tongue when he faced Paul Van Ryn.

"Let me make sure I understand. You are turning away an unconscious patient. Did I hear you correctly?"

The nurse, he saw, was no fool. By now, she had realized he was not the fruit tramp he resembled—yet she continued to bar the entrance.

"I've told you there's no doctor here. In those circumstances, I'm refusing you admission. Can you find Lower Street by yourself? If not, I'll send an orderly with you."

"I'll manage on my own." Turning on his heel with a curt nod, Mike hurried back to his car. Before he could swing into the driveway, the door to admissions had clicked shut behind him.

A half hour later, standing before Dr. Artemus Coxe's X-ray-view box in the darkroom of the cottage hospital in the Old Town, Mike was still warning himself not to make a hasty judgment of New Salem Memorial. It was quite possible that no qualified doctor had been present on his arrival—residents were rare nowadays in non-teaching hospitals. In that case, the nurse-in-charge could accept new patients at her discretion, or refer them elsewhere.

Fortunately, no harm had been done in this case. Sandra West had regained consciousness while Mrs. Bramwell, Dr. Coxe's nurse, had been undressing her and Mike had ordered a hypodermic of Demerol, certain now that the head injury was not important.

The break, revealed in the X ray, was a simple one, involving only the large bone of the lower arm, the radius. When he returned to the old-fashioned surgery, the patient was asleep from the medication and Mrs. Bramwell had washed the dirt and gravel from her face, arm, and the small cut in her scalp. A brief examination gave no evidence of any more serious injury, confirming his original estimate.

"I fixed the Novocain tray you ordered, Mike," said Mrs. Bramwell. "Or should I call you Doctor, now?"

"Mike will do nicely, Emma. Think I should wait for Dr. Art?"

"He may not be back for hours."

"Have I your permission to treat a patient in his absence?"

"You don't need anyone's permission to practice here, Mike Constant. Don't forget I know your whole history."

He scrubbed at the basin in the corner, and put on the sterile gloves the resident nurse had opened. Mrs. Bramwell steadied the injured arm while he made a series of Novocain injections in the skin above the fracture area. After he had raised a mound above the broken bone, he thrust the needle deeper, continuing the injection until he felt the point touch the fracture itself.

When Mike drew back the plunger of the syringe, a drop of dark blood appeared, pulled through the needle into the clear Novocain solution. It told him he was inside the hematoma, the small bleeding area formed at the broken ends of the radius as blood seeped from the break in the marrow. Here, he injected a half syringe of Novocain. Then, moving the needle a second time to the surface above the break, he made a final injection to block off the nerve branches in the periosteum, or outer lining of the bone.

While he waited for the Novocain to anesthetize the area of the break, Mike closed Sandra's scalp wound with the skin clips the nurse had provided—an effective way to join the edges so they would heal without a noticeable scar. Then, taking the arm in both hands, he snapped the break together. The patient moaned under his hands—but the Demerol, plus the Novocain, had done its work well. She hardly stirred as the ends clicked neatly into place.

"Dr. Coxe was right," said Mrs. Bramwell. "You chose the proper trade, Mike."

"Save the blarney, Emma. Any intern can set a broken radius." Even as he refused the compliment, a warm glow filled his heart. For the first time today, he knew that he had come home. "Plaster ready?"

"The bandages are soaking now."

Using a dripping bandage impregnated with chalk-white plaster of Paris, Mike unrolled a strip nearly two feet long and several layers thick. With the nurse's help, he covered it with cotton padding, repeated the process with a second bandage—and applied both strips, with the arm snugly between them. An ordinary bandage, wound in tight spirals, anchored the dressing. Taking the now-splinted arm between his palms, Mike molded the plaster so it would fit smoothly against the skin. Until she wakened, he had done all he could for Sandra West.

"Did you notify her relatives?"

"There's only her brother left. I called the Gate House when I admitted her—but he didn't answer."

"Is he well enough to come to the phone?"

"Jason West has been *too* well lately—if you know what I mean."

"He was a champion pub crawler when I was in Los Angeles," said Mike. "I hoped he'd discontinue the habit in New Salem. Is it true he has a chronic heart condition?"

"It's more than that," said Mrs. Bramwell. "I'd call his trouble Actor's Complaint. My guess is he's come home to sulk, because they don't write his kind of parts any more."

Mike did not pursue the topic. Emma Bramwell was an excellent nurse—and an incurable gossip. For once, he suspected the rumor she had just passed on was accurate. Looking down at the sleeping girl, as they wheeled her to a bed in a private room, he wondered if she would have confirmed it. Sandra West, he reflected, was facing trouble at more than one level.

"You'd better ring the Gate House again, Emma."

"Don't fret, Mike. Jason West will hear the news. Our grapevine still functions—in and out of saloons."

"Can you keep Sandra here for a few days?"

"Dr. Coxe will be glad to get a patient. We don't have many, since *your* flossy new hospital opened. Incidentally, you still haven't told me where you found her—or how. I'll need the facts for our records."

"She had a fall," said Mike. "I happened to be passing, and picked her up. I can't give you the circumstances, because I don't know them." The evasion, he told himself, had its elements of truth. Perhaps he would never have the whole story.

"Keep her secret, if you feel you have to," said Mrs. Bramwell. "I'll know it soon enough."

Dr. Artemus Coxe lit his pipe, settled comfortably in the broken-back chair that stood behind the desk in his cluttered office. The old doctor was heavier than Mike remembered, and his china-bald head suggested an irate kewpie. The twinkle in his eye was unchanged when he faced his younger colleague across a familiar welter of lab reports, unfiled histories, and unpaid bills.

"I'm glad you waited, Mike," he said. "I'll try to answer your questions in order."

"Don't blame me for being confused, Dr. Art."

"I don't blame you in the slightest. You've had a violent introduction to your native heath—beginning with Aaron Zeagler."

Mike grinned through the rising smoke screen. "I'll admit *he* was shock enough, for one afternoon. If I could, I'd have put off Paul and Sandra until tomorrow."

"I'm glad you approve Zeagler's motives—if not his methods."

"Surely he realizes he can't win over New Salem while the Duchess reigns at Rynhook."

"He's done his best, Mike."

"Did he think his daughter's marriage would help?"

"It may be hard to accept, but that was his hope, at first. There was a time when an alliance between the two families seemed possible. I don't have all the facts—but Paul met Anna in New York, and married her after a headlong courtship. For a while, Zeagler was sure he'd turn into a prince consort. Even an heir apparent—"

"I gather he soon admitted his error."

"The error was admitted—on both sides," said Dr. Coxe dryly. "Marcella Van Ryn was furious when she found a daughter-in-law on her doorstep—especially a girl of Anna's faith. Zeagler wrote off his son-in-law as an artist with a taste for extramarital adventures. There the matter rests."

"What would you call it—an armed truce?"

"The term's as good as any other. You'll soon see how it operates."

"I promised Zeagler I'd call on the Duchess. Do you think she'll want to see me—when she learns I saw him first?"

"Marcella is eager to learn how you've fared. She said as much, when I visited her last week and told her you were coming back. So far, I'm the only doctor who's allowed on Bearclaw Point. She has nothing but contempt for New Salem Memorial. To her mind, it's a command post in the enemy camp."

"If she's one of your patients, you must have a prognosis of her condition."

"It's too general to help much," said the older doctor. "The clinical picture's clear enough. Arteriosclerosis, of course, with some degeneration of the brain; that's to be expected, at her age. The real pathology goes deeper—the kind of thing so many older people develop, when they've always had their way. Treatment won't help, so there'd be no point in committing her. The touchstone of her existence is the fear of change—and the need to keep her son at heel."

"Does that suit Paul?"

"It suits him perfectly. He knows her good moods by heart—and he can anticipate her lapses. He trades on the first to get cash. When her mind clouds over, he takes off for New York, and hits the tomcat trail."

"Where does this leave Zeagler's daughter?"

"In their tower suite, living with the Van Ryn ghosts. Alcohol has been her chief solace for some time."

"I can't picture Paul's wife too clearly."

"I'm convinced she loves him, in her fashion," said Dr. Coxe.

"Does her father know about her drinking?"

"Aaron Zeagler's a strange man, where his daughter's concerned. He has a streak of the patriarch in his make-up, even though he's a citizen of tomorrow. It's quite possible that Anna married Paul to further his interests. I'm sure she was putting the best face she could on the marriage—when she elected to live at Rynhook and refused the house he offered them. Now she's made that election, he doesn't see her often."

"Does he spend much time in New Salem?"

"Not with factories from here to Tel Aviv. His second wife is an international hostess. The place he built on Mohawk Knoll is one of a half-dozen residences. As of now, I'd say he's playing a waiting game, with his son-in-law—and reining in his temper. You must have seen he suffers from hypertension."

"I gathered that anger's an emotion he can't afford."

"Few of us can these days," said Dr. Coxe. "You saw what it did to Sandra on the Overlook."

"I'm waiting for your estimate of that explosion," said Mike. "From my car, it looked like an attempted suicide, after a lovers' quarrel."

"Put it this way, Mike. We both know how long Sandra's eaten out her heart for Paul. It could be a trauma she'll never outgrow."

"I'd buy that diagnosis, if she didn't know Paul so well. Obviously, she sees through him, as clearly as you and I."

"When a girl's in love, she always hopes for the best from her man, and closes her eyes to the worst. Sandra West is a fine, level-headed person: she's proved that by the way she's cared for Jason. I doubt if she has more control than the average female, when it comes to the grand passion. And Paul's a past master at fanning that sort of flame."

"What's happened between them, since I've been away?"

"She made a real success of nursing in New York. She could have had a career job at St. Luke's, if he hadn't appeared on the scene again."

"*After* his marriage?"

"Paul isn't the type to be slowed down by a wife. Nor, I regret to say, is Sandra. She's been a perfect St. Luke's nurse, so long as he stays in Rynhook. Whenever he drove that fireman's-red roadster to New York, she played the game by his rules."

"I'm not sure I want to hear more, Dr. Art."

"Naturally, there are two sides to the coin. Paul's departure from Rynhook has the same effect on Anna. I've seen it happen, time and again. She turns into a good citizen overnight—puts away the bottle, and pitches in at a children's clinic her father gave her, at Bear Creek Crossing. The reform lasts—until her unrepented husband's had enough outside dalliance, and returns to his easel. *Then* Anna goes back to the hopeless business of forgiving him, and loving him. And drinking again, because she *knows* it's hopeless."

"A psychiatrist would call that pattern self-destructive."

"It is—with the compensating elements I've mentioned."

"So Anna Van Ryn is killing herself by inches. If I can believe my eyes, Sandra tried to do the same job, in one installment. Will she thank me for my intervention?"

"You can ask her yourself, Mike. When I came in just now, Emma told me she was conscious."

"I'm not looking forward to the interview."

"Take my opinion, for what it's worth. Sandra West isn't the type who'd kill herself for love. She has too much courage, even when she's behaving like a fool."

"Are you suggesting it was an act?"

"Women are great performers, when they have a special end in view. You saw how badly Paul was shocked. Perhaps it's all she meant to accomplish."

"She shocked me far more."

"Are you still in love with her?"

"I'll always love her, Dr. Art. That's *my* trauma, if we're still being clinical."

"Why return to New Salem, then—if you're as unhappy as you sound?"

"Perhaps I felt I owed something to you, and the town. Perhaps I only wanted an excuse to punch Paul's jaw. Right now, I can't wait to see the inside of a hospital that would refuse an emergency admission."

"Don't judge New Salem Memorial by what happened at the ambulance entrance."

"How can I help myself?"

"Try to keep an open mind, Mike. You'll find other things there you won't like. Nothing's wrong on Indian Hill a good man can't set right—if he's working from the inside, and has friends in court."

"I'm not sure I'm that man."

"Promise me one thing, Doctor. Make no decisions until tomorrow, and don't blow your top in the meantime. We'll have a second talk when you're ready. And don't be *too* hard on Sandra, please. A woman is always fighting a losing battle, when she's in love with the wrong man."

The room where Sandra West lay had been shuttered against the afternoon sun. The girl was resting in a propped-up bed, with her hair like a red aureole on the pillow. She seemed to be dozing when Mike entered—but her eyes opened as he bent above her, and there was no welcome in the level glance she gave him.

"So we meet again, Mike Constant." Her voice had an ironic overtone that chilled him instantly—a sound that was a far cry from the girl he remembered. "It seems I'm luckier than I know."

"We can agree on that much." His own voice was harsher than he had intended. It seemed unfair of her, to put him on the defensive so soon.

"I'd heard you were coming home to improve the general welfare. Somehow, I didn't expect you to begin with me."

Mike controlled the retort that had almost escaped him. While he checked the plaster splint, he put on his professional manner—along with the surgeon's prerogative of silence during an examination. The routine was entirely defensive. A glance had assured him that his patient's injuries would heal themselves.

"Do you always behave like a doctor when you're mad?" asked Sandra.

"This afternoon, you *needed* a doctor."

"Then what Emma Bramwell says is true. You saved my life."

"You needn't feel indebted to me."

"Why should I—when you practically pushed me off the tor? The least you could do was bring me back." Her voice had broken on the mockery. For an instant, she covered her face with her uninjured arm, and gave way to a wild fit of laughter.

"You can't deny you were quarreling with Paul."

"It wasn't a quarrel. It was all-out war. We have those battles often. This one was worse than usual."

"I saw you run to the cliff's edge. Naturally, I assumed you meant to jump—"

"Suppose I'd done just that? What right had you to interfere?"

"The right of one human being to save another."

"It's my life. From your viewpoint, I've wasted most of it. Why shouldn't I end it as I saw fit?"

"Then you *were* thinking of suicide."

"I was *not,* Mike Constant. That last remark was meant to test your crusader's instinct. In the future, I hope you'll suppress it, where I'm concerned." For the second time, her voice broke in a spasm of laughter she made no attempt to control. "Incidentally, how did you get me back from the ledge?"

"We used Paul's slacks, and my trousers, to make a sling. I went down after you. He pulled us both up."

Sandra's laughter continued, but there was a new note to her mirth—and something close to contrition in her eyes.

"That must have taken courage."

"I didn't have time to be afraid. Not until it was over."

"Who brought me here? You, or Paul?"

"I did. Paul seemed to have business elsewhere. He couldn't leave the tor fast enough."

"So he's deserted me again," said Sandra. "Now that I recall the language I used, it's no more than I deserved."

"I'm still not sure I believe your story."

"Look at my shoes, if you want proof. They're on the dresser."

Mike turned to the chiffonier to examine the two pumps. One of the spike heels, he noted, had been wrenched from the sole. Sandra had been standing in loose rock—dangerously close to the edge—when he had given that unwise shout of warning. The shoe was a mute witness of the obvious. Startled by the impact of a new voice, she had been thrown off balance—breaking the heel, and starting her near-fatal plunge.

"Well, Dr. Constant? Are you ready to admit a crusader can wreak havoc, when he enters a battleground without a map?"

"I'll buy you a new pair of shoes," he said. His back was still turned to the bed, while he waited for the thud of his heart to subside. "I'll also instruct Emma Bramwell to send me your bill, since the fault was mine."

"Your generosity's accepted," said Sandra. "Right now, I'm a bit short of funds."

"Surely you had *some* motive in dashing to the edge. Were you trying to upset Paul?"

Sandra hesitated, before her good hand reached across the bed to press his quickly. "Forgive me for teasing you, Mike," she said. "Didn't Dr. Art explain why I returned to New Salem?"

"To nurse your brother?"

"Jason's been in a bad way lately. I made him come home, to pull himself together. For the past month, we've been living at the Gate House. This last week, he seemed almost well. He'd begun talking of Broadway offers. Yesterday, he even called his agent to sound out the best prospects. I let myself believe I'd done all I could for him—and gave Paul the date he'd been asking for."

"Don't tell me this was your first date with Paul since his marriage."

"No, Mike. And it won't be my last."

"Even after what happened on the Overlook?"

"When I finished training, as you must know, I tried to settle in New York. After Paul married Anna, I did my best to forget him, to lose myself in work. I even thought of writing you—"

"I wish you had, Sandra."

"It's well I didn't. Two months after his marriage, we knew it was an utter failure."

"*We?*"

"He said he needed me, more than ever. I believed him. I still do—even when we quarrel."

"Do you still expect him to desert his wife and marry you?" Mike made no attempt to hide the sarcasm in his voice.

"Don't think I'm without shame, please. I know how helpless he's been—tied to the Duchess, with only his painting to sustain him. Year after year, I've told myself he'd break the silver cord. Leave Rynhook, and give Anna a divorce."

"Isn't that a rather forlorn hope by now?"

"Not when he's free of his mother—and can be himself. This afternoon, I was sure he'd have the answer to my prayers."

"Apparently, he disappointed you rather badly."

"Only a month ago—in New York—he said he was never meant for marriage with a rich wife. He said he'd been a fool, to let his mother rule him all these years. He swore he'd leave them both, and get a job—so *we* could marry."

"And you believed him?"

"He meant it then, Mike. I'm sure he did. Today, I learned he'd looked over the field, and found nothing that suited him. Besides, how could he hold a job, and go on painting? At Rynhook, he could do as he liked, if he kept out of the Duchess' way—"

Mike shrugged. The dead-level tone of Sandra's recital had shocked him far more than her avowal. "In other words, he prefers to go on as before."

"Until he's found himself, as an artist. He can handle his mother. Anna takes care of money problems. Why should he trade a studio in New Salem for a desk in New York? When he said *that*, I jumped out of his car, and ran to the cliff."

"Apparently I spoiled your big moment, Sandra. I'd apologize, if I could."

"I still love him, Mike. I have, since I was in pigtails. I'll always insist there's hope—for us both—once his painting is recognized. *Now* do you see why I used a—a rather shabby trick to hurt him?"

"Perhaps he wasn't quite so hurt as you hoped. He might have let you jump, and not turned a hair."

"Even if that's true—and it isn't—I can't afford to listen."

When he turned to leave the room, Mike's heart had never been heavier. The image of Paul Van Ryn's face swam before his eyes—the fixed stare, the hands that had all but loosened their hold on the sling. While the evil mirage lasted, it was more real than his own heartbeat—yet he had no way to share it with the girl in the hospital bed.

That afternoon on the Overlook, tottering on the brink of eternity, they had been as helpless as two marionettes whose lives hung on a demon's whim. . . . The image faded, as he left Sandra's bedside, without another word. Every instinct he possessed was urging him to speak the truth—but today, at least, he knew the truth would fall on deaf ears.

THREE

The new surgeon's first glimpse of his hospital had been too obscured by anger to register clearly. Driving again through its gateposts, Mike Constant admitted that he liked what he saw. Even the flamboyant wings of the central building, and the chromatic arc of firebrick that framed the main entrance, seemed integral parts of New Salem Heights. So did the crisply uniformed nurse pushing a wheel chair across the velvet lawn, the whirl of a power mower barbering another stretch of greensward that already seemed smooth as a putting green. . . . New Salem Memorial, he thought, might seem too severely functional to the layman's eye. At the moment its aseptic face was almost welcome.

Mike parked his vintage Ford in the section marked FOR DOCTORS ONLY, noting the three Cadillacs and two sleek Triumphs that already stood there. In the lobby—a pastel-hued, floodlit rectangle that could have served as the foyer of a luxury apartment building—he found a handsome girl receptionist behind an all-glass desk. Her face lighted in a smile when he gave his name.

"I'm Alice Jenks, Doctor. We've been expecting you all day."

"Is the director here?"

"I'm afraid this is Dr. Melcher's afternoon for golf. But Mr. Pailey's in his office."

The girl led the way to an alcove, opening to a wall of pressed glass and the grilles of the cashier's cage. The administrator's department, Mike observed, was bathed in neon light, and efficient as the cabin of a space ship. The youngish, balding man who had just bounded from his chair with his hand extended was part of his background. Save for the rimless glasses that formed a natural extension of his nearly naked brow, he might have passed for a full-back who still observed training. The suit he was wearing had a New York cut; his handshake, firm but not aggressive, suggested the disciplines of ivied walls.

"Ralph Pailey, Dr. Constant. Glad to have you aboard. You couldn't have arrived at a more opportune time." He signaled through the grille, to a girl engrossed in the operation of a check puncher. "Mark Dr. Constant present on the daily record, Miss Cole. Our contract with the County is now in force."

"The New Salem County Hospital?" Mike asked.

"We're taking over its patients, now it's closing. The change-over will be a blessing for the town, Doctor. In its last days, the County was even more decrepit than you would remember. We'll cost a bit more, of course—but the city fathers decided our fees were far cheaper than building a new hospital."

Mike studied Pailey more carefully. The man's welcome had seemed genuine. Why, he wondered, did he feel he was addressing a machine?

"You said the contract was now in force. How does that concern me?"

"One of its clauses provides for a surgeon in residence. We've just fulfilled that provision, since you'll be quartered upstairs. The patient transfer began yesterday, on my assurance you'd arrive before nightfall. Now, praise Heaven, we can collect our first per-diem stipend."

"Couldn't you get a fill-in doctor while you waited?"

"It's difficult to fit a temporary resident into our type of operation, Dr. Constant. Especially since New Salem Memorial's yet to be accredited by the Joint Committee."

"Haven't you made the grade in three years?"

"Not with the red tape the committee requires," said Pailey, too smoothly for Mike's approval. "Of course we've weathered the preliminary evaluations. Now *you're* here to lend us prestige, our troubles should be over. Actually, the post you're about to fill has been our only real stumbling block. Until you accepted our offer, the best we could turn up was a series of foreign graduates—all of them fresh from their internships. Dr. Melcher vetoed their applications, to my relief."

"We had some excellent foreign doctors on the Coast."

"In California, you'd have a choice we lack here. I'm only explaining why it won't be practical to supply you with an assistant at the moment. You'll get regular time off, naturally. Our attending surgeons will work out a rotating system, so you can have equal hours away."

"I'm used to the routine, Mr. Pailey. I'm aware I must be available at all times."

"Dr. Melcher should be back in the next hour. May I show you around in the meantime?"

"If you aren't too busy."

Pailey chuckled, as though Mike had just made a joke. "It's no trouble whatever. You're a VIP, doctor—starting this minute. Where did you leave your baggage?"

"It's all in my car."

"If you'll give me the keys, I'll have an orderly take it to your quarters. You'll be the California license, I suppose?"

"And ninety-six thousand miles on the speedometer. He'll have no trouble finding me."

The administrator guffawed. Mike found himself disliking the sound; in his ear, it seemed as false as applause on television.

"We'll start with the business office. Not that you'll spend much time there." Pailey led the way to an extensive work space behind the grille. Three secretaries were busy here, in addition to the girl at the punching machine—one at a conventional set of ledgers, the others at the controls of automatic bookkeepers.

"I use only the latest equipment in my billing," said Pailey. "These machines are expensive—but they earn their keep when we classify a patient."

"As a medical or a security risk?"

This time, Mike's attempt at humor went unnoticed. "We have very few of the latter, Dr. Constant. Our collection rate last month was just under ninety-eight per cent—and each item was fully recorded. You'd be surprised how much a hospital can lose when it fails to list every charge."

From the foyer, an elevator lifted them to the operating suite on the second floor. Mike noted with approval that it was situated in the central building block. The equipment, though not elaborate, was adequate. The orderly at an autoclave seemed to know his job. So did two nurses, working at top speed to prepare one of the two operating theaters for a patient who waited, drowsy from preoperative medication, on a wheeled stretcher outside.

"Our average time between major operations is ten minutes," said the administrator proudly.

"Ten minutes is very good indeed."

"You'll get expert assistance here. Miss Searles is an outstanding O.R. supervisor. Here she is now."

In the second of the two operating rooms, Mike found himself facing the girl he had encountered at the ambulance entrance. At the moment, she was instructing another nurse in the technique of an electrosurgical unit—the so-called electric knife used in brain operations.

"Dr. Constant, Miss Hubbard—and Miss Lenora Searles. Lee is the supervisor in our surgical section. You'll be working closely together."

Lenora Searles was wearing a cap over her dark hair, and a scrub gown—a one-piece garment that appeared to have been tailored to her measurements. Mike saw her eyes narrow as they met his—but she gave no overt sign of recognition.

"Miss Searles greeted me earlier this afternoon," he said. "At the ambulance entrance."

"Were *you* the one who tried to bring in an emergency patient?"

"Yes, Mr. Pailey. And this is the nurse who refused me admission."

The attack had been instinctive—and Mike regretted it at once. As his sense of fair play took over, he could admire Miss Searles' aplomb.

"I'm sure you'll understand, Mr. Pailey," she said coolly. "When Dr. Constant appeared, we had no physician attending. Unfortunately, he didn't choose to identify himself."

"You caught us at a bad time, Doctor." Pailey, Mike observed, was fast on his feet when it came to fielding hot grounders. "Now you're one of us, we won't have the same problem again. You'll forgive us, Lee, if we whip through the recovery room without you? I can see you and Miss Hubbard are busy."

Lenora Searles had kept her eyes on Mike—a level, attentive glance that had not wavered. There was no enmity in her expression, and no acceptance.

"When Dr. Constant's ready," she said, "I'll be glad to bring him up to date. Both of us live in the hospital. He can choose his own time."

Mike made no comment as his guide led him swiftly through the second surgical unit. Here, they descended to the combined clinical and pathological laboratory, located in the hospital basement for easy access to the morgue. A single technician was on duty, in a room that seemed, to the newcomer, far too small for a hospital of this size. Pailey marched on, past an autopsy table, which an orderly was scrubbing with antiseptic; Mike could not help smiling, when he saw the administrator's nose crinkle at the familiar, faintly sinister odor of formaldehyde.

In a glass-walled alcove beyond, a man in a long-skirted white coat sat at a microscope. He was speaking into a dictaphone as he studied a slide, and did not look up until he cut the switch.

"Dr. Garstein, this is Dr. Constant." There was a wariness in Pailey's manner that caused Mike to study the other doctor carefully. Garstein gave him a quick handshake, without rising from his lab stool. He was a wiry man, on the runty side; a brace was attached to his left shoe and a pair of aluminum arm crutches were propped against the desk. The face thrust up from the microscope was ugly in a simian fashion, but the dark eyes were luminous with intelligence.

"Glad to see you in the flesh, Constant," he said. "There's been a great deal of talk here about our new wonder boy. I hope you live up to it."

Pailey's voice cut in smoothly. "I'll take you through the wards, Doctor, and the private wing. Then I'll show you to your quarters."

"Let him catch his breath, Ralph," said the pathologist. "I'll show him the rest later. You can resume your love affair with that brand new computer."

"If you don't mind, Dr. Constant–"

"Of course he doesn't mind," said Garstein. "Don't get your tail in a vise. I won't show him the family skeletons."

"Louis is famous for his wit," said Pailey. "You'll adjust to it in time, Doctor."

"Not that we couldn't use a skeleton in this outfit," said the pathologist. "I'm sure some of our nurses began their training at a veterinary hospital."

The administrator departed–with more haste, to Mike's mind, than Garstein's remarks had warranted. The man at the microscope used one of his hand crutches to push a second lab stool near the table.

"Sit down, Constant," he said. "Don't mind my left jabs. That walking Univac brings out the worst in me."

Mike smiled as he took the offered seat. He had conceived an instant liking for the pathologist; the man's sharp tongue was a welcome change from Pailey.

"You can take off the disguise, Dr. Garstein," he said. "I've met you before, in another form."

"That's hard to believe."

"Not at all. Every hospital has its *enfant terrible.* I can see you've elected yourself for the part at New Salem Memorial. You can't be so bad as you sound."

"That's where you're wrong. Frequently, I'm a good bit worse–like most cripples who are soured on the world. I'm sure you've noticed my disability by now."

"Of course I noticed. I can also see there's nothing wrong with your mind."

"Save the milk of human kindness," said Garstein. "Not that I won't purr at first, if you pet me. Just remember my claws will be ready for your back, the moment it's turned. One of my hobbies is seeing the color of a man's blood."

"I can save you the trouble, in my case," said Mike. "It's red, not blue. I was christened Mikhail Constantinos. My father dropped the last four letters when he sold his fruit cart and opened a grocery."

"On the wrong side of Bear Creek," said Garstein.

"Naturally."

"I know all about your origins. Are you ashamed of them?"

"No, Dr. Garstein. I'm proud to be a Greek."

The lab man's grin told Mike that he had liked the answer. "It may interest you to learn I'm partly responsible for your being here. For some odd reason, they put me on the selection committee, when they were combing the woods for a surgeon. Art Coxe and I are old drinking companions. After he showed me your record in California, I advised the committee to look no further."

"I'm grateful, Doctor."

"Repeat that in three months, and I may believe you. New Salem Memorial's a long ways from Johns Hopkins—but you'll find you can practice good surgery here. Naturally, you must learn to ignore the animals outside the O.R., and their habits."

"How did you happen to locate here?"

"The job suits me. They pay me a good salary. I earn it—taking care of the pathology for smaller hospitals in our area. I'm also useful, in another field. Where else can you find a pathologist who can double in anesthesia? Besides I'm Aaron Zeagler's brother-in-law—but that's beside the point."

"The combination is certainly unusual."

"Actually, I'm related to Aaron through his first marriage—when he was still Orthodox."

"Don't you approve of Jews, Dr. Garstein?"

"I'm proud of my race, just as you're proud of yours. Zeagler's a prime example of our breed. A good man who's lived his success story. I'm just trying to place myself in the scheme of things here. Pailey and Melcher know I can do my job—and they know the owner's behind me. That's why I can sound off when I'm in the mood, and run no risk of being fired."

"Of course I knew Zeagler built this hospital as a community unit," said Mike. "Does he sit on the board?"

Garstein shook his head. "That isn't Aaron's way. This is a special enterprise, needing special skills. He's left its actual management to others."

"People like Pailey—and Dr. Melcher?"

"It's a pattern tract builders follow these days," said the lab man. "They include a hospital in their development, then lease it to doctors who live there. It gives the added attraction of medical care on the homeowner's doorsill; that's worth a lot to people who choose this way of life. The original builder writes off the hospital against taxes. The medical group that runs it cleans up—and everyone benefits."

"Hospitals aren't usually run at a profit."

"This one is. Why else would our walking Univac look so happy?" Garstein gave Mike an appraising glance. "Surely you knew we were in the proprietary class?"

"Only that you were organized by a board of doctors. I didn't stop to examine the details."

"Were you so anxious to locate here that you came in blind?"

"It was Dr. Art's letter that brought me. He said I was needed in New Salem—so I decided to give the job a year's try."

"Art Coxe expects you to make some changes here—all of them for the town's good."

"Like convincing the Joint Committee you should be accredited?"

"That among others," said the pathologist. "The way he built you up, you may be the boy to clean out the stables."

"Is the metaphor justified?"

"I'll leave that decision to you—when you've seen our whole setup. If you succeed, it will be a nice mark on your record." Garstein studied Mike for a moment; the eyes under his knitted brows were still coolly mocking. "You're also aware that Aaron expects a certain amount of personal service outside these walls?"

"He mentioned his problems too."

"Did you promise to turn Paul Van Ryn into a normal citizen? Or to take my niece Anna off the sauce? Will you turn your charm on the Duchess, and persuade her to sell the foundry?"

Mike shrugged off the questions. Stated with such bald sarcasm, they made his half promise to Zeagler seem little short of fantastic.

Yet he sensed that Garstein was on his side, regardless of the shield he held between them.

"Don't cast me as a miracle man," he said mildly. "Let me hang up my hat and get my bearings."

"Just prove you're a doctor, Constant—and I'll stop my prodding." The lab man selected a slide from his rack, and placed it on the stage of the microscope. "You could still be one of those hotshots who came home to get rich."

"If you thought that, would you let down your hair with me?"

"Maybe you're for real. There's one way to convince me." The pathologist pushed his mobile stool away from the table. "Look through the lens there, and tell me what you see."

"You've an odd way of testing applicants."

"Odd but effective. Not that I'll flunk you, if you fail this test. It isn't easy."

Mike studied the slide carefully, moving it about on the stage to bring different areas into view. The tissue was easy to identify: the section had been cut across a small, solid cylinder that could only be a human appendix. There was the usual opening in the center—marked by a line of mucous-membrane cells, wrinkled into hills and valleys. Outside the cylinder was the thin peritoneal layer that covered most abdominal organs. The wall between showed clusters of characteristic, dark-stained cells, suggesting that it had been spattered with bird shot.

At first glance, the slide seemed a textbook demonstration. Mike needed the closest scrutiny before he observed that part of the mucous membrane had lost its pattern and started to run wild. The explosion was centered in a small area—but it was enough to give him his diagnosis.

"Come, Dr. Constant! Surely you recognize a normal appendix when you see one sectioned."

Mike's grin expanded into an outright laugh. "You know damned well this tissue isn't normal. It's one of the earliest carcinoids I ever saw, but it's typical."

"They did a good job of raising you at Stanford," said the lab man. "A lot of pathologists would have missed that one."

"I had a year in your first specialty during my surgical internship —and a half year in your second."

Garstein rose on his hand braces, stumping with remarkable agility to the far end of the alcove, to restore a test tube to its rack. His eyes were still narrowed when he turned to face the new staff surgeon—but Mike had not missed the gleam of respect behind the lids.

"Listen carefully, Doctor. Or may I call you Mike, now we've nearly come to blows?"

"Please do, Louis."

"You'll probably be wasting your time here—even if you *are* an ex-slum boy who wants to prove he's arrived. If your hands are as good as your brain, you can make five times your New Salem salary in city practice."

"At the moment, I'm not interested in big money—unless that's too un-American to suit you."

"Obviously, Aaron has convinced you that you can help the natives see the light. And Art Coxe has sold you a bill of goods on improving our routine here. I still insist you're the wrong man—for *both* rat races."

"I'll decide that for myself—if you don't mind."

"I don't mind in the slightest," said the pathologist. "In fact, that was test number two. I was positive you'd pass it." The phone was ringing on the desk. He growled into the mouthpiece, then hung up with a laugh that ended in a snort. "Your next test is coming up. That was the director's office. Larry Melcher finished his golf game early, and wants to see you."

Dr. Lawrence Melcher was still under fifty—a deep-tanned, athletic figure whose professional manner was as faultless as his smile. He opened a humidor to offer a cigar—and, when Mike refused it, selected one himself and pierced it expertly with a spike. The trinket, Mike noted, had a gold handle. It was attached to a watch chain, besides Phi Beta Kappa and Omicron Delta Kappa keys.

"Ralph Pailey tells me he didn't have a chance to update you on how we're organized."

"Not yet, Dr. Melcher."

"You know, of course, that New Salem Memorial's been leased to a corporation, of which I'm president."

"Do you operate as a group clinic?"

"We considered that method and decided against it. Group practice tends to create hard feelings among outsiders when it takes over a whole hospital. Inevitably, the doctor who hasn't joined complains that group patients get better care than his own. It's also said—with some justice—that beds are hard to find at short notice."

"I can see your point," said Mike. "It's a problem I didn't encounter in California."

The director of New Salem Memorial studied the ash on his cigar. The smile had been replaced by a frown that was too well bred to be called a scowl.

"Practice at this level is somewhat different," he said. "We decided we'd get better results by forming an eight-man board. All of us are doctors except Ralph Pailey. We guarantee operating expenses, and open our doors to all qualified physicians. Since we're in complete charge, we can expand our medical coverage at an hour's notice. Our acceptance of County Hospital patients is a case in point. All Ralph needed was your presence to make the contract valid."

Perceiving the flattery, Mike had no choice but to accept it. "I'm sure your surgical facilities are adequate."

"Physical equipment isn't the whole story. I'm tremendously relieved to have a highly trained surgeon on hand. Without you, I'd never have taken over the County list."

"Couldn't your present staff do the job, if need be?"

"Most of us have more practice now than we can handle, Dr. Constant. A number of New Salem g.p.'s do surgery, of course; it's the rule these days, when no big-city center is nearby. Two of these men are members of our group."

"How near are they to certification?"

"For the past year they've been assembling their qualifications for the College of Surgeons. Naturally, approval of New Salem Memorial by the Joint Committee would speed their acceptance."

"I take it you mean the Joint Committee on Accreditation of Hospitals."

"The examining board of the American College of Physicians, the American College of Surgeons, the American Hospital Association, and the A.M.A." Melcher rolled the resounding titles on his tongue as though he enjoyed their flavor. "Having you in charge of surgery should do a great deal to clear the way."

"Meanwhile, I'm to look after your county patients—and take over anything that's too complicated for the others to handle?"

"That's about it, Doctor. We won't bother you with routine stuff. There'll be a fee each time you're called in as a consultant; Pailey will collect it and credit it to your account. When patients start coming to you on their own, you'll receive those fees as private practice."

"It sounds like a workable routine." Mike tried to strike an enthusiastic note—and knew his voice was too dry to be quite convincing. He was relieved that the director, absorbed in his recital, had accepted the remark at face value.

"All of us have been happy in our three-year association," he said. "Of course Zeagler's factory personnel has been our backlog from the start."

"Don't you get Old Town patients?"

"Not so many as we'd have liked, while the County Hospital was operating. You're a New Salem boy, Doctor. You know how slow these Hudson River communities are to welcome newcomers—especially when they've existed on a one-industry base for centuries. From now on, of course, the Old Town must come to us if it means to stay healthy. There isn't another hospital within twenty miles, except Dr. Coxe's place—and he's on the verge of retirement." Melcher took a typed form from his desk drawer. "Here's a permanent contract, dated to expire one year from today. It will supplement the tentative letter of agreement you signed in California. Look it over, and let me know if you find it in order. Have you seen your quarters?"

"Not yet. I've been visiting in pathology, with Dr. Garstein."

The flicker of annoyance that passed over Melcher's face was fleeting but definite. "Louis Garstein's quite a fellow."

"I've already made that discovery, Dr. Melcher."

"A bit warped, of course, because of his disability. But he's a capable man, in both the lab and the operating room. We're extremely lucky to have him." Melcher rose from his desk. "Take your time about settling in, please. We have you down for emergency duty tonight, but there aren't many cases, as a rule."

The interview was ended. It had been pleasant, instructive—and entirely friendly. Mike could not explain why it had left him unsatisfied. He stifled a feeling of uneasiness while he crossed the rotunda to meet the orderly who would take him to his quarters. A new job always contained elements of trial and error: his own specialty, by its very nature, was more exacting than most. . . . He held out his hand to the orderly, pleased by the man's firm grip, his easy Southern drawl.

"You're in the east wing, Dr. Constant. I think you'll like the setup. My name's Wilson. Most everybody calls me Will."

"Are you on the surgical service too, Will?"

"I do what needs to be done, Doctor."

"How did you stray so far from Georgia?"

"It's West Virginia, Dr. Constant. I worked at the foundry, and stayed on when it folded."

The orderly led the way down an upstairs hall to a well-planned suite—a living room that opened to a terrace commanding a fine view of the valley, with a bedroom and bath on its far side. There was a built-in television—and, to Mike's surprise, a small bar. His baggage and book cartons had arrived from the parking lot; he saw that Wilson had taken his suits from the Val-A-Pak and hung them in the wardrobe.

"You share the terrace with two ladies, Doctor. Miss Ford, the night supervisor; and Miss Lee—I should say, Miss Searles. All this floor is staff. You won't be lonesome."

Mike studied Wilson for a hint of hidden meaning—but found none. It was too soon for direct questions, he told himself. He had already found a useful ally in Garstein; the orderly might prove another. There were many worlds under a hospital roof—and few bridges between them.

"Thanks for the unpacking, Will. I'll see you later."

It was only when the door had closed behind the orderly that Mike saw the note propped on the desk. The spidery hand that had written his name on the envelope was still familiar. He had seen it on a hundred grocery lists he had picked up on the kitchen stoop of Rynhook.

Dear Michael Constantinos:

I am informed that you have returned to New Salem. Please call on me this afternoon at five.

Marcella Van Ryn

Mike had not expected so prompt a summons, but he did not consider refusing it. Less than an hour after his arrival at Indian Hill, he left the hospital in his car, to negotiate the steep downhill road that led from the modern highway to Bear Creek. From this point, it was only a short drive to the bridge spanning the dam that had once served the Van Ryn Foundry.

The bridge had been shaky in his youth, when he had crossed it with his delivery cart. Today, he could feel the planks rattle under his wheels, and cut his speed to a crawl before he gained the far shore. He was careful to park on the shoulder of the private road that led past the fences of the dead foundry. Beyond were the gates that opened to the estate proper. It seemed both natural and logical to make this last lap of his approach on foot, allowing a more detailed survey of the terrain.

To his surprise, the tall, wrought-iron portals were freshly painted and free of rust; the lawns had been mowed, and the once-famous boxwoods were neatly trimmed, though they had lost their resemblance to dragons and pagodas and jousting knights. Behind their screen, the turreted mansion rose against the sunset on the river. In that light, there was something primeval about its stony bulk: the square granite Gate House—where the Van Ryn factors had once dwelt—was part of that bleak image, an outpost of a special universe that obeyed no laws but its own.

There was no sign in life in either building, no obvious change save for the studio skylight in the north tower of the castle. The feeling that he was entering history by the back door persisted as Mike walked gingerly through the half-open gates. Had a helmeted pikeman sprung from the shadows to bar his path, he knew he would have turned back, without daring to state his errand. . . . Despite the chill that had descended on his spirits, he smiled when he found he was following the flagstone path that led from the driveway to the kitchen. It was time to ignore the memory pictures that surrounded him, to march beneath the porte-cochere and ascend the front steps of Rynhook.

In the doorframe, he squared his shoulders before lifting the brass knocker—a mailed fist, with the family motto above it: *Nemo me impune lacessit.* Generations of patroons, Mike thought, had fulfilled that defiance. Few of the family enemies had dared to strike at its entrenched power. Those who had dared had regretted the impulse.

The door was opened promptly by a Negro maid. Mike remembered her as a former kitchen helper—a descendant of the slaves who had made Bearclaw Point a stop on the Underground Railroad, before the Civil War.

"Good evening, Nellie."

"Come in, Doctor. Madame's in the parlor."

The son of Spiros Constantinos had been allowed only a few glimpses of the mansion's lower hall. Expecting dusty bareness, he found the massive set pieces in place—the Sargent portrait of Nicholas Van Ryn (the Duchess' husband and the last forge master), the matching painting of old Peter Van Rynsteyne, the first patroon. Ten years had not diminished the ferocity of their frowns, or the funereal gloom that surrounded them. . . . The whispering passage of a cockroach across the floorboards was the only sound that broke the silence. Nellie's instinctive move as she put her shoe on the insect set the final seal on the emptiness.

"How is Madame's health these days?" Mike's voice had dropped to a whisper. It seemed appropriate to that graveyard hush.

"Like all old folks, she has her bad days," said Nellie. "This one's been good, so far." She pushed through the tall doors that gave to Rynhook's main parlor—a huge room with a groined ceiling, baronial fireplace, and niches that had once held suits of armor. Today, the desert of parquet was barren of furniture, save for a Queen Anne armchair that stood before a television set, whose volume had been tuned down to exclude the sound. On the dark-paneled wall behind it, a pair of hunting rifles were mounted on brackets. Like the television, they seemed an anachronism in a room that belonged to another century—until Mike remembered that both Nicholas Van Ryn, and his wife, had enjoyed hunting in their younger days.

The woman who sat with her eyes on the television screen redeemed its intrusion. Marcella Van Ryn, Mike reminded himself, was now well over seventy—and the light streaming through the uncurtained casements did nothing to disguise her age. Her hair was done in a pompadour that belonged to another era; the serenely proud face beneath it was timeless. She was still wearing the widow's weeds she had put on at her husband's death—and continued to wear, so town gossip went, in penance for the wastrel that same husband had sired. Mike knew she had chosen their meeting place deliberately. He wondered if he should ask Nellie for a chair—but the girl had vanished, with the ease of a phantom that could move through walls at will.

"Come in, Michael Constantinos," said the Duchess of Rynhook—and her voice had all of the deep resonance he recalled so vividly. "I'll never understand why your father shortened his name."

"He always said no one at the bank could spell it."

"Even as a boy, you were brash as they come. I can see you haven't changed."

"Nor have you, madame." The salutation came to his lips without thought. Van Ryn servants had always used the formal address; the grocer's son had only echoed it.

Marcella Van Ryn cut off the television set with a flick of gnarled fingers. When Mike had last seen those hands, they had blazed with jewels: there had been diamond pendants in the Duchess' ears, and an emerald choker to hide her wattles. Today, the bareness of that parchment-yellow hand put another footnote to the story of Rynhook.

"At this hour," she said, "it soothes me to see the world march by —from a safe distance. That's why I bought this absurd machine. Naturally, I only *watch* the people it brings me. I can't bear the sounds they make." Her eyes left the screen, to move in Mike's direction at last. For a moment more, she stared at him in silence, as though she could not quite believe in his presence. "I'm not offering you a chair, Michael. If memory serves, you've yet to sit down in my house."

"Never, madame." Knowing the slight had been deliberate, Mike kept his temper. Already, he was beginning to enjoy the welcome discovery that the mistress of Rynhook seemed in reasonable possession of her wits.

"I sent my summons an hour ago," said the Duchess. "Apparently you received it promptly."

"The moment I arrived, madame."

"It's true, then? You're the latest employee of that Jew named Zeagler? The man who bought my pasture, after it went for taxes?"

"I work for the hospital—not for Mr. Zeagler."

Marcella Van Ryn dismissed the correction with a wave of her hand. "You realize he's using you as an entree to Rynhook? That he hopes to bore from within? To persuade me to sell my land?"

"If you're willing, madame, Mr. Zeagler would like to make peace. To work with you to help New Salem—"

"The Van Ryns can have no further contact with Zeagler. He will never enter this house while I live—or set foot on foundry land. He persuaded my son to marry his daughter. That was insult enough."

"Do you think the marriage was arranged?"

"I'm sure of it, Michael. So sure that I did my best to have it annulled." Again the Duchess dismissed a digression with an impatient flick of her fingers. "Not that I asked you here to discuss a family feud. How long are you going to work at the hospital?"

"I'm about to sign a year's contract."

"Did you come home, hoping to marry Sandra West?"

The question seemed ingenuous—but Mike answered it carefully. "At the moment, I have no marriage plans."

"That's a pity. You're the sort who should have a wife and children. Why don't you pocket your pride and ask her?"

"I'd oblige you if I could. Unfortunately, Sandra wants no part of me." Wondering if the Duchess had already heard the story of his encounter on the Overlook, Mike was careful to say no more.

"You're here to practice medicine, then? There's no other reason?"

"None, madame. A long time ago you advised me to make the most of myself. I've done my best to follow your suggestion."

The eyes under the massive pompadour studied Mike keenly: they seemed bright and cloudy by turns—like a wild-bright sky in March. "It's good to have you back, Michael. Even if you don't marry Sandra. I may need your help later. Promise me you'll come at once, if I send for you?"

"As a doctor? Or a citizen of the Old Town?"

"As a native son. Never as an employee of that man Zeagler."

"I've told you I'm employed by the hospital."

"Keep that distinction in mind. I may never require your services—or I may need them tomorrow. I'll expect you at once, when I send for you."

"Was I ever late with your groceries, madame?"

"Never, Michael. I'm sure I can depend on you. In the meantime, tell Zeagler that my door remains closed. His daughter forced her way in, six years ago. I've learned to accept her presence, so long as she remains upstairs. There will be no more intruders. *You* will be admitted, if I have need of you. So will Artemus Coxe. I think that is all I have to say."

The parchment-yellow hand lifted in a gesture of dismissal, before it made contact with the tuning knob of the television. As he tiptoed from the room, Mike stole a glance at the screen. The Duchess of Rynhook was watching a soundless ball game at Yankee

Stadium, her lips curled in a faint smile at a spectacle beyond her ken.

When he had closed the doors of the double parlor, Mike paused to collect his thoughts. Already, the interview seemed a figment of his imagination. He was still puzzling over the Duchess' reason for summoning him, when he heard his name spoken in the dusk-dimmed hall—and realized a figure had detached itself from the shadows.

"May I talk to you for a moment, doctor?"

The girl was tall and blond; she was wearing a maroon-red housecoat—and she swayed, ever so slightly, before she gave him her hand.

"I've been at the keyhole," she admitted. "I'm Anna Van Ryn."

He had not expected to meet Paul's wife this easily. Nor had he pictured a woman so untouched by the eroding side effects of life at Rynhook. Then, as they moved under the great fanlight of the door-frame, he saw that Anna Van Ryn was balanced (like all expert drinkers) on the hairline that divides lucidity from open intoxication. The flushed cheeks, the too-bright eyes were part of that general euphoria. So was her smile when she crossed the foyer—and opened a wall panel, to reveal a compact elevator shaft.

"My contribution to Paul's welfare begins here," she said. "I don't like stairs—nor does he. Will you join me in a drink, Doctor?"

"I'm due at the hospital in another hour."

"Then you'll have time to spare. You must have been badly confused by what you've just seen and heard. Perhaps I can shed a little light."

The lift was just large enough for two. Anna Van Ryn did not speak while it rose smoothly to the top story of the mansion—but there was no sense of strain in her silence. When the door slid back on well-oiled casters, she stepped out briskly—then stood aside to give Mike an unimpeded view of a small but beautifully furnished living room. The contrast to the haunted bareness downstairs was startling.

"How long has *this* been part of Rynhook?"

"Since Paul brought me here—after our wedding trip. My father insisted on building us separate quarters, before he'd consent to the marriage. It was his present to us both." Anna led the way through a bijou dining room, and opened a french door to a terrace commanding a panoramic sweep of the Hudson.

"I thought Paul used the tower as a studio."

"He does. This is part of the old servants' wing. I had it roach- and ratproofed when I put in the lift." She moved to a side door and listened at the keyhole, her lips framed in a mischievous smile. "Paul's at his easel—and it's going well. If it weren't, he'd be cursing like a trooper."

"I'm not sure I should be here uninvited."

"*I* invited you, Dr. Constant. And this is my home." Anna moved to a bar in a corner of the dining room, filled her own glass without measuring, and poured bourbon on ice for Mike. He was careful not to question this impromptu hostess again while she led the way to her terrace, settled in a canvas chair, and motioned him to another.

"I promised to explain what goes on downstairs, didn't I?"

"Tell me first how you managed these changes?"

"The Duchess complained bitterly, of course—but my wish was still law to Paul. For once, he faced her down and had his way."

"Does she come here?"

"It's been a long time since she's left the ground floor, Doctor. She broke her hip five years ago, and Dr. Coxe advised her to move as little as possible. Nellie takes good care of her: she won't let me hire a nurse. When that downstairs panel closes, she can pretend I don't exist."

"What about Paul?"

"He visits her daily, like a dutiful son and heir. Not that there's much to inherit beside the land. Her trust fund dies with her; it's barely enough for her creature comforts. I pay Nellie's salary, and keep up the grounds. I can't risk doing more. The Duchess doesn't notice much these days—what she *does* observe, she sees clearly."

"Would you call today a lucid interval?"

"You're the doctor, not I."

"She seemed in possession of her faculties. I can't say that she made too much sense."

"Why should she bother to make sense? She has the past for company."

"No mind can live in the past and survive."

"The Duchess has done nicely so far—with some lapses. Besides, she has her son to console her."

"How can *you* bear to go on living here?"

Anna Van Ryn drained her glass. "Life in this tower isn't so bad as it seems. As you see, I have my special consolation. I'm sure you've already heard me described at some length. Are you too startled at what you see?"

"Frankly, I didn't realize Paul was so lucky."

"I'm not sure that's a compliment, Doctor—but I'll take it as one. What do they call me in the Old Town?"

Mike smiled down at his glass. "Don't forget I only arrived this afternoon."

"The heir's wife, who spits snakes at her mother-in-law? The long-suffering millionaire's daughter, who thinks her artist-husband can do no wrong? Or the spineless lush, who won't stand up for her rights? There's some truth in all those slanders."

"I won't accept the last."

"You will if you stay in New Salem much longer," said Anna Van Ryn. "Get me another whiskey, please—without water." She lay back in her chair, with her eyes on the river, while Mike went to the bar. The voice that pursued him was still firm—and as clear cut as its owner's thoughts. "I don't often have a chance to speak my mind. You deserve the full treatment, since you're in my father's camp."

"Don't put me there too soon," Mike warned. "So far, I'm committed to nothing—except a year at the hospital."

"You'll fight this war on all fronts, Dr. Constant—and you'll be on the Zeagler side. I learned that much at the downstairs keyhole." Anna took her glass from his hand, grimacing at the size of the drink he had poured her. "Shall I take up the pictures New Salem's drawn of me, and explain what's behind them?"

"Please do."

"First, the wife who hates her mother-in-law. That one's both true and false. I *did* hate the Duchess, for the way she's borne down on Paul. Once I'd settled in here, I found she had her reasons. She's convinced he'll be a great man someday, once he's developed his talent. She's tried to shield him from the world—to provide the right climate for creation."

"Do you mean his talent as an artist?"

"I do, Doctor. Are you beginning to see why she permitted me to give him this tower studio?"

"Do you share her belief?"

"It's all that's kept me here—plus the fact I still love him. It excuses everything. His fits of temper. The way he leaves me for distractions outside—"

"Does his mother know of those distractions?"

"He never leaves Rynhook—until she has what Nellie calls her bad days. At those times, she remembers nothing. Paul can take off when he likes."

"With no protest from you?"

"I've given up protests long ago. Like his mother, I'm sure his work will be recognized someday. Our belief is more important than the fact he's ceased to love me—if he ever did."

"You've given him six years of your life. What has he accomplished so far?"

"A great deal. You'll find one of his paintings above the mantel."

Anna Van Ryn did not stir while Mike opened the glass door to the living room, and touched a light switch to illuminate the picture that hung there. At first glance, it seemed only a wild splash of color, exploded on canvas by a tool stronger than a brush. To Mike, the whorls of paint were pure abstractions—and yet, as he continued to study the painting, he admitted to a genuine stir of emotion, a quickening of the pulses from a cause he could not yet define.

"What does it say to you, Doctor?"

He turned with a start, to find his hostess swaying in the terrace doorway. Seeking to put his feeling into words, he could only grope for phrases.

"It stirs me," he admitted finally. "I can't tell you why."

"Nor could I," said Anna. "Paul's in another world when he paints. I couldn't join him there, even if he'd let me. Sometimes, when I've had a great deal to drink, I feel I might understand his canvases, if I really tried. So far, I've been much too afraid."

"Of what?"

"Of what I'd find—if my husband and I could communicate."

"Forgive my rudeness, but can you be sure this painting is art?"

"I *feel* it, with all my senses. Isn't that enough?"

Anna, Mike reflected, had expressed his own reaction perfectly. One could smell and taste those wild whorls of color—and he knew, in his heart, it was the taste and smell of evil.

"Has he shown his work to experts?"

"Not yet. Sometimes I think he never will."

"The gossip was right when it said you were long-suffering."

"Don't think that's why I drink, Dr. Constant. Alcohol is only a drug to ease the pain of my own failure."

"Just how have you failed?"

"First, as an actress. I spent years at the Academy—and fell on my face, when I tried out in a show with Jason West. You must have heard that story too."

"Your father mentioned it."

"I thought I'd lived that fiasco down when I married Paul. I told myself I could at least help an artist, even if I could never be one."

"Surely you've done that."

"I've given him a studio—and put a door between him and his mother. But don't think, for one moment, that he wants me for myself." Anna had moved to the terrace rail. With an impulsive sweep of her right arm, she flung her empty glass into space.

"Have you thought of divorce?"

"Sometimes—when he's left me for weeks, and I can guess just where he's gone. Then he comes back, swears he can't paint again without me—and we go on as before."

"You just said he didn't need you for yourself."

"Needing me as a wife is one thing. I'm still useful as a buffer, when the Duchess begins rampaging."

"You still haven't explained why she sent for me."

"Will you settle for *noblesse oblige*?" Anna asked.

"The chatelaine of Rynhook, keeping track of her subjects? You could be right."

"Of course you were summoned for a practical reason. Dr. Coxe is getting old. She'll want a younger doctor handy when she faces a real crisis here. A man who'll come running when he's called—"

"What does *crisis* imply?"

Anna moved to the bar for a fresh drink. She was weaving now, but her tongue had not slurred a syllable. "I don't care to answer that, Doctor—for the same reason I refuse to lose myself in Paul's painting."

"I've promised to help the Duchess, if I can. Would you be offended, if I made you the same offer?"

"You've helped me already," said Anna. "Twenty minutes ago, when I spied on you downstairs, you were a stranger. You could have been an enemy—sent here by my father to spy on my marriage."

"You know better now."

"Yes, Mike. I'm going to call you that, since I'm sure we'll be friends."

"Please do, Anna."

Paul's wife had moved closer. He saw that her eyes were filled with the facile tears that are a frequent by-product of alcohol. When she put a hand on his shoulder, there was no mistaking the appeal in her heartbroken smile. Resisting the impulse to comfort her with something as dangerous as a caress, he turned toward the lift panel, with a murmured word of good-by.

Seconds later, he was glad he had restrained that all-too-human impulse. Across the living room, the studio door had just opened. Paul Van Ryn stood on the threshold.

The artist wore a paint-daubed smock and carried a palette knife —poised, like a conductor's baton, in his hand. His brows were knitted in a frown Mike would ponder later. It was gone at once, replaced by the tentative smile one offers an unexpected visitor whose name one does not remember. When Paul spoke, his voice was a model of well-bred surprise.

"Sorry, Anna. I didn't know we had a caller."

"Surely you remember Mike Constant." If Anna realized Paul's pretense was deliberate, she gave no sign. The presence of her husband in the room had aged her visibly. Her shoulders drooped—and she stared down at her drink as though her dearest wish was to drown there.

"Of course—the new doctor at the hospital." Paul was crossing the room to offer his hand. "Welcome to New Salem."

Forcing the handshake, Mike controlled a mounting anger. Incredible as it was, he knew this monstrous egotist had blotted their earlier encounter from his mind—along with the sorry part he had played.

"I'm hardly a newcomer here—"

Paul had already turned to his wife, with the air of a man trapped in a situation he cannot explain with logic.

"Dr. Constant has probably told you we were classmates at Cornell. I hardly expected him to remind me. I'm still the nobody he left behind ten years ago. *He's* our returning hero."

Mike could not help admiring the other man's aplomb. He could hear the grudging acceptance in his tone, when he forced himself to answer in kind.

"As they say in the Navy, there's no need to apply the grease."

Paul laughed. There were urbane overtones in his mirth, a charm an outsider would have accepted without question.

"Does this mean you accept a mere artist as your equal? Even when he has yet to do a stroke of honest toil—as the word is used among the Philistines?"

Mike saw he must force the issue, if he meant to pin this quicksilver personality to earth. Anna, it was evident, had decided to withdraw from the contest. She had wandered to the far side of the room, devoting full attention to the fresh drink she was pouring.

"I've been visiting downstairs with Madame Van Ryn," he said quietly.

Paul nodded: his bright-eyed stare was unwavering. "That's as it should be in New Salem. The Van Ryns and the Constantinos are definitely Old Town—"

"May I have a few minutes with you—now I've come this far?"

"Of course. Shall I make us a drink?"

"I have mine now," said Anna. Her voice, Mike noted, was muted to the vanishing point; her whole being seemed concentrated on the need to leave the room. "If you'll both excuse me, I'll see about dinner." She left in haste. A few seconds later, the crash of a falling pan announced her arrival in the kitchen.

"Pay her no mind," said Paul. "It's part of her make-believe to pretend she's tight—when she really isn't. She'll prepare an excellent dinner, and serve it promptly. Can I persuade you to join us?"

"Thank you, no." By now, Mike found that he could almost match Paul's airy manner. "Shall we talk here, or on the terrace?"

The artist glanced toward the kitchen. "The terrace would be better, I think." He moved toward the french door, then stood back courteously to let his visitor precede him. "Not that I mind if my wife listens. There's little I can tell you she doesn't already know." He led the way to the far end of the terrace, and sat down on the balustrade. "Fire away, Mike."

"Why did you pretend I was a stranger?"

"To test your reaction," said Paul. "In your place, I'd have been much angrier."

"You made the same pretense on the Overlook."

"I was a bit unnerved, there. As you saw, I had good cause."

"Sandra has told me the sort of game you've been playing with her. Must you go on pretending?"

It was the first score. Mike was sure of it when he saw the red glow in Paul Van Ryn's eyes, the tightening of his too-handsome mouth. The flash of rage was short. While it lasted, it had been less than human.

"I'm hardly surprised that Sandra's made you her confidant," he said. "You were created to serve as some woman's wailing wall. Were you offering Anna your shoulder to cry on, when I came in? Or was that only her six-o'clock hysterics?"

Mike pressed hard upon the balustrade—before his fist could crash into that smiling mouth. "You might answer my question first."

"To be perfectly candid—I'm not at all pleased to find you in New Salem. When I saw you on the Overlook, in your usual role of hero, I liked your presence even less."

"You'll admit I saved Sandra's life?"

"True enough—with substantial help from me. Unfortunately, our rescue apparatus forced me to hoist you both. Otherwise, I'd have dropped you without a qualm." Paul's easy grin had lost none of its power. "I hope Sandra wasn't too badly hurt."

"A broken radius, and a small head wound. She'll recover from *those* injuries fast enough."

"But not from the heart wound I've inflicted?"

"Try answering that yourself."

Paul shrugged. "When my own welfare's at stake, I refuse to wrestle with moral issue. I suggest you adopt that philosophy, and cease intruding."

"Have I intruded, so far?"

"In the worst way. First, at the cliff's edge. Second, in the parlor downstairs—where you never set foot as a delivery boy."

"I was invited by your mother."

"Never mind your credentials. I'm warning you, in the strongest terms, to keep out of my way."

"Sandra expects you to marry her—if your wife divorces you."

"Of course she does. My alliance with the Zeaglers interrupted our affair six years ago. It seemed the easiest way to eat my cake and have it too."

"Then you admit that you were lying?"

"Why not? You see, I'm in the enviable position of having both a wife—*and* a part-time mistress. Each of them loves me to distraction, and both accept my lies as gospel."

"Does your wife know about Sandra?"

"Anna is an understanding soul—and a submissive one. She realizes a creator can't obey the laws of the herd."

Mike turned his eyes toward the sunset light on the Hudson. Had he faced that placid smile a moment more, his control would have snapped.

"Even if you are a genius—and it's yet to be proved—you're abusing your privileges."

"By your code—not by mine. You see, I *have* no code—no rules, beyond the moment's need. When I want a certain tone on a canvas, I blend paint to suit my fancy. When I need a woman to distract me, I take her."

"I'm going to keep you from taking Sandra."

"Believe me, Mike, I'm leaving her in peace tonight. In fact, I'll promise to stay clear, until she sends for me."

"Don't be too sure she will."

"She'll regret our quarrel, long before that broken arm has healed. When she does, she'll try to phone me—that's always her first maneuver. I won't be here to receive the call. By midnight, I'll be in New York."

"Will your mother let you go?"

Paul accepted the mocking question easily. "I know the Duchess' emotional timetable perfectly. After the shock of seeing *you* again, she's bound to slip over the border."

"I could repeat this conversation to Sandra."

"You could—but you won't. Even with your romantic notions about women, you know she won't listen."

Mike had long since realized that Paul had prolonged this encounter for his own enjoyment. One possible way remained to crack his armor.

"I'm sure that *you* are too divorced from reality to hear what I'm saying." He breathed deep, and forced himself to speak slowly. "It's still my duty to warn you that you're a sick man—"

"Really, Dr. Constant?"

"Yes, Paul. The sort of psychotic who should be certified."

Again, he caught the quick, hot light in Paul's eyes, as though a furnace door had opened in his brain. When he shrugged off the attack, his armor was in place again.

"I've been called worse names in my time, Mike. Your diagnosis doesn't impress me."

"The pattern's complete. It explains every move you've made, since you fouled your first man in high-school football. It explains your way of life in this haunted house—including those cyclones of paint above your mantelpiece. You're living in the shadow of paranoia. Do you know what the word means?"

"I've a vague idea, Doctor. As I told you, I've been called mad in several languages."

"The shadow will deepen, if you don't submit to psychiatric treatment. Already, it's blighted two women's lives; I'm sure it's hastened your mother's decline. Don't wait until it destroys you as well."

Mike left the terrace without pausing for a reply. In the living room, he pressed the lift button with all his strength until the panel opened; it was the only compensation for the iron self-control that had kept his hands from Paul Van Ryn's throat. . . . Just in time, he remembered the palette knife the artist had brought from his studio, but he refused to turn. When he entered the elevator, his body was still braced for a blow that had not come.

A final shock awaited him in the lower hall.

In the lift, he had had time to be ashamed of his outburst, to curse the too-quick temper that had made him forget a doctor's duty to keep silent, when dealing with a disease he cannot cure. The downstairs hall was thick with dusk. For an instant, he was positive the huddled shape on the parlor doorsill was another, deeper shadow, that its sobs were an echo in his still-heated brain. Then, as he drew closer, he saw the weeping figure was Marcella Van Ryn.

Nellie had rolled a wheel chair from the parlor before Mike could reach the door. She lifted the Duchess of Rynhook by the armpits and settled her in the chair, as casually as though she were the crumpled doll she resembled.

"Dr. Coxe tole you not to walk, by yourself, madame," she said. "Why you run from Nellie when it's bedtime?"

Mike found his voice. "Does she need help?"

"No, Doctor. Once she takes her medicine, she'll sleep like a baby."

"Who's that stranger in the hall?" The doll in the wheel chair had

almost screamed the word. Mike took another step forward, but Nellie waved him off.

"It's Dr. Constant, madame."

"Nonsense. There's no Dr. Constant in New Salem. I know him now. It's Michael Constantinos, from the market on Lower Street. He's just delivered the groceries. Give him a quarter."

The tableau held. A coin changed hands as Mike held out his palm above the armchair. He did not need Nellie's warning gesture to leave Rynhook, at a walk that was almost a run.

FOUR

Driving down the southbound thruway at a speed well above the legal limit, Mike breathed deeply of the fresh night air—and waited for the tumult in his brain to settle. Reason returned at one level when he saw the food-and-fuel sign ahead, remembered he had not eaten for several hours, and turned in for hamburger and coffee. While he ate, he told himself it would have been wiser to dine at the hospital and cement new contacts. Until he could sort out the revelations at Rynhook—and convince himself that the warring phantoms he had met there were flesh and blood—he was in no mood for contact with his fellow man.

A half hour later, when he had retraced his route, he was calm enough.

Paul Van Ryn, he told himself grimly, remained an unpredictable menace—but Paul would depart for New York tonight, now that Sandra was beyond his reach and the Duchess had retired to her private world. Warped though Paul might be—and Mike had meant every word of his warning—he was sure his diagnosis had registered in the man's sick brain. Sandra would be safe, with more than a hundred miles between them—and he could plan ways to protect her before Paul's return.

Dr. Coxe was away when Mike stopped at the cottage hospital on Lower Street—but Mrs. Bramwell reported that Sandra was resting quietly, with an ampoule of Demerol to insure a sound night's sleep. He was crossing the reception room when a visitor emerged from the corridor, en route to the porch that opened to the street. The room was dimly lighted, but Mike had a quick impression of debility—a sharp contrast to the man's almost-youthful clothes and the Malacca cane he carried. The sagging shoulders and uncertain gait completed a picture of near collapse. As Mike watched from the office doorway, the visitor swayed violently, and saved himself from falling with both hands braced on a chair back.

"Can I help you, sir?"

"Thank you, no. Whatever help you could offer is too late."

The orotund sentence had been declaimed rather than spoken; the Malacca stick had already lifted, like a knight's lance, to hold Mike off. Even with the cane between them, the gust of alcohol that reached the surgeon's nostrils was overpowering. *This is your night for drunks and demons,* he told himself—and pushed the cane aside to ease the man to an armchair.

"Catch your breath, Mr. West."

"You know me?"

"I recognized your voice at once."

Jason West rested a leonine head against the faded antimacassar of the armchair. In the half-light, he resembled his own death mask —but Mike was not seriously alarmed. Sandra's brother, it seemed, was a performer who made no real distinction between the footlights and the everyday.

"I'm grateful for your recognition," said the actor. "It's cheering to find that one's public still exists—even in this unlikely corner. Were you surprised to find me still among the living?" He swept on, without awaiting an answer. "Of course, I use the word advisedly. At this moment, I am drunk as well as dying, so the thought of tomorrow is endurable. *The stag at eve had drunk his fill,* as Sir Walter would have it—though he had more salubrious waters in mind."

"May I take you home?"

"Again, the answer is no. By the way, who are you?"

"Dr. Michael Constant."

"The man who saved my sister's life. I have just been in her hospital room, to admire your handiwork. Fortunately, she was too deeply drugged to note my presence."

Unwilling to leave while Sandra's brother seemed unable—or unwilling—to rise from the armchair, Mike let the rich, well-modulated voice roll on. He tried, with no success, to avoid staring. As a boy, he had admired that now-ravaged profile from a gallery seat. He had seen the same profile (older but still handsome) on a score of movie screens, on a television serial that had once enjoyed the highest rating of its network. . . . It was a grotesque trick of time that this declamatory figure should be the Jason West he remembered.

"You're sure you don't need help, sir?"

"Help, Dr. Constant? Why should I need help, when my course is so clearly charted?"

"I'll call Mrs. Bramwell—"

"Bring me water, please. I have my own medicine, and it isn't what you think."

When Mike brought a paper cup from the hall cooler, Jason West was waiting with a tablet on his palm. Even on the edge of oblivion, he managed to swallow it with a flourish. Minutes later, the color had returned to his cheeks, and his eyes had cleared. He seemed ten years younger, and almost jaunty.

"As you see, Doctor, there are other sovereign remedies besides alcohol. Don't ask me to give this one a name; a cardiac man in Hollywood prescribed it when I could still afford such expert attention. And please don't tell my sister I visited her bedside in my deplorable state. Only that I asked for her, and was pleased by your report."

"I'll be glad to take you to the Gate House."

"There is no need. My car is outside, my indisposition is behind me—and I'm en route to an appointment."

"Shall I follow, to make sure you arrive safely?"

Jason West shook his head. It was a tragedian's gesture, made in the grand manner.

"You are the sworn enemy of the individual I am meeting, Doctor. The appointment I mention is in Samarra."

"I hope you'll defer it tonight."

"Perhaps I will, Dr. Constant. I may even decide to lie in wait and shoot Paul Van Ryn through the heart. If I did, would you applaud the deed?" Once more, the magnificent voice swept on, before Mike could answer. "The answer's no, of course. Your task is to heal, not to destroy. Even when the destruction would benefit the human race—to say nothing of the honor of its women. Do we agree on that item, at least?"

The actor had risen with the query, his cane raised in a parody of a fencer's *en garde*. Mike found himself chuckling at the pose. A moment ago, he would not have believed that Jason West could lift his spirits.

"We're in complete agreement—though I can't admit it officially."

"Set your conscience at rest, then. Much as I'd enjoy the result—in the case of the Rynhook cad—I lack the courage to cause his death. Just as I lack the courage to go on living. May I wish you good night, on that note of paradox?"

The cane-turned-sword thrashed upward, in a swift thrust and parry. With the motion, it became a walking stick again. Whirling it gaily, the actor vanished into the darkness.

It was nearly eight when Mike left his car in the doctors' parking lot on Indian Hill. Melcher and Garstein had long since departed, and Pailey's computers were locked behind their grilles until morning. With a single lamp burning above its entrance desk, and its corridors wrapped in shadows, New Salem Memorial seemed a replica of the world the new staff surgeon had left in California. Tonight, it was sheer relief to don a white coat again, to take the report of the three-to-eleven supervisor and check the technicians' notes in the clinical lab. . . . When he started his rounds, Mike knew there would be little time for soul searching until morning.

He began on the lowest floor of the hospital, a partial basement because of the steep pitch of Indian Hill. In most hospitals, the area would have been used for storage. Here, the long, low-ceilinged room had been converted into a ward, to accommodate the newly arrived County patients. Mike saw that not an inch of space had been wasted. Ventilation was by window fans, and beds and furnishings were obvious war surplus—but he could find no real fault with these economies. Already, he had realized he must accept a standard of service quite different from his experience.

The ward attendant was a licensed practical nurse, judging by the LPN on her cap, but with a capable supervisor on the floor above he could hardly criticize the delegation of authority. In most small hospitals, he knew, such nurses had taken over many of the tasks once performed by the more rigorously trained RN—now in woefully short supply and badly needed for more important duties.

Noting with approval the reassuring odor of pine-oil antiseptic, Mike began a bed check of the County patients who had arrived in the day's transfer. None of the cases was serious: the charts showed him that accepted practices were being followed in the treatment of three heart patients, a pair of postoperative varicose vein cases, a broken rib cage, and several admissions for jaundice. In the female ward, he examined a fractured hip, now in its fourth week of bed rest. The X-ray films in the chartroom showed the break had been nailed none too expertly—but the patient was mending and could soon be transferred to a wheel chair.

On the private surgical floor above, he was surprised to find that at least half of the patients were postoperative abdominal cases. Before he could complete his rounds, he had counted ten hysterectomies, six hernias, and five appendectomies. Each of the operative histories was remarkable for its brevity—and almost every prognosis indicated the patient would be discharged in record time.

Only one case could be called critical—a gastroenterostomy, performed by a Dr. Bradford Keate, who had admitted his patient for a duodenal ulcer. Reviewing the surgeon's curt summary, Mike attached a reminder to question the director in the morning. Dr. Keate's procedure had been largely abandoned in favor of subtotal stomach resection—or, in some cases, vagus nerve cutting, with plastic enlargement of the pylorus. Both these approaches, though more serious, had proved much more effective.

All in all, the new staff surgeon concluded, bed care and surgical techniques at New Salem Memorial were not too much below average—though the facilities at the disposal of nurses and orderlies had been held to an absolute minimum. The most serious fault was the doctors' own write-ups of their case histories: in over a score of folders he examined, the operative descriptions, resumés, and marginal comments were sketchy to the extreme. He was too tired to read further, in an effort to pin down the worst culprits. . . . Melcher had stressed the hospital's need for the Joint Committee's seal of approval. Obviously, the files were far below the standards of that all-important reviewing board.

It had been a long day—and Mike was glad to turn out the lights in the record room and ascend to his quarters. It was a relief to slip between the sheets at a good hour, knowing that his training as intern and resident would guarantee a dreamless sleep.

When his bedside phone rang, the luminous hands of the clock stood at a few minutes past midnight.

"Dr. Constant speaking."

"This is Miss Ford, Doctor. I'm the night supervisor. We've just admitted Mrs. Van Ryn to a private room in Section Two. I think you should see her right away."

"The Duchess?" The question had been instinctive while he struggled toward wakefulness.

"No, Doctor. Mrs. *Paul* Van Ryn."

Shaking himself from sleep, Mike moved toward the hospital whites he had laid out before retiring. As always, the act of dressing was both swift and automatic. When he descended to the lower floor, Wilson was crossing the corridor with an empty wheeled stretcher.

"They brought her in by ambulance, Doctor."

"From Rynhook?"

"The maid put in the call. She's in Number Twenty-four. Looks pretty sick."

The night supervisor, a tall, gaunt figure in a fresh-starched uniform, waited at the door to the private room. Mike took instant comfort in Miss Ford's rocklike assurance. Like himself, he knew she had lived through these vigils before.

"She's in great pain, Dr. Constant—and advanced shock."

Anna Van Ryn lay on the white-counterpaned bed, her ashen face pressed hard against a pillow. Her breathing was hurried. Despite a dilation of the pupils, there was hardly a trace of alcohol on her breath. A considerable bruise beneath the left eye was her only visible injury.

"I'm sorry they brought me here, Doctor," she said. "There was no real need."

"Let's just make sure of that."

The patient attempted a smile—not too successfully, Mike noted. "It was one of those stupid accidents you can't explain afterwards. I wakened an hour ago, and couldn't sleep. The light was out in the kitchen, when I went there for a—a glass of milk. I tripped and fell down the service stairs. Nellie found me and phoned for the ambulance."

"Where is the pain?"

"Just below the ribs. I must have struck something pretty hard."

With Miss Ford's help, Mike wrapped the cuff of a sphygmomanometer around the patient's arm and began to inflate it. A clinical pattern was already forming in his mind—but he warned himself to proceed with caution, in view of Anna's seeming reluctance to help with the diagnosis.

"I'll take your blood pressure before I examine you."

The stethoscope, pressed over the brachial artery at the front of the elbow, confirmed his suspicion of the primary cause of the shock. Systolic pressure was at eighty-eight—a hurried, thready beat that warned of severe blood loss. Anna's mention of the source of her pain, plus the absence of other external evidence, told him that blood must be pouring from a broken artery or arteries, somewhere in the abdominal cavity.

At Mike's nod, Miss Ford moved forward to expose the patient's body. There were a few superficial bruises on the chest wall—but it was the abdomen that Mike studied first, noting the failure of the muscles to move with respiration, and the way they tensed when his exploring fingers merely brushed the skin. There was a patch of discolored flesh just below the left side of the rib cage. He was not surprised to hear Anna's gasp of pain when he touched it.

A second exploration with the stethoscope assured him that lung function was still normal, the heartbeat steady, though very rapid.

"Did Paul leave for New York?" he asked casually.

"He drove down earlier this evening." Anna had still refused to meet his eyes. Her whole being seemed concentrated on the need to suppress further evidence of pain.

"Your father's flying to Europe tonight. Is there any way I can reach him?"

"I'm afraid not. He's already en route."

"What about your stepmother?"

"They left Idlewild together, Doctor. Is this something *bad*? It seems to be only a bruise."

"I will have to operate immediately," he said. "You have a serious internal injury—a rupture of the spleen. The hemorrhage must be stopped, but I'll need your permission to proceed—since I can't reach Paul, or your parents."

"What if I refuse it?"

Mike looked across the bed at the night supervisor. "Dr. Garstein is the patient's uncle, Miss Ford," he said. "Will you ask him to come at once, for an emergency?" He did not speak again until the nurse had hurried from the room. "I don't think you quite understand the situation. Your spleen is ruptured, and you're losing ground rapidly. Unless we operate, you'll die."

"Suppose that's what I want, Doctor?"

"I won't listen to such nonsense. Idlewild will give me your father's flight number; I can reach his plane by radio."

"Don't do that, please. He has a heart condition. The shock might kill him."

"Will the shock be any less—if I let you die?"

Anna's eyes met his directly, for the first time. Reading the stark terror there, he was sure now of its cause.

"Do what you wish, Dr. Constant," she said. "You have my permission."

Miss Ford appeared in the doorway. "Dr. Garstein's on the phone."

When Mike took up the receiver in the hall, the lab man's voice seemed oddly detached. It was almost as though he had anticipated the summons.

"You're sure of this diagnosis, Mike?"

"Positive. How soon can you be here?"

"In fifteen minutes."

"How do I get to your blood bank?"

There was a short pause on the wire. "We don't have one. Generally we line up donors."

"There's no time."

"We should have a few flasks of Type O in cold storage. You can use that."

"Has your niece been admitted here before?"

"This is her third accident. The others weren't so serious."

"Get over here as fast as you can. I'll start a transfusion at once."

Miss Ford was waiting outside the patient's door when Mike returned from the phone. He noted with approval that she had already stationed another nurse at the bedside. It meant that she had anticipated his next orders.

"How soon can we be ready for a splenectomy?"

"In thirty minutes, Doctor. Maybe less."

"Dr. Garstein will be here by then. Is there someone on the staff who can assist me?"

"Miss Searles usually assists our surgeons. She was off duty tonight, but I heard her come in a moment ago."

"Will you ask her to set up at once? I'll want citrate solution for an autotransfusion, if we need it. What about a scrub nurse?"

"One is always on call, Dr. Constant. I usually circulate at this hour."

"I can see you're well organized, Miss Ford. Will you give the patient an ampoule of Demerol and a hundred and fiftieth of atropine, by hypo?"

"Yes, Doctor."

"I'll want a flask of Type O blood from storage. We'll start the transfusion in the operating room."

A half-hour later, in an operating suite, his hands and forearms still tingling from their antiseptic bath, Mike surveyed his domain from the scrub-room door and found it good.

It was true that New Salem Memorial, with profit as its watchword, had cut corners; what he had seen so far, in wards and private wing, had shown that this hospital lacked much of the equipment found in the best institutions. A careful spot check had just told him that the operating theater was prepared for the task ahead—and he could see, with keen satisfaction, that his surgical team was thoroughly familiar with its job.

Lenora Searles, already gloved and gowned, was completing her sponge count at a table covered with a sterile sheet. As he watched, she began arranging a battery of instruments and dressings there, while she gave low-voiced instructions to a second nurse, who would stand beside her during the splenectomy—threading sutures and supplying sponges and pads. The surgeon's first hemostats and scalpels were already arranged on a smaller table, which would be placed across the patient's body after it was draped.

Anna Van Ryn lay in the bright cone of the operating-room lights, already half asleep from her preoperative medication. The transfusion of stored blood was going smoothly. Louis Garstein, resting on his hand braces, stood clear of the table while Miss Ford propped the patient's left side with sandbags, to give the surgeon better access to the operative area. When the preparation was completed, Garstein moved to the head of the table to start the anesthetic; his hands were swiftly competent as he placed the mask over the patient's face, twirled the controls on the tanks, and inflated the breathing bag.

"She's in fair shape," he said. "But I'd like to keep this short. She's obviously lost a lot of blood."

"I hope the transfusion's helping. It was the only Type O flask on hand."

"So Miss Ford told me. I asked for more a week ago, but Pailey's been on another economy kick. We've got a pint of plasma—and that's all."

Surgeon and anesthesiologist exchanged a grim look while Mike slipped into the gown and gloves the scrub nurse held for him. Type O blood—a class to which some forty per cent of the general population belonged—could be stored for weeks under refrigeration; it seemed incredible that an adequate supply had not been kept in stock, when no regular blood bank was available. He added another black mark to the list of complaints he would present to Dr. Melcher in the morning.

Lenora Searles passed Mike a sponge stick, with a square of gauze clamped in its jaws. Dipping it in the scarlet antiseptic solution used to sterilize the skin, he painted the patient's left lower chest and upper abdomen—using quick, smooth strokes, and applying a second layer above the first.

Sterile towels came into his hands as he outlined the rectangle where he planned to make the incision. When they were clipped in place, the surgical nurse helped him drape the entire field with a windowed sheet, centering the opening upon the scarlet-stained area exposed by the towels. At the surgeon's nod, the circulating nurse adjusted the main operating lamp until its shadowless beam was centered perfectly on the operative field. In that white glare, the bruise was much more noticeable.

Lenora Searles swung the movable instrument table across the patient's body. "I think we have everything you'll need, Doctor."

"Everything looks perfect, Miss Searles."

The nurse acknowledged the compliment with the briefest of nods; it was hard to judge her true reaction, since only her eyes and a bit of forehead showed between her mask and the nunlike hood she wore. Mike saw that she was already prepared for his first need, with a sponge in one gloved hand, a hemostat between the fingers of the other.

"I'll use a transverse incision," he said. "Scalpel, please."

The scrub nurse slapped the knife into his extended palm; he was glad to note the speed of her response. Whatever the deficiencies of New Salem Memorial might be—and the lack of a blood bank was a drastic one—its surgical department seemed well organized. Already, he could sense that its efficiency was due to the poised young woman who awaited his next order across the table.

"How's the blood pressure, Louis?"

"Stabilized at a hundred."

Mike's first knife stroke was extensive—beginning a little above and to the left of the navel and reaching to the flank. The steel bit deeply, opening skin and fat down to the tough, white-fibered fascia sheathing the muscles. Lenora Searles caught each bleeder expertly in a hemostat; as her flying fingers kept pace with the knife, she sponged the area clean, permitting the surgeon to complete the initial incision with no visible pause. In a moment more, another knife stroke bit through the fascia, to expose the reddish-muscle layers beneath.

The technique was a precise one, baring one of the two long muscle strips that lay on either side of the midline. The knife cut partially through this left-hand strip, exposing it inside its sheath to make room for the blunt, rakelike retractor Mike slipped into the wound. When he pushed the handle of this instrument toward Miss Searles, she retracted the muscle toward the midline, exposing a medium-sized blood vessel beneath it, which the surgeon clamped and cut. Bleeders of this sort were difficult to control if they got loose during a major abdominal operation. The measure was a precaution careful surgeons followed.

Working with knife and knife handle, Mike separated the grid-like layers of muscle extending across the flank and exposed the peritoneum, the lining of the abdominal cavity. Glancing at his assistant, he saw that she understood the significance of the dark, clouded look of that normally translucent membrane. It was a sure sign that the cavity beneath it was filled with blood.

"It's the spleen, all right," he said. "I'll have it in a minute, I hope. Is the patient holding up, Louis?"

"She'll do," said Garstein. "A third of the transfusion still to go."

Lenora Searles had already poised a hemostatic forcep above the wound. When Mike tented a small area of the peritoneum with a thumb forcep, she caught it with the hemostat, taking care to avoid the intestine, which could be seen clearly beneath it, moving with each of the patient's deep, snoring breaths. Mike slit a tiny opening in the membrane, then tented the peritoneum higher while he widened it.

"Catch all the blood you can when I go in," he said. "We may need it later for an autotransfusion."

Miss Searles, moving with fluent speed, lifted a basin to the edge of the incision, while the instrument nurse held another ready. Surgical scissors came into Mike's hand unasked. He slit the peritoneum in both directions, for almost the full length of the incision. The wound was now large enough to permit him to insert his whole hand into the cavity.

Dark blood welled through the opening instantly, a copious portent that advertised the extent of the hemorrhage. The surgeon held the wound wide, permitting the nurses to catch the greater part of the blood, much of which had already clotted, in the two basins.

"Put that aside for now, please. Add some of the citrate, so we'll have no more clotting." The sight of those brimming basins told its own story. They had gotten to Anna Van Ryn just in time. In another half hour, perhaps even sooner, she would have bled to death within her own body.

The rest of the approach, though delicate, was routine—and Mike followed it confidently. A self-retaining retractor opened the gaping wound still wider. Sliding his left hand beneath the rib cage, he reached for the spleen in its isolated hiding place, well beneath the left side of the diaphragm.

Normally, this organ was a wedge-shaped mass, whose function was thought to be the destruction of old red blood cells. Not necessary to life, it rarely caused trouble—except when damaged, or enlarged after some blood disorder, such as malaria. Its elusiveness, as he groped to define its shape, was a final proof of its rupture. When his fingers closed on the organ at last, it had lost its semi-fibrous consistency. Sight unseen, he could tell that it had literally exploded after a violent blow—so completely, that its remnants had the amorphous shape of a handful of crushed berries.

"It's a multiple rupture," Mike said. "I'll try to expose the pedicle."

The stalk of the spleen contained the complex of vessels that nourished it—the entering artery, the departing veins, and the ligaments that held it in place beneath the rib cage. The bleeding would cease once it was controlled—but the approach was difficult, since he was forced to depend on his left hand, while his free fingers handled the needed instruments.

"Pad, please."

A square of quilted gauze came into his hands, damply warm from the saline basin where it had been soaking. A tape was fastened to one of its corners with a metal ring—to facilitate its extraction when it had served its purpose and to remind the surgeon of its presence before he closed the incision.

"Spatula."

With the broad metal strip, he pressed hard on the pad, to expose the damaged organ—a red, pulpy mass still thick with blood. His fingers closed firmly on the pedicle, and the steady drip of blood slowed to an ooze, then ceased entirely.

"Suction, please."

The instrument Lenora Searles placed in the wound was ingenious—a metal tip, from which a length of tubing ran back to an electric pump. Before the minute hand of the operating-room clock could finish its second sweep, Mike had removed the surplus blood from the abdomen, as neatly as a vacuum-cleaning housewife.

At this point in his approach, he could see the entire field—but his eyes remained fixed on the spleen, now clearly visible in its hiding place, thanks to the gaping transverse incision. When he was sure the hemorrhage had ceased, he held out his right hand for a long-armed, racheted forcep—an instrument with an arclike curve at its end, permitting its jaws to fit naturally round the still-elusive pedicle. A second forcep was inserted to reinforce the first. When both were clamped, there was no danger of further bleeding. It was now a simple matter to cut away the blasted organ, and drop it into the basin held by the scrub nurse.

"We'll use a braided-silk ligature."

The handle of the needle holder was slapped smartly into his palm. Miss Searles steadied the two pedicle clamps while he drove the needle through the stalk, caught the point on the far side, and drew the ligature through. A double loop of the tough black thread tied off the area above the first forcep. When the instrument was out of the wound, Mike added a second and third knot, cutting the ends, but leaving a short section free. The technique was repeated behind the second forcep, an added precaution to forestall further bleeding.

"We're ready to close, Dr. Garstein."

There was no reply from the anesthesiologist. When the silence persisted, Mike broke his iron concentration on the wound to look over the wire-draped sheet separating Garstein from the sterile operating field. The tips of the stethoscope were in the other man's ears, and his hand had just moved along Anna's chest beneath the drapery. No words were needed to tell Mike that Garstein had just placed the metal disk of the instrument above the patient's heart.

Suspecting what had happened, the surgeon inserted his hand into the abdominal cavity, touching the spot where the aorta and the inferior *vena cava*—the great artery and vein controlling the blood supply to the lower half of the body—lay in front of the spinal column.

The artery had ceased its pulsation. It was a chilling warning that the heart had stopped.

Cardiac arrest was a damning term that no surgeon uttered willingly. The splenectomy had gone through without a hitch. A moment earlier, there had been no warning—however slight—that a normal circulatory system would kick back in this baffling fashion, causing the heart to cease its beating. Surgery and anesthesia, of course, were the most frequent predisposing factors. Mike had met the crisis before at the close of an operation. This was the first case when the patient was his sole responsibility—and he lacked the resources of a great medical center.

Behind the sheet, he could hear Garstein manipulate the breathing bag, an effective means of artificial respiration that increased the flow of pure oxygen to the lungs when the heart was beating. Even this vital element was useless now, since it could not reach the brain cells unless the blood stream kept moving. In a matter of minutes, lacking that essential flow, they would be damaged beyond repair.

"Drop out and get a cardiac pacemaker, Miss Searles," Mike said quietly. "Dr. Garstein will place the electrodes."

The pacemaker was an instrument that had come into use during Mike's internship, a literal shocking machine to combat cardiac arrest. Placed on the victim's chest wall, it administered rhythmic jolts of electric current that usually stimulated the heart, forcing it to contract at a tempo roughly resembling its normal rate. Mike had seen the miracle machine in action too often to doubt its value. Older methods required the surgeon to open the chest at top speed, then massage the heart under direct vision. The pacemaker, which could be connected in a moment, bypassed such Draconian remedies. Most large hospitals were equipped with the device, and the surgeon had issued the order without conscious thought.

Now, packing gauze pads into the incision to keep its contents in place, he was conscious of a stillness in the room—and looked up in time to catch the frightened dilation of Lenora Searles' pupils. It was the first emotion she had shown in his presence—save for her flash of anger at the ambulance entrance.

"We don't have a pacemaker, Mike," said Garstein. "Pailey wouldn't approve the expense."

"In that case, we'll use adrenaline. Miss Searles will help you with the injection, while I massage the heart through the diaphragm."

Wasting no time on recrimination, Mike moved round the table as he spoke, taking the nurse's place. She had already hastened to the instrument cabinet, to prepare a long, slender needle for direct penetration of the heart. From the right side of the table, it was a simple matter for the surgeon to slide his hand into the incision and feel his way upward, until his fingers touched the diaphragm—the dome of muscle that formed a flexible partition separating the abdominal and chest cavities.

While Garstein had kept Anna Van Ryn under artificial respiration, the partition had remained almost immobile; in normal breathing its contractions and relaxations created a flexible working space where the lungs could perform their function. Thanks to this immobility, the surgeon soon found the base of the heart, outlining it with his fingers through its own coating, the pericardium.

Anatomically, the heart sat upon the diaphragm, near the center of the chest cavity—like a right-angled triangle with its base and lower angle pointing to the left. Mike could have slit the diaphragm to reach the organ directly—but the immobility of the partition permitted this more conservative approach.

Wrapping a portion of the diaphragm around the heart itself, he began a rhythmic massage. Miss Searles and Garstein had already folded back the draperies to expose the patient's chest, while Miss Ford continued the steady pulsations of the oxygen bag. Working at driving speed, the anesthesiologist swabbed the chest with antiseptic, then drove the slender needle boldly downward, until the red stain in the barrel of the syringe told him it had penetrated the heart wall, and the blood-filled chamber beneath.

"Save half of it, Louis," said Mike. "And try to put it directly into the cardiac muscle. It will do more good there."

Garstein nodded—and drew the needle back slightly until no more blood spurted into the glass barrel, showing that the point was now in the heart muscle itself. Here, he injected the remainder of the adrenaline, then withdrew the needle.

"Put on fresh gloves, Miss Searles," said Mike. "I'll need your help, if I have to make a chest incision."

As he gave the order, he felt a sudden wriggle under his fingers—and knew the stalled heart, under the double stimulant of drug and massage, was attempting, however feebly, to resume its function. Automatically, he glanced up at the wall clock; he had checked it when he first touched the aorta, for time was the most precious factor in this last-ditch procedure. If present stimuli failed, he would have no choice but direct approach—either via an incised diaphragm, or through the chest wall itself.

"Still under two minutes," said Garstein. "I think she's responding."

"So do I, Louis." Mike had just felt a second contraction, and a third, each stronger than the one before.

"Are you still massaging?"

"Yes, until we're sure."

The surgeon's hand remained anchored at the diaphragm, with the apex of the heart loosely in his grasp. Only when the beat had steadied, and the rhythmic pulse of the breathing bag told him normal respiration had resumed, did he slacken his hold. Hard-won knowledge warned him that it was too soon to rejoice. Life had asserted its sway again, before the patient could pass beyond all help. The splenectomy could be called a success in another moment, providing there was no fibrillation, the strange phenomenon that was the bane of all heart surgery. Mike had seen too many hearts thrash their way to death, in useless, uncontrolled contractions, to abandon his watchful waiting.

Fibrillation could best be described as a seizure of the heart muscle; at its height, the heart, for no visible reason, seemed to go berserk. Normally, the condition could be corrected by jolting the organ with electrical charges, until the maverick muscle was forced to resume its normal pattern of expansion and contraction. With no defibrillator at hand, the surgeon had but one choice left: to open the chest above the heart and apply Novocain directly—a procedure that offered scant hope for the patient.

"She's coming round," said the anesthesiologist. "I can feel the pulse."

Mike waited until the second hand of the wall clock had made another sweep, then moved to his former place as Lenora Searles came up to the table in fresh gown and gloves. With her expert help, he closed the peritoneum, and began the repair of the muscle wound by suturing the fascia with catgut.

He knew that he could rely on Louis Garstein to watch the patient while he completed the closing. The crippled man's behavior under pressure had confirmed his first impression. Whatever it might lack in equipment, this was a crack operating team.

"How's she doing?"

"Responding steadily. Pressure's around a hundred again, and pulse slowing. We're over the hump, Mike."

The last stitch was in place less than forty-five minutes after the first scalpel stroke. Pulling off his gloves, Mike strapped the dressing in place and stepped back from the table to shed his gown. It had been a long time since he had felt quite so weary—or so happy in the calling he had chosen.

"You can discard the whole blood, Miss Searles. We won't risk a transfusion reaction by giving it."

"Very good, Doctor." Now that the crisis was over, Mike saw that the nurse had resumed her impersonal mask. In its way, it shielded her as completely as the square of surgical gauze she had just discarded.

"I'll give her some myself, if she needs more," he said.

"*I'm* available as a donor, Dr. Constant."

Mike nodded his appreciation. "Somehow, I don't think either of us will be needed."

"Nor do I," said Garstein.

"One thing more. This was a tough one—but it turned out well. I'd like to thank all of you for a fine job."

Lee Searles smiled faintly at the exchange, but gave no other sign of pleasure as she transferred the patient to the wheeled stretcher Will had just brought to the O.R. door. Mike moved forward to help, saw he was not needed, and stood aside as Anna Van Ryn was wheeled back to her room.

In the hall, he was aware that Louis Garstein had kept pace with him. "Stop by the chartroom, will you, Mike? I'm pretty sure you'll find a transatlantic call waiting."

"For me?"

"Why not? I've got a brother-in-law named Zeagler, remember?"

"Anna said he was airborne."

"So he was—two hours ago. He's been grounded in Madrid, by bad weather."

"How much should I tell him?"

"The best news he could want—that Anna has survived another fall."

Mike glanced at Garstein sharply. "All I did was save a patient with routine surgery."

"The patient happens to be his daughter. And heart massage at the climax of a splenectomy is hardly routine."

Mike hesitated at the chartroom door. The facts behind Anna's injury were far reaching—and he was glad that Garstein had not pursued the topic. Zeagler still deserved a report on the actual operation.

"I'll talk to him now, if he's still in Madrid."

The overseas operator in New York was ready to connect New Salem with Spain. In a matter of minutes, Aaron Zeagler's voice boomed into the receiver. He listened attentively while Mike described Anna's emergency admission, the procedure that had saved her, and the hopeful prognosis.

"I can't begin to thank you, Doctor." The industrialist's voice was hoarse with emotion—but there was no hint of the excitement Mike had feared.

"The surgery was simple," he said. "Our big break was getting the case in time."

"I'll fly back at once, if I'm needed. I can't reach my wife. She's gone on to Egypt."

"There's no need to alter your plans. After ten days here, your daughter will be good as new."

"Perhaps she'll be *better* Dr. Constant. This isn't her first fall after she's been drinking. Where's her husband?"

"Paul's in New York," Mike said carefully. "I'll inform him tomorrow, when we track him down."

There was a pause on the wire. Expecting an explosion, Mike was startled by Zeagler's measured calm when he spoke again.

"You say Anna will be hospitalized for ten days?"

"Roughly that. It might be longer."

"Don't let her leave, until you hear from me—and don't let her touch a drop. In ten days, I'll have a plan of action ready."

"Can I do anything more in the meantime?"

"You've more than done your part, Dr. Constant. Tonight's work calls for a special fee. Do you want to name it?"

"Emergencies are part of my job, Mr. Zeagler."

"I insist."

"Suppose we compromise on a thousand dollar donation—for essential equipment."

"What sort of equipment?"

"A cardiac pacemaker and a defibrillator. I needed the first badly tonight. Eventually, we're bound to need the second."

"I'll wire the amount to Pailey. You're sure a thousand's enough?"

"More than enough, sir."

"Won't you take another check for yourself?"

"I'd prefer a fully equipped operating room."

"You're an unusual man, Dr. Constant—as well as an unusual surgeon."

"I happen to love my work, as much as you love yours, Mr. Zeagler. By the way, I've had no success whatever *outside* the hospital—though I've talked to all the people you mentioned."

"We'll discuss that angle when we meet again. I may have information that will interest you."

When he hung up the chartroom phone, Mike sat at the desk for a moment to ponder the things he had left unsaid. He was glad Garstein had put through the call—and he was still puzzled by Zeagler's quiet acceptance of his news. It was useless, of course, to speculate on the man's last cryptic statement. Zeagler would make whatever moves he saw fit to make—and discuss their import later.

Returning to the private wing, Mike found Miss Ford at Anna's bedside. "Dr. Garstein's gone home, sir. He said he'd see you in the morning."

"I'll watch her for awhile, if you have work to do."

"We've started a flask of glucose. A special nurse is on her way."

"Do you have Mrs. Van Ryn's admission folder handy?"

"It's on the bedside table, Dr. Constant."

When the night supervisor had departed, Mike checked the patient's condition and found it satisfactory. Anna was still unconscious from the anesthetic—but her blood pressure had risen steadily, and the pulse curve was still downward, showing that her circulation was rapidly resuming its normal state.

Once he had added his own comments to the chart, he was ready to examine Anna's record. As he had expected, the history was on the meager side—but the scanty notations told him more than enough. . . . There had been two previous admissions: one, for a suspected skull fracture that had proved a false alarm; the other for "multiple abrasions" whose exact nature was unspecified. Both admissions had been signed by Dr. Bradford Keate; both injuries were listed as aftereffects of a fall.

The third admission was now on the bedside chart—and Mike carefully attached the over-all case history. Hurried though the early notations were, they made a distinct pattern. Dr. Keate had been too cautious to suggest that Anna Van Ryn had been intoxicated when she fell, but the inference was plain. Apparently he had not paused to ask himself if such injuries were the normal side effects of excessive drinking.

Mike wrote:

Alcohol cannot be ruled out entirely as a contributing factor. It is regretted that no precise tests were made at the time of the first two admissions, to determine its presence or absence. While it is true that heavy drinkers are subject to falls, they rarely injure themselves seriously, because of body relaxation.

His own entry had ruled out drink as the cause of the patient's injury. She had been sober when the ambulance collected her. . . .

Mike sat up in the bedside chair, and shook his head quickly, realizing he had dozed over the chart. In the bed, Anna had stirred faintly. He sensed that she had been speaking for some time in her drugged slumber. It was the sound of her voice that had wakened him.

"Don't, Paul!"

The surgeon bent above the sleeping figure. Anna's face, smoothed of all strain by the medication, gave no clue to the subconscious gyrations of her brain.

"Please, Paul—! I can't stand any more!"

The special nurse was waiting in the doorframe when Mike left the room—and Anna's muttering had long since faded into silence. Back in the chartroom, he took up the record sheet for a final notation. It was a long time before he could choose the right words.

When they came to him at last, he wrote them down in a numbed detachment that had nothing to do with his weariness.

> *This is Mrs. Van Ryn's third admission for accidents she describes as the result of a fall. The patient's explanation of her injuries seems at variance with the clinical picture. Investigation by the police will be requested, to determine their true cause.*

FIVE

The bedside phone had been ringing for some time when Mike wakened from one of the soundest sleeps he had known. Hot spring sunlight, beating on the terrace blinds, told him it was midmorning.

"This is Miss Sturdevant, Doctor. Did I waken you?"

"I'm afraid you did."

"I'm Dr. Melcher's secretary. Could you come to his office at once?"

Despite his drowsiness, the staff surgeon could detect the note of tension. "We had an emergency last night. I'll need time to dress."

"I know, Doctor." The secretary spoke in blurred tones—presumably to the director himself—then her voice cleared again. "If you don't mind, Dr. Melcher will join you in your room."

Mike was nearly dressed when he heard the discreet rap on his door. Lawrence Melcher looked fresh as the spring day. He was wearing a lab coat, and carried a file folder under his arm.

"I should have let you sleep longer, Dr. Constant. The morning report said you and Louis Garstein were keeping late hours."

"I didn't turn in until four."

"Your first surgical job for New Salem Memorial was a brilliant one."

"We saved a life. No great brilliance was required."

"I've talked to Louis; he told me the whole story."

"I don't think Dr. Garstein knows everything—though I'm sure he has a few shrewd suspicions. After all, this was the patient's third accident report."

"Are you questioning our admission records?"

"I question them strongly, Dr. Melcher. In fact, I was planning to give you my complete findings on Mrs. Van Ryn, before I report them to the police."

The director opened the file he was carrying. It was the case history Mike had left at Anna's bedside. "As you see, I've saved you the time. Lee—Miss Searles was making a routine check on Anna when she found this report. She brought it straight to me. Of course, it must go no further."

"Obviously the patient was holding back," Mike said. "Last night's injuries were the result of a beating. So, I'd assume, were the others. Is it the hospital's policy to withhold such information?"

It was the first time he had seen Melcher at a loss. For a moment, he could almost feel sorry for the medical director of New Salem Memorial.

"I'm sure Anna didn't authorize this notation."

"Naturally she didn't. Just as she held her tongue on other occasions, when her husband beat her up."

"The patient's an alcoholic," Melcher protested. "She's fallen before. Your own note mentions a roll down the kitchen stairs, after she tripped on her housecoat."

"I was reporting the patient's story. I don't believe it. When I was interning at San Francisco General, I admitted a dozen similar cases —from beatnik pads on North Beach, *and* Nob Hill. Social position's no bar to this syndrome, Dr. Melcher. Sometimes, I think the so-called upper classes have an edge in the sweepstakes."

"You mentioned a syndrome—"

"The A.M.A. articles dealing with the battered-child syndrome set the general picture. Sometimes, the victim's a helpless elder relative, or a wife."

The director's reaction was all Mike needed to confirm his original estimate of his character. Lawrence Melcher, he felt sure, was a competent doctor—and an honest one. It was his misfortune that—as president of a corporation operating a hospital—he had been cast as a mediator as well. Faced with an unfamiliar problem, his exclamation of disbelief had been instinctive.

"I know the battered-child syndrome is an established symptom pattern," he said at last. "I'll admit it exists, at all levels of our society—"

"But you won't admit Anna Van Ryn's a badly battered wife? Or that her husband's almost surely responsible?"

"Have you the right to jump to that conclusion?"

"The basic story's in that file," said Mike. "When she was admitted last night, Anna was too frightened—and too proud—to tell us the truth. Why was Paul absent on two previous occasions, when Dr. Keate admitted her? Why did he take off for New York before her third admission? And why was Anna so desperate she almost refused to let me operate?"

"All of this is circumstantial, Dr. Constant."

"How would *you* explain her terror?"

"She'd been badly injured—in a natural state of hysteria."

"There's nothing natural about her kind of fear, Doctor. Next time, she may be killed. It's our duty to report her condition to the police."

"I still can't believe this of the Van Ryns."

"I can understand your reluctance. Slandering a Van Ryn, in this town, is beyond the pale. But they're still subject to due process, if they've broken a law."

"It could have been someone besides Paul."

"That's possible, of course—but highly unlikely. It's best to let the police decide."

"Are you suggesting that Anna's husband is psychotic?"

"The family is the oldest in these parts—and the most inbred. The Duchess has always been an eccentric. Paul's the end of the line. Psychotic isn't too strong a word to apply to his recent behavior. I've already seen enough to insist that ordinary precautions be taken."

"*Insist* is a strong word, Dr. Constant."

"Will you go to the police, or shall I?"

"Anna's admission history is still part of our records. Until there's more proof, I refuse to release it. The least we can do is wait—until we learn what Aaron Zeagler wants done."

It was Mike's turn to hesitate, as he recalled the transoceanic phone call, and Zeagler's promise of action. "Do you think *he* suspects Paul?"

"I'm sure no love is lost between them. Perhaps he'll insist on a divorce. Will that satisfy your sense of justice?"

"A potential criminal would still be at large. Paul Van Ryn should be under treatment now."

"Dr. Constant, you're no psychiatrist and neither am I. What should be done with Anna's husband remains a matter of opinion."

"A police investigation could change it to a matter of fact."

"You can't be sure of that—from what we know so far. Anna is safe, while she's under our care. Meanwhile, Zeagler will find some way to deal with his daughter. He owns this hospital; if he wished, he could dissolve our whole operation. We must learn his intentions before we make a move."

"In other words, you'll suppress the evidence, and hope for the best."

"Let's say I'll keep the Van Ryn name out of the tabloids, and await a peaceful solution of Anna's marriage problem." Melcher picked up the file and closed it. "Shall we leave things there—and forget this conversation?"

"You won't mind if I talk with Dr. Garstein?"

"Not at all. Louis is Zeagler's brother-in-law. I know how he'll advise you." The director's manner was almost jovial as he turned toward the door. "He's gone to Albany, but he'll be back later in the day. Will drove him there this morning—to get a pacemaker, and a defibrillator."

Mike's eyes opened wide at the news. Zeagler had promised him a check on the phone; he had not expected it so soon.

"Zeagler's agent in Switzerland wired us the money," Melcher added. "It was here when Ralph opened his office. I'm glad you put that order through. We mustn't be caught short again."

"Thank you for your co-operation, Dr. Melcher."

"Larry will do from now on, Mike."

"Believe me, Larry, I've no wish to upset the applecart my first day." Mike felt his voice was too dry to match the other man's warmth—but the chance to drive home a point could not be ignored.

"We may never need a pacemaker again—or we could need one tomorrow. I prefer the extra insurance when I operate."

"No one can blame you for devotion to your calling." Melcher tapped the folder with another smile. "All you've told me about this case may be gospel. We'll risk nothing by adopting an attitude of watchful waiting—"

"—and keeping the *other* case histories updated?"

"Have our doctors been neglecting their files?"

"The records are barely adequate, Dr. Melcher. As I see it, your number-one objective is to get this hospital accredited. We'll need real spadework in that department to get a passing grade."

"You've a point there. I won't deny it's a vital one."

"Another point's even more important, now that we're bearing down on the records. If present trends continue, I'm afraid the Joint Committee would find far too many hysterectomies on your admission list. And I'm sure Louis Garstein is too honest a pathologist to put down malignancy or fibroid where none exists. A close look at some of those cases could be pretty embarrassing to your surgeons."

"Anything else?"

"I noticed a gastroenterostomy in the men's ward. It isn't anything to make a federal case of—but duodenal ulcers are usually treated differently these days."

"I can see that your first tour of duty was a thorough one, Mike."

"Isn't that the reason I'm here?"

"Of course. If we're to improve our over-all procedure, we'll have to let you set the pace." The director of New Salem Memorial extended his hand. "Starting today, we're a reform committee of two. I'll expect you to lay down the law in earnest at our next staff meeting."

When the other doctor had left, Mike slowly finished dressing. Part of his mind insisted that Melcher had been sincere, according to his lights. Another, more cynical part could not help wondering if he'd been treated to one of the finest snow jobs in the medical repertory.

The staff dining room, Mike found, was excellent—its coffee fresh-brewed and scalding hot, its eggs and bacon cooked precisely to his order. At another time, he might have wished that some of this attention to the comforts of personnel had been extended to the wards. This noon, he was much too hungry to ponder the contrast—and far too concerned with the aftermaths of his meeting with Melcher.

He was on his second coffee when Ralph Pailey bustled in, drew a cup at the urn, and moved to join him.

"I've a bone to pick with you, Dr. Constant. Do you mind mixing business and food?"

Mike made room at his table. A broken sleep had done nothing to change his first impression of the administrator.

"You have the floor, Mr. Pailey."

"Mrs. Van Ryn's father has already wired me a check for the operation you performed last night."

"So he promised, when we talked on the phone."

"A thousand dollars—with an equipment tag attached. Louis Garstein has drawn against it, and taken the money to Albany."

"I'm aware of that as well."

"You should have let *me* do the billing, Dr. Constant."

"It wasn't a bill," said Mike, not too patiently. "The money was a donation to my department."

"Permit me to differ. The patient was admitted as an emergency. She'd have been charged for the service later—regardless of the fact her father owns the hospital. Now the check's gone through, I can hardly send a second bill."

"Why should you? I think we've been amply recompensed."

"Recompensed!" The administrator had turned Turkey red; the popeyes behind his rimless glasses seemed to swell in their sockets. "Under your contract, patients who come to us for treatment are cared for by you, with no added fee. It's my function to send out the bills, not yours."

"Have I questioned that?"

"Don't you see my point, man? After what you did for Anna, I could have gotten five thousand from her father. *Ten,* if I'd played my cards properly—" Pailey broke off his tirade as Mike exploded with laughter. "Have I made a joke, by any chance?"

"I was laughing at myself, not at you," said the surgeon. "Ever since we met, you've puzzled me. Now I know why. You look like a man—but you're a robot, with silver dollars circulating in your blood stream. I couldn't feel sorrier for you in your affliction. Especially when you try to deal with human beings."

"I'm not interested in your pity." Pailey's voice was just under a shout. "I *am* concerned with a fair return on our service."

"You just said a thousand dollars was too low a price for a woman's life. It was all we needed to save last night's patient."

"What does that mean?"

"We were dangerously short of stored blood, Mr. Pailey. Dr. Garstein tells me it's because you didn't put through his requisition for an extra supply. We could have lost the patient, if she'd needed a second transfusion. Point two, her heart stopped beating on the table. With up-to-date equipment, I could have started it again—but we didn't have that either. Suppose Anna Van Ryn had died—and Zeagler or her husband sued us? Have you any idea how the verdict would have gone?"

"We carry liability insurance."

"Is that all a needless death means to you, Pailey? I see you wear a wedding ring. Do you have children?"

"Two boys and a girl."

"Suppose I'd had one of *them* on the table—and lost him? Would you write it off as an insurance risk?"

"That's a loaded question."

"Loaded or not, you answered it. I owe this town a lot. Last night, I paid off a little of the debt. Obviously, it's the kind of obligation that doesn't interest you."

"We both have our jobs, Doctor. Mine is to protect the interests of the men who hired you."

"Are you one of them?"

The administrator had recovered his poise—and his temper. Before he replied, he drew himself up proudly in his chair. Again,

Mike smiled inwardly. Pailey, it seemed, was one of those self-created wonder boys who could strut even when sitting.

"I brought the New Salem Hospital Corporation together. I was paid in stock—so I'm a voting member."

"Why did you go into hospital administration? Couldn't you get rich faster in Wall Street?"

"At the time, I was a real estate promoter for the Zeagler interests. When he planned his New Salem plant, he decided to add a hospital to the housing development."

"I thought the idea was yours."

"The medical angle was part of Zeagler's blueprint. I took care of the details—and organized the doctors' group that signed the lease."

"Did you know Dr. Coxe wanted to build a voluntary hospital—using the old County buildings as a base?"

"That plan's been on the drawing board for years," said Pailey contemptuously. "The Old Town didn't have the cash to swing it. Once I found the right doctors, our deal went through in a month."

"On a proprietary basis."

"Why not, if we serve the community?"

"You've done business here for three years. If your ideal is service, why haven't you been accredited?"

"We give far better care than the County Hospital ever dreamed of."

"That wasn't my point. Have you compared your service with voluntary hospitals in the state?"

"Our problems are special. You can't measure us with the same yardstick."

"I doubt if you have any yardstick besides profit. What's your average return on invested capital?"

"So far, roughly twenty per cent."

"Because Zeagler Electronics gave you a liberal lease—and a ready-made list of patients?"

"I don't think that's your concern, Doctor. This is a well-run institution. Our patients are satisfied with their care."

"Would they be—if they compared New Salem Memorial with hospitals that aren't run for profit?"

Pailey had begun to sweat; the flush had crept from his collegian's collar to his well-fed jowls. "I defy you to find a single thing amiss in my books. We've been passed by the State Hospital Board—"

"But not approved by the Joint Committee."

"That's why you're here, Constant—and why we're paying you a top salary. If there's something you want done, ask for it. You'll get your request, if it's within reason."

Mike put down his cup. "Let's make a bargain. Run the business end of this outfit as you like. Just don't tell me what I need or don't need to practice surgery."

"That suits me," said Pailey. "In the future, I'll handle all fees for patients. We'll give you an office for your private practice—when you develop one. *They'll* be billed to your account, and I'll ride herd on your collections. Could I be fairer than that?"

"I suppose not," said Mike resignedly. "Will you leave the argument there?"

"Gladly—if we understand each other."

"We do. I'll stay out my year—if *you'll* stay with your bookkeeping, and the staff plays ball. I think you will, now we've cleared the air. After all, you've the best of reasons for giving me a free hand. Unless you're accredited, Zeagler will probably cancel your lease when it comes up for renewal."

"I'll admit the threat exists," said the administrator stiffly. "It's something we've faced from the start."

"You want the approval of the Joint Committee. I'll do my best to see you get it. Just stop pushing while I do. I don't push easily."

When Louis Garstein returned from Albany with his operating-room equipment, Mike had made his rounds and recovered from his anger. He found the pathologist in the surgical storeroom, gloating over the precious instruments an orderly had just brought upstairs.

"How is Anna, Mike?"

"I just came from her room. She's doing nicely."

Garstein lifted one of the electrodes from the neatly coiled wires of the pacemaker and weighed it on his palm—as lovingly as though the small metal plate were a gold ingot.

"Odd, isn't it, that we had to risk losing a patient to bring this beauty into the shop? By the way, I hope you don't mind my using a bit of our windfall for anesthesia. We needed some intratracheal tubes and a laryngoscope."

"That's what the money was for, Louis."

"I suppose Pailey gave you hell for taking a gift without consulting him."

"He tried."

"Judging by that Cheshire-cat grin, you outshouted him."

"It wasn't hard," said Mike. "Not when I realized how scared he was underneath. He's skating on thin ice here. If things had gone badly with Anna, he could have sunk without a trace."

"I'm glad you cut him down to size," said Garstein. He closed the top of the pacemaker, and stowed it carefully in a glass-front cabinet. "Don't make the mistake of letting him climb on your back later. He'll drive you mad."

Pathologist and staff surgeon walked into the utility area dividing the two operating theaters. One of the staff doctors, a bulky man whose iron-gray crew cut, spiky mustaches, and black-browed scowl suggested a general in the *Wehrmacht,* was putting on a gown to begin a herniotomy—with the patient under low-spinal anesthesia and a nurse watching blood pressure.

"*That's* Bradford Keate," said Garstein. "Keep your guard up when you're around him, too. He's the kind who hits first and argues afterwards."

Keate, Mike recalled, was the doctor who had cared for Anna's first two admissions, and accepted her story of a fall, without question. He paused at the observation window until the surgeon had made his first incision, saw that the man's scalpel stroke had been both curt and sure, then moved on—a little ashamed that he had yielded to the compulsion.

"All in all, Louis, I've had quite a day. Melcher began it, when I wanted to take Anna's case record to the police."

"I was afraid you'd smell a rat, Mike."

"It's standard practice, where the surgeon has doubts about an accident report."

"Not in this town. You should know that better than I."

"Even the Van Ryns aren't above the law."

"We both know Paul beat his wife insensible, then kited off to New York. I'm sure Larry Melcher half suspected it—but thoughts of that nature don't sit well on his tidy mind. How did you leave matters?"

"Nothing will be done while Anna's still hospitalized. The next move will be Zeagler's."

"You didn't relay your suspicions to *him*?"

"Of course not. He mentioned her other accidents—and said he'd have plans for her when he returns. Do you think he suspects Paul has been beating her?"

"No, Mike. Anna and her father aren't that close. She'd never confide in him, and he's too busy empire building to ask questions. At the same time, he cares for her deeply, in his Napoleonic fashion. If he could plan her happiness with another blueprint, he'd give it top priority."

"He must realize the marriage is a failure—and that Anna's only staying at Rynhook because of pride—"

"Plus the fact she believes the *schlemiel* she calls a husband is an artist. I'm sure Aaron would break up the marriage tomorrow, if he could think of a way."

"Then you feel it's wiser, for Zeagler's sake, to suppress the facts?"

"Absolutely. With that blood pressure he's carrying, the truth could kill him. Larry Melcher wasn't being timid when he refused to take Anna's chart to the police."

"We can't play this score by ear forever," Mike warned.

"We can for ten days. Aaron may return from Israel with a revelation—a latter-day miracle, where this town's concerned. Perhaps he'll buy Paul out, and salvage Anna from the wreckage. It's been done before."

"You don't buy out a Van Ryn, Louis."

"Not even if he's a cad and a coward?"

"I don't think Paul is either. He's just a megalomaniac wl be locked up."

"You'll never pin that charge on him—and make it sti Duchess would defend him. So would Anna—God forgive he stein steered Mike back to the corridor, where nurses and cians were converging on the staff dining room. "Put the pr out of your mind for now, and join me for dinner. There's nc more we can do until we hear from Aaron."

"If you don't mind, I'll drive into town. Can you cover for next few hours?"

"Of course, providing you get back by eleven. Will you be visit your patient in the Old Town?"

"If Dr. Art hasn't discharged her by now."

On Lower Street, Mike parked at the side entrance to Dr. Coxe's hospital, and entered the building by the emergency door, a short cut that permitted him to head for Sandra's room without facing Mrs. Bramwell. The door was ajar; before he could knock, he heard the girl's voice raised in argument—and drew back when he realized she was on the long-distance phone. Hating himself for eavesdropping, he lingered a few seconds in the corridor, then strode on, with a shrug of despair. The target of Sandra's fury was a hotel clerk in New York. Mike had already heard enough to know she had tried to reach Paul Van Ryn in the city—and still refused to believe the clerk's patient insistence that he had checked out.

Before he could turn the corner of the hall, Mike heard the receiver bang down behind the half-open door. It would have been sheer folly to face Sandra in her present mood. . . . A moment later, he was seated in Dr. Coxe's office, studying the latest X ray of his patient's arm.

"That was a nice reduction job," the old doctor said. "In six weeks, the bone should be good as new."

"I wish we could say the same for the patient."

"Sandra's still depressed—and who can blame her?"

"Apparently she's well enough to make phone calls."

"I could hardly object to that. She plans to start nursing full time

when her brother leaves. Naturally, she has to keep up her contacts."

"Business and social," said Mike. "I quite understand."

Dr. Art gave him a searching glance, but did not pursue the topic. "How was your day on Indian Hill?"

"Crowded. In fact, I've been almost too busy to think."

"At times, Mike, that's a healthy state of affairs. The whole town's buzzing over the way you saved the owner's daughter."

Dr. Coxe puffed serenely on his pipe while Mike described the splenectomy, and the touch-and-go techniques that had pulled the patient through. His mentor's matter-of-fact questions had quieted his nerves. When he told the story of Melcher's agitation, his row with Pailey, and Garstein's reactions, he found he was almost calm again.

"Baptism by fire may be too strong a label," he said. "I do think I've run the gantlet. Frankly, Dr. Art, it left me stunned."

"You've a right to feel numb, until the effect wears off. Yesterday I warned you New Salem Memorial wouldn't be one hundred per cent to your liking. Now, I suppose, you'd call that a gross understatement."

"Yes and no. There are some things I like very much indeed. My surgical team is tops. And I'm sure Lawrence Melcher is a good man, under that Ivy League front. At least he isn't all opportunist, like Pailey."

"Pailey's an extreme example of his breed," said Dr. Art. "Larry's chief fault, up to now, has been delegation of authority to the front office. After last night, he'll listen to your ideas, and act on them."

"He turned me down on bringing charges against Paul. I still think we should have nailed him."

"Sometimes it's wiser to move slowly in these borderline cases."

"What's borderline about three obvious beatings? Wouldn't you close in, if you were me?"

"Of course—if I thought the police could help. You say Paul is a paranoid. Having observed Rynhook over the years—including the behavior of the Duchess—I'm in complete agreement. But would Chief Wharton buy the idea—with no relative to sign commitment

papers, and Anna swearing each of those injuries was an accident? You couldn't even sell it to a psychiatrist, once Paul was on his guard."

Mike was silent, as the logic of Dr. Art's words sank home. As an intern, he had studied his quota of disturbed patients. He had observed foaming madmen, schizophrenics who changed their moods like agile chameleons, catatonics wrapped in a stony silence that rejected all outside contact. These were the extreme forms of inbalance. Paranoia was an inclusive term for a mental illness embracing a whole field of bizarre symptom-patterns. It was difficult to diagnose correctly, even under optimum conditions. Precise evaluation could be impossible if the patient were aware of the doctor's intent—and hid behind a mask of sanity he could assume at will.

"Face the realities, Mike," said Dr. Art. "Louis was right. You have ten days of grace with Anna. Perhaps her father can persuade her to leave Rynhook—or consent to a divorce."

"What about Sandra? Suppose Paul turns on her?"

"Paul may be a psychopath; we've yet to prove he's a monster. It's common knowledge that his form of mental illness hits out at the nearest object—a mother, a wife, or a child. If they'll speak up, it's easy to bring in the law and a strait jacket. But you'd be surprised how often the people who've been hurt most will cover up—from fear, or love, or a blend of both. If those same fists start swinging *outside* the home, it's another story."

"Meaning that Sandra would hit back?"

"I don't think she'd submit as tamely as Anna has. If you like, I'll tell her the whole story while she's here—and warn her to cut Paul out of her life."

"She'd only think you were lying, Dr. Art."

"Exactly. Which means the situation's unchanged. She must fall out of love with Paul in her own way. There's nothing either of us can do—until she sees him as he really is."

"You can keep them apart, as long as she's your patient."

"Paul Van Ryn knows better than to show his face here," said Dr. Coxe. "If he does, I'll throw him out myself. For all we know, Sandra may do likewise. Her plan to return to nursing seems a good augury."

"Perhaps you're right." Mike had done his best to disguise his low spirits. It was no time to mention his eavesdropping—and the note of anguish in Sandra's voice, when she had failed to reach Paul by phone.

"Forget a problem you can't solve," Dr. Art advised. "Take a fresh look at one you can. Are you going to stay on at New Salem Memorial—after what you've seen there?"

"I mean to try."

"I hoped you'd say that, Mike. By this time you have a general idea of the hospital's faults, and its good points. You know that Larry Melcher's the brain of the operation, and the dynamo that keeps it running. You were quite right to call him a good doctor. He's fully qualified in internal medicine. Johns Hopkins and Columbia. F.A.C.P.—"

"Fellow of the American College of Physicians is an impressive rating."

"Louis Garstein's a first-rate pathologist—and a Rock of Gibraltar in anesthesia. You don't get that combination often. Now *you've* joined the team, the front is complete."

"I don't care for that word, Dr. Art. Is there something I don't know yet?"

"Have you ever heard of a hot-bed hospital?"

"It sounds vaguely immoral."

"It is—but not for the reason you're suggesting. I refer to a hospital that's run for profit. All the traffic will bear."

"Is that immoral, by present-day standards?"

"Hospitals rarely show a profit operating on a voluntary basis. They make ends meet with endowment funds, or community donations. It's another story in the proprietary field."

"Private enterprise is the cornerstone of our system. After all, doctors form groups for mutual gain."

"I didn't say the system was wrong, per se. New Salem Memorial is almost certainly better than most of the city or county hospitals you'll find in this enlightened land—where graft is added to the over-all cost, and both patients and public suffer. The trouble starts when private enterprise changes to private greed—when an operator like Pailey sells the public an up-to-the-minute façade, with nothing solid inside."

Mike hesitated before he spoke. Dr. Coxe's indictment was too sweeping for his taste. Even as his memory brought back the crisis at his operating table, the open-and-shut cases in both ward and private room, and the single flask of blood available last night, he found himself arguing for his own.

"Are you accusing Pailey of cheating the patients?"

"The answer's a qualified no, Mike. It's still a fact that the public is conditioned to buy the package these days—without unwrapping it. No one can find much fault with the sort of care Larry Melcher gives the *average* patient. It's an integral part of the Zeagler living-pattern, and it's streamlined for service."

"Like his split-level houses, and his push-button Food Mart?"

"Make all the remarks you like about supermarket culture. It's here to stay in every small-town setup; it's entrenched even deeper in the green-belt suburbs of our big cities. Eventually it's going to justify its existence."

"Providing the doctors and the hospitals keep the customers healthy?"

"You've made my point for me," said Dr. Art. "New Salem Heights is an encouraging example of American social evolution on the march. The factory itself is one of Zeagler's best. Its employees are tops in their class, whether they're white collar or blue. Join their buying power to the five-figure executives, and you'll know what's kept our country prosperous, in the first decades of the atomic age. All of these lucky toilers enjoy their lot. They're ready to pay the asking price—whether the bill comes from the liquor store, the garage that services their car, or Ralph Pailey."

"In other words—a prefabricated Eden?"

"Yes, if the merchants are honest. The liquor store can't sell bootleg booze. The garage must give top service: too many of their customers are good mechanics. It isn't so easy to check on the scalpel wielders or the pill pounders."

"You're saying that's my function, aren't you?"

"It could be—if you're the same Mike Constant who once worked with me. I'm not going to condemn you if you don't agree. You can go back to Indian Hill, and forget all I've said so far. Practice good surgery, make friends with your staff, and ignore what happens outside the O.R. door. You'll have more than enough to keep you busy."

"Go on, please. I know that was only a teaser."

"Aaron Zeagler believes in his hospital," said Dr. Coxe. "He has faith in Larry Melcher; he's sure you'll round out the staff, and keep production booming. Like all good businessmen, he knows he must delegate authority. He won't interfere with Melcher's methods—unless something goes really wrong."

"I'm still waiting for your indictment," said Mike.

"First let's examine the bright side of the coin. A proprietary hospital can be a gold mine in a community of this sort. Its patients are provident. They have the last word in insurance, financed with the company's help—so bills are paid on the nose. Pailey has no headaches over collections, no charity service to speak of—"

"What about the new County patients?"

"Even there, New Salem has been forced to move with the times. When we couldn't keep the old hospital open any longer, we had to take Larry Melcher's offer. On paper, it's reasonable enough. We've yet to see whether he can deliver the care he's promised."

"Have you a valid reason for doubting him?"

"Personally, no—even if statistics over the country are against him. As I've said, New Salem Memorial may be the exception that proves the rule. If so, I'll be glad to eat this lecture."

"Meaning your principal worry is the type of service, not the personnel?"

"Yes, Mike. For example, it's a proven fact that proprietary hospitals have a far higher incidence of staphylococcus infection."

"Hospital staph can turn up anywhere."

"True. But a recent survey in the West uncovered twenty-three proprietaries that failed to keep up minimum standards—including clean kitchens and proper sterilization in surgery. It's also a fact that many such hospitals attract doctors who practice substandard medicine. I've got a New York City survey in my desk, rating a cross section of hospital patients, by their doctors' own standards. Thirty-nine per cent in proprietary hospitals received what the examiners called 'good' care. The figure was sixty-four per cent at nonprofit institutions in the same area."

"I never realized you were an authority on the subject, Dr. Art."

"I wasn't—until I started fighting to save the old County, and lost. We accepted the alternative—New Salem Memorial—because nothing else was available. Medicine for profit is a trend that's always been in the making. Perhaps it isn't fair to blame its recent rise on the proprietaries—but they've been the worst offenders."

"With no previous experience, I won't argue the point."

"In California, you were working for institutions that functioned on the highest plane. In that type of hospital, a patient's ability to pay had no bearing on the service he received. It's always a shock to a young doctor to learn that—outside the big, university-sponsored hospitals—not many of the others, even the so-called best, operate entirely on such principles."

"What's the real villain? An ignorant public? Or our easy-money era?"

"I'd say a little of both. Most well-paid workers have a plethora of medical coverage nowadays. When a patient needs expensive diagnostic service, his doctor usually sends him to a hospital to have it done. The patient gets the best science available. The doctor collects an office fee without lifting a finger. The hospital makes money from an admission that needs no nursing care. In the long run, of course, it's the patient who pays—when his insurance service is forced to raise its rate."

"Then you're saying the Hippocratic oath's gone out the window?"

"It isn't a question of bad medicine, Mike. Actually, the diagnostic racket has become a matter of economics. If you forget the cost, you can see that these medical-insurance patients get a better laboratory work-up than they'd receive elsewhere. Naturally, such blessings don't extend to the small, hot-bed hospital. Pailey can't afford the personnel, and pay back Melcher's colleagues at twenty per cent on their investment."

"I'm beginning to understand the term *hot bed*," Mike said. "I can also see why New Salem Memorial doesn't cater to emergencies."

Dr. Coxe nodded. "We both know how long a severe accident can tie up a bed. There's also a payment problem—when you admit a patient before you see his credit cards."

"Won't Pailey have that problem with County patients?"

"Not with the taxpayer footing the bill. *This* doctors' group has friends in high places. They made sure funds for indigent cases and police pickups were on hand before the contract was drawn."

"What about the space tie-up? Especially with police and terminal cases?"

"If you've made your rounds in the basement, you know there are plenty of ward beds. They're adequate, even though they are Army surplus."

"Dr. Art, if all these things are true, why saddle me with this job?"

"Because I figured you'd be a Grade-A trouble shooter, Mike. If things get worse, you can ask Zeagler for a crackdown. If I'm a calamity howler, you're the man to do the upgrading—enough, at any rate, to get the hospital accredited."

"It's obvious I can't do much alone."

"I'd pitch in if I could, Mike. But I'm *personna non grata* at New Salem Memorial—for good reasons. They haven't forgotten the part I played at City Hall, when they were fighting to keep a new County Hospital off the drawing boards."

"Who'll support me—if there's a stand-up brawl?"

"Garstein will be in your corner. And Larry Melcher will back you, once he's seen the light."

"What about the other members of the staff?"

The older doctor frowned at the bowl of his pipe. "I've nothing against half of them. They're pillars of New Salem—but they're also run-of-the-mill doctors who prefer to stay out of quarrels. When they do join a fight, they side with the heavy artillery. The rest are the timeservers you'll find in any profession. Especially the surgeons."

"Why bear down on my specialty?"

"You'll see why, when you check their performances. They're

the sort who account for half the needless hysterectomies performed in profit hospitals. They do the chronic appendix removals, the uterine suspensions, and the floating-kidney anchorings. Bear down on those diagnoses every time. They'll be a revelation."

"Any particular villain I should look for?"

"The ringmaster is a man named Bradford Keate. He's a competent carpenter, who loves to break down the human anatomy and watch it tick—even when the spare parts he removes are healthy."

"I saw him at work this afternoon."

"He's well trained, Mike—and he's dangerous. Bypass him when you can. His mind was closed to logic twenty years ago, when he got his diploma."

"I've met the type before. I won't mind trading punches, if it helps the cause."

"When you do, go into the ring with bare knuckles, and use every trick in the book. In his bulldog way, Brad Keate sums up all I've been saying. He's the type who retires at fifty-five, with a half million in taxproof bonds—bought mostly with cash collections that never appear on his federal return. And *that's* because he accepted twice as many patients as the average surgeon—and processed them twice as fast."

"Isn't someone trying to fight the racket?"

"You and I are making a start, in New Salem. There are plenty like us who are tired of watching our profession change into a vending machine. So are review boards in our up-and-coming states. If New Salem Memorial were being built today, I could probably marshal enough figures to block its license."

"And you're *still* asking me to work there?"

"Yes, Mike—if you think such a fight is worthwhile. So is Melcher, for the same basic reason. And so, in his dollar-sign fashion, is Pailey—I'll say this for him, he worked hard to become an expert in his field. Maybe you can build up the lab and improve the records. You may even drive out the Keates. If you can, I'll be the first to cheer."

"It's ironic that a boy from Lower Street should get the job of making a New Salem hospital respectable."

"There's still time to back out."

"Not any more," said Mike. "I signed a permanent contract for a year, right after I talked with Melcher."

"Why then?"

"It's hard to say, Dr. Art. Maybe I was sorry for him, and wanted to see him gain ground. Maybe I decided he was a man—in spite of his bedside manner. Besides, who ever saw a Greek turn pale before a battle? Have you forgotten Salamis and Thermopylae?"

When he left the hospital, Mike was careful to avoid the hall that lead past Sandra's door. Postponing his return to Indian Hill deliberately, he drove north until he reached the steep pitch of Division Road, a business artery that descended to the Hudson and the slum-clotted blocks of Lower Street.

There was a bar halfway to the river, and he parked at the curb just beyond the entrance. Ordinarily he would have passed up so obvious a temptation, even though he was off duty at the hospital; drinking to escape one's troubles had always seemed illogical, in view of the greater trouble alcohol could sow in its wake. Tonight, burdened by the task Dr. Art had assigned him, and the despair that settled like a cloud when he allowed his thoughts to veer to Sandra, his mood demanded release.

The room inside the frosted-glass doors was dimly lit. When Mike took the first barstool, he seemed to be the only occupant, save for the heavy-jowled custodian of the bottles, who sat at the cash register, immersed in a racing form.

"Bourbon on the rocks, please. Make it a double."

When the drink came he downed it, feeling its potency spread through his being with consoling heat. The consolation, he told himself, was a short-term thing—but he was still glad he had paused here, to avoid the treadmill of his mind.

"Dr. Constant, I presume?"

The well-modulated voice had boomed from a wall booth. Even before its owner rose from the shadows, Mike knew it was Jason West—complete with Malacca cane, half-empty glass, and tragedian's smile. Tonight, the actor was wearing a beautifully cut suit.

There was a gardenia in his buttonhole; his graying hair had been freshly cut and glistened with pomade. Curiously enough, the grooming made him seem even more forlorn, though his manner was bright enough.

"Will you join me?"

"Gladly, Doctor—much as it surprises me to find you here. I'm afraid our friend Stevenson wouldn't approve. Not the U.N. statesman, the author of *Treasure Island.* Surely you're familiar with his tribute to your profession?"

"I'm afraid my acquaintance stops with Long John Silver."

Jason West lifted a peremptory arm, as the barman chuckled.

"Silence, Barney, while I quote: *There are men and classes of men who stand above the common herd. The soldier, the sailor and the shepherd infrequently. The artist rarely. More rarely still, the clergyman. The physician, almost as a rule. Generosity he has, such as is possible to those who practice an art, never to those who drive a trade. Discretion, tested by a thousand embarrassments. And, what are more important, Herculean cheerfulness and courage.*"

"You're right," said Mike. "That *is* quite a tribute. Don't forget it was written years ago. I wonder if Stevenson would have repeated it today?"

"I think so—with your example to inspire him. In our brief encounter yesterday, I approved what I saw. Now I've observed you in action—or, to be precise, had reports I could trust—I approve still more."

"I'm not sure I follow."

Jason West glanced down the bar, saw that Barney had moved to serve another customer, and leaned closer.

"I owe you a great debt, Dr. Constant."

"Mike would be better."

"Thank you, Mike—for saving someone very dear to me. A pearl among women, richer than all her tribe. Like the Bard's base Indian, I threw this jewel away, when it could still have been mine. That was the greatest folly of my life."

"If you mean Anna Van Ryn—?"

"Who else would I mean? Last night, you saved her with your healing knife. I had the whole story from my sister, who had it from her nurse."

"Surgery's my job, Mr. West. I deserve no special credit." Mike had flushed with pleasure at the words. It was not the compliment that had pleased him—but the fact that Sandra had heard the story and repeated it.

"I am still in your debt. If Anna had died last night, I could not have borne the loss." The actor's face was etched with pain: for the first time, Mike glimpsed the being who existed behind the posturings, the tag ends of poetry and melancholia. With that glimpse, he had a revelation: the secret of Jason West's art lay in the man himself, in his need to give love, to be loved in return. It was an emotion he had always shared with his audiences, lifting them out of their everyday selves, compelling them to share a better world until the curtain fell. . . . Had that same sharing been possible offstage with Anna Zeagler—before her own folly had changed her name to Anna Van Ryn?

"I knew that you and Anna had acted together." Mike spoke the first words that came to mind; bemused by his view of the real Jason West, he could not yet think clearly. "I never realized you were more than acquaintances outside the theater."

"It's a familiar story, Mike. Anna's father financed her training as an actress. He backed the play in which we both appeared. I'm sorry to add the show closed in tryout; it convinced Anna that her love for the stage was not matched by her talents. *Her* talent was plain for all to see. Even then, she stood ready to save me from myself. Had I taken that priceless gift, I would not be a burnt-out husk at forty-seven. Of course I feared her father would brand me as a fortune hunter. Also, I was a four-time loser at the altar—and convinced myself I would only lose again. The day our show closed, I accepted a Hollywood offer and left her."

"Your paths must have crossed again in New Salem."

"I've been careful to avoid that risk. It wasn't hard. Sometimes, I had a distant glimpse—from the Gate House window, when she walked among the boxwoods. She seldom leaves Rynhook, when her husband is there."

"Isn't she the real reason you came back?"

"The question's indiscreet, Mike. You've no right to ask it. I have less right to answer."

"I have the answer now. The fact you're here, with only an estate wall between you, is positive proof you want to go on living."

"Didn't they teach you as an intern not to make a snap diagnosis? I seem to remember that from a movie role I played once."

"You've admitted you're in love with something outside yourself—even if it's only a might-have-been. So long as there's a chance you can come together—a hope, however faint, that Anna still loves you—you'll cling to life. This talk of self-destruction is a screen you hide behind—an excuse to wallow in self-pity."

"Even for a doctor, you're abusing your privileges."

"What I've said is true, Mr. West."

"Call me Jay, please. All my friends do. So do my enemies. At the moment, I'm not sure of your category."

"Why? Because I say that any man's life is worth living—including what's left of yours?"

"I had no idea doctors were this romantic. Actually, it's only an ironic coincidence that Anna and I are both in New Salem."

"I don't believe that, Jay."

"The facts will bear me out. I'm in the Gate House because I have nowhere else to turn. Six weeks ago, I collapsed on Hollywood Boulevard. For the past year I had been, as we say in the theater, at liberty. Being without funds, I was taken to a city hospital—until my sister rescued me. A charity ward isn't the best place in the world to die."

"So we're back at death again?"

"I've told you the truth, Mike; I'm a man at the end of his tether. Naturally, I've tried to keep the truth from Sandra; I've even spoken of returning to the stage again. It wasn't difficult to deceive her, when her thoughts were elsewhere."

"In New York—with Paul Van Ryn?"

"Your perception does you credit. Even then, she was trying to reach him by phone. She loves that unspeakable bounder—more's the pity. Her love seems to grow with each of his betrayals. If it's humanly possible, she means to steal him from Anna."

"Is there no way to stop her?"

"A bullet between Paul's eyes would do the trick. I'd put it there, if my hands would stop shaking. I'm afraid there's no other way to arrest the march of fate."

"Sandra may come to her senses in time."

"*That*, my dear Mike, is the most romantic illusion of them all. I have thirty years of philandering to prove it."

"You didn't philander with Anna."

"True. She was the one love of my life. That's why I've no intention of witnessing her present misery firsthand. My sister's folly is burden enough." Jason West drained his glass and got down from the barstool. He swayed slightly, until he steadied himself with a foot on the rail. "I'll bid you adieu—having shown you the secret places of my heart. I fear it was an unrewarding glimpse."

"Not for me, Jay. At least I know there's real hope for you."

"Wrong again, Mike. There's just one cure for *my* long illness. Therefore, it's time I began plying the needle."

"Another quotation coming up?"

"How did you guess? I must resume *sewing at once, with a double thread, a shroud as well as a shirt.* The lines are from Thomas Hood, a minor British poet. Their meaning should be obvious."

Still swaying, the actor left the barroom, saluting Barney with a flourish of his cane as he passed through the outer doors. Mike drained his own glass, and put a bill on the cash register.

"Does he drink like this every night?"

"Mr. West isn't loaded, Doctor. He's been nursing that glass for an hour. Don't let his staggers fool you. It's a bad ticker that brings 'em on, not my whiskey."

"I'd better follow him home, then."

"He's left this way before, and made it. But there'll be a first time —when he won't."

Jason's car, an ancient Cadillac that was an heirloom from his palmier days, had just swung away from the curb; he was halfway to Lower Street before Mike could start his own engine to pursue it. From a distance, the actor seemed to be driving normally. It was only when he shot through a red light that his pursuer had the first twinge of alarm. He had no choice but to follow, if he meant to keep the Cadillac in view.

A hundred yards beyond, the street emerged from the shadows of the tenements to open ground along the creek. Directly ahead was the bridge to Bearclaw Point, with the spillway of the dam below its pilings. Jason bore down on his objective at a reckless speed; Mike gave a futile shout of warning when the Cadillac swerved sharply, just as he reached the bridge.

Braking his own car, he was sure the Cadillac would crash through the fence that separated Lower Street from the artificial lake created by the dam. Instead, it came to a jarring halt, with two wheels in the ditch beside the road.

The Cadillac's horn had begun to bleat before it ground to a stop. It was still raising echoes (and several irate householders had appeared on their porches) when Mike coasted up beside the stranded car. When a man with a flashlight crossed the street to investigate, the beam showed Jason slumped across the wheel, his head and shoulders pressed down on the metal half circle controlling the horn.

A dozen people had clustered at the curb before Mike could push into the group.

"It's that drunk from Rynhook Gate House—"

"Again?"

"Is he really Jason West?"

"The one and only. Would you think *he* ever starred in pictures?"

"It's the same fellow, all right. I saw him last week, on the late-late show."

Mike raised his voice above the murmur. "Hold that light steady, please. I'll lift him off the horn."

"Better leave him be, mister. You can get in trouble—fooling with drunks before the cops come."

"I'm a doctor. There's no need for the police."

When Mike lifted Jason, he noted that the motor was still running.

Apparently the actor had felt himself losing control in time to make this panic stop. His lips were blue—and Mike was startled by the slowness of his pulse.

"I'm taking him to the hospital. Will someone drive this car, while I support him?"

The man with the flashlight slid under the Cadillac's wheel, as willing hands pushed the car from ditch to pavement. Another neighbor brought up the rear in Mike's Ford. It was less than a five-minute drive to the ambulance entrance of New Salem Memorial. This time, there was no wait as he pressed the buzzer, and Wilson hastened out with a wheeled stretcher.

A quarter hour after the actor's collapse, Mike had undressed him on a private bed with Wilson's aid, clothed him in a hospital nightshirt, and applied the mask of a portable oxygen inhalator. By now, the evidence of cyanosis was unmistakable. Even the patient's earlobes were blue.

"He looks bad, Doctor," said Wilson. "Think you can bring him back?"

"We've a fair chance. Bring me the cardiac pacemaker. It's on the top shelf in surgical stores."

Miss Ford had come into the room while they worked. At Mike's nod, she took over the oxygen machine, permitting him to bare the patient's chest and percuss the shape of the heart beneath the bony wall. To his surprise, it was roughly normal in size. The stethoscope told him the rate was half the normal figure, but there were no significant murmurs. When the pacemaker came, he was ready to place the two flat metal electrodes directly over the laboring organ.

"Switch on the current, Will. Thank God we got this today."

The effect was striking. Stimulated by the minute jolts of electricity now coursing through the heart muscle, the actor's sluggish pulse changed to a normal beat. Less than five minutes after the first touch of the electrodes, it had steadied under the surgeon's fingers—and the bluish tint had begun to fade from his lips and earlobes.

"What happened, Doctor?" Miss Ford asked.

"It looks like a Stokes-Adams attack from heart block. He fainted at the wheel when it hit him. The heart wasn't beating fast enough to supply the brain with blood."

"How soon will he come out of it?"

"Not for several hours, judging by his present reaction. He had a drink or two this evening; I hope they'll make him sleep awhile, even with the pacemaker going."

"I'll have someone stand by, in case he wakens before morning."

"When he does, call me. I'll stop the current, and we'll see if his heart can hold the same rate without it. Have you admitted him before?"

"Not that I know of."

"He's a medical case—but there's no point in bothering Dr. Melcher tonight. He can examine him tomorrow, and take an E.K.G. Then we'll see what's causing the picture."

Dawn was breaking when Mike returned to the actor's bedside. Jason West had begun to regain consciousness, after passing a tranquil night. While the surgeon was taking his blood pressure, he opened his eyes in sleepy wonder.

"So the men in white have closed in again. Unless, of course, you're an archangel, welcoming me to a better world."

"You're in New Salem Memorial, Jay," said Mike. "Apparently you decided to go on living. I'm glad my prediction was justified."

"Did you fish me from the pond?"

"You stopped in a ditch on Lower Street."

The actor shrugged. There was elegance in the gesture, despite the coarse-grained nightshirt, the elevated hospital bed.

"Trust me to fluff my big scene, Mike."

"Then you *did* know what was happening?"

"Of course. If you had help at the dam, you were told I've stopped there before. Last night's try was closer than most."

"Did you decide on suicide, and then faint?"

"It seems the wish brings on the attack, Doctor."

"Of course it does. It's further evidence that my diagnosis is accurate. You want to go on living."

"You don't believe I tried to crash the fence?"

"Nothing could be easier than smashing that rotten barrier," Mike said severely. "Your subconscious mind refused to carry out your plans for a grand finale."

"You've probed my psyche, and decided I fear death more than life. Have you also diagnosed my physical illness?"

"You had an attack of syncope. One of the more common failings of the heart."

The actor rolled his eyes to heaven. "As a two-time Oscar winner, I refuse to admit I suffer from a common ailment."

"With the proper treatment, you need suffer no longer."

"What treatment exists for coronary thrombosis—with an infarct?"

"If you can describe the trouble that exactly, you've had medical attention before."

"I had expert help—after my first attack, when I could still afford a specialist. Dr. Branch of Beverly Hills gave me the rundown. I was too low in my mind to listen closely."

"The anatomical picture's simple," said Mike. "A portion of the heart muscle is deprived of blood—and degenerates. In time, it's replaced by a fibrous scar."

"*My* scar is small, according to Dr. Branch. There was never much pain—and few coronary symptoms." The actor rested his head among the pillows; his manner was supremely detached, as though he were discussing another man's illness. "Apparently, the vital difficulty is the location of my *bête noire*."

"I'd guess your infarct originally involved the interventricular septum."

"That sounds formidable enough."

"It's the region where the internal nerve supply of the heart is located. In that area, the fibers act like telephone cables. Roughly eighty times each minute, they carry a message to the rest of the heart, from a center in its upper segment—the part called the pacemaker—telling the muscle to contract. Each of your heartbeats is initiated there. Just relax, and we'll see if it's functioning again."

While he spoke, Mike had been disengaging the electrodes of the pacemaker, which had remained attached to the patient. Now, he lifted the apparatus from the bedside table, and placed it on a stand in the corner. Applying a stethoscope to Jason's chest, he listened carefully to the regular *lupp-dupp* of the heartbeat. The rate was only a little more rapid than it had been last evening—but, with the demand now reduced to a minimum, the patient's color was good and he was obviously comfortable. Only an electrocardiogram, and other precise tests, would determine the extent of the permanent damage—and the chances of correcting it.

"This mumbo jumbo is most impressive," said the actor. "Did the gadget on my breastbone see me through the night?"

"Call it a safety factor that wasn't needed, once you recovered," said Mike. "Right now, your heart is running like a Swiss chronometer—if you can imagine a clock working at two thirds its usual speed. Fortunately, you have a second pacemaker in the lower part of the heart. It sets the rhythm, when the impulse from above can't get through the scar."

"The stand-in, I take it, is sometimes a bit lazy—hence my fainting spells."

"It's the precise picture of a syncope. Fortunately, there's a way to prevent its recurrence."

"Surely not by surgery?"

"The surgery itself is simple. All that's required is the placing of two electrodes in the heart muscle."

"To me, that seems anything but simple."

"In this operation, the mechanic is the healer, not the man with the knife. After we place the electrodes, we connect them to a device that generates pulses of electric current—a miniature version of the pacemaker we used on you last night. You wear it as you would a hearing aid—only it's under the breastbone, not attached to the ear. Once it's in circuit, it causes the heart muscle to contract at normal speed, even though your own cardiac system has failed. Instead of collapsing, as you did last night, you'd continue to be up and about."

"It sounds like a miracle, Mike. One you can turn on and off."

"They must have mentioned it to you in Hollywood. Several years ago at Stanford, I did experimental work with electric-battery pacemakers. By now, the technique's well understood."

"Something of the kind *was* mentioned. I refused to listen."

"Why? Did you have the death wish, even then?"

"I knew I was only half a man," said Jason West. "A few wires in my hide might lift the percentage to three quarters. It still isn't enough."

"Last night at the dam, the half man snatched your body back from death. With a pacemaker on your side, there's no reason why you couldn't act again."

"I'm no longer in demand as a star."

"There are other good parts available. I'm sure you'd get offers—if your friends knew you were available."

"Of course I'd be offered contracts," said Jason. "Could I accept a new role, when I'd be sure to let my producer down?"

"Not with a built-in battery to keep you ticking."

"Could I get drunk when I liked—and make love?"

"Not as you did at thirty. But you'd be leading a full life otherwise."

Jason West closed his eyes, and shook his head slowly. Watching from the foot of the bed, Mike saw he was enjoying the self-created suspense—as much as he had enjoyed yesterday's flirtation with eternity.

"Suppose I told you I'm an all-or-nothing man, Dr. Constant?"

"I'd call you a damned fool. No man can have life on his own terms."

"*I* did—until my heart gave out."

"And you refuse to compromise now?"

"One more quotation will drive home my point."

"Do you always think in quotes?"

"It's an occupational hazard of my trade. This one is really obscure. A poem called 'Let Me Live Out My Years,' by a fellow named Neihardt. It has overtones that would appeal only to an actor."

Eyes still closed, Jason West lifted a pontifical arm—and recited slowly, in a bravura tone, with lingering emphasis on each word:

Let me live out my years in heat of blood
Let me die drunken with the dreamer's wine
Let me not see this soul-house, built of mud
Go toppling to dust—a vacant shrine!

And grant that when I face the grisly Thing
My song may trumpet down the gray Perhaps.
Oh, let me be a tune-swept fiddle-string
That feels the Master-Melody—then snaps!

The actor opened his eyes, and smiled. "*Quod erat demonstrandum*, Doctor. When a man has touched the stars, he can hardly be asked to walk the earth again."

"Just as you like, Jay. As I told you, we can't even be sure the experiment would work, until we test you thoroughly."

"May I have a hypo to make me sleep? Or are you afraid I'd get hooked?"

"You've been a failure as an alcoholic," said Mike, with a grin. "I can't say that a *homme fatal* is one of your better roles—and you were an outright flop as a suicide. I'll send Miss Ford with the needle."

The roosters were crowing in New Salem Heights when Mike sat down in the chartroom to update the history of Jason West—not for the hospital records, but to evaluate his own thoughts.

It was a chore he could have postponed—but he knew he would not sleep until he had put his conclusions in order. Using a semi-shorthand he had perfected as a student, he filled a page with no pause for reflection. When he had read back his notes, he felt his nerves relax. The actor himself, he reflected, could not have spoken in a more oracular style.

Last night, another prodigal was admitted to the fold. The most spectacular prize, so far—the once-famous actor, Jason West.

His cardiac condition, while serious, is not half so dangerous as his wounded spirit—which refuses to adjust to the inroads of middle age, the loss of his former matinee-idol status. Therefore, he continues to play Hamlet to an audience of one—himself. He is the star-crossed mortal, still asking man's eternal question: is it better to be, or not to be?

Last night, at the Van Ryn dam, Jason went through his suicide ritual once again—a well-rehearsed performance, that takes him to the brink, but not beyond.

Someday, of course, his make-believe could backfire. Last night, syncope and the resultant cyanosis almost killed him outright. At best, without prompt help, the brain damage could have been irreversible.

Will this brush with death mark his turning point? It would be presumptuous to say yes. It is still my hope that he will consider the pacemaker surgery I suggested. A man of his attainments need not leave the stage when he is no longer the central figure.

Mike took up his pen. The image of Jason West he had just sketched with such freehand ease was a wish projection, with little relation to the derelict across the hall. . . . Again, he filled a page with shorthand, making no effort to sort his words.

What of the prodigal who remains under her doctor's care, in loco parentis?

Sandra West's brother, by his own admission, has come home to give up the ghost. Sandra herself has returned to New Salem—with her defiance intact—to live outside its accepted codes. Last night, I made the bitter discovery that a woman possessed (*the term has a special meaning only a trained psychiatrist could explain*) *will stoop to any end to win the object of her desire.*

As for Anna Van Ryn, her patience, so far, has been infinite.

I cannot escape the conviction that she, too, will return to Paul if he summons her. Like Sandra, her eyes are opened wide to his depravities. Yet she continues to believe the image he has created—the thwarted genius who still needs her help. . . .

The pen lifted from the sheet, as Mike stifled a yawn. The demands of the wearied body, he told himself, could sometimes be more useful than the vagaries of an overactive mind. Fascinating though it was to dream of altering a man's destiny, he could hardly avoid this collision with truth.

What had he done, so far, to save Jason West from his touch-tag with death? Could he prevent Sandra from surrendering to Paul Van Ryn, at a time of his choosing? Blocked by the iron codes of New Salem, could he spare Anna from the next assault of Paul's fists—while Anna herself seemed almost eager for punishment?

A line remained at the foot of the second page. He printed two sentences there, and stared at them a moment more, before he shredded both sheets into Miss Ford's wastebasket.

> *Aaron Zeagler—to whom it is second nature to play God—has promised action on his return. How would* you *stop Paul, if you had Zeagler's power?*

Dr. Artemus Coxe had once expressed regret that he had not strangled the last of the Van Ryns at birth. The solution was an attractive one. Mike Constant needed a determined effort to drive the evil fantasy from his mind.

Zeagler's promise, he knew, had not been an idle one: he could hardly hope for so forthright a solution. . . . *You're thinking like him again,* he told himself. *Get back to your job with no more lost motion.*

With a final yawn, he reached for a fresh work sheet—and began to set down the clinical notes on Jason that Dr. Lawrence Melcher would read that noon.

SIX

The note taking at dawn had also been a soul searching. In the fortnight that followed, Mike was glad he had destroyed the inconclusive evidence. Fearing new alarums and excursions, he had been gratified to find the basic situation unchanged—thanks to Paul's continued absence from Rynhook, and the fact that his three patients, involved in their respective cures, seemed content with an uneasy status quo.

The day after Anna's admission to the hospital, Paul had sent roses from Washington, along with a telegram expressing his concern over her accident and his pleasure at her recovery. The wire stated that he would report later on the results of his mysterious journey—but there was no explanation of the reasons that brought him to the nation's capital.

Anna's postoperative progress had been satisfactory, though the patient herself remained on the listless side. Jason West's prognosis was still reserved—pending a more precise evaluation of his electrocardiogram (which showed a definite heart block from a coronary scar) and his response to several drugs Dr. Melcher wished to try. The actor had been docile when informed that he must submit to several days of bed rest—but Mike was not deceived by this apparent co-operation. Jason, he knew, was biding his time. The questions raised on the night of his syncope remained unanswered.

Sandra had made a sickbed visit the day after her brother's admission, her arm in a light plastic splint Dr. Coxe had molded at Mike's suggestion to replace the original cast. Her poise had been complete when she thanked Mike for saving Jason's life. It was hard to believe this was the girl who had answered him without shame when he had questioned her plans for the future—and harder still to face the memory of her fury on the long-distance phone when she had failed to make contact with Paul.

Mike could only wonder if that contact was now established—or if there was another, healthier reason for Sandra's apparent serenity. It was encouraging to note that she had entered her name on the hospital's roster as a registered nurse who would be on call as soon as her arm was fully healed. . . . This, after all, was Mike's own province. He could question her safely, even though the questions skirted forbidden ground.

"Does this mean you'll remain in New Salem for the present?"

"I've got to—for Jason's sake," she said. "There's no choice—now that you've told me what's really wrong with him."

"I'll have to admit he can be treated as effectively in New York."

"The city's no place for him, in his present frame of mind."

"Suppose he consents to pacemaker surgery?"

"Do you think he will?"

"He knows the score, Sandra. Semi-invalidism—or a return to his career, on a limited basis."

"Jason has yet to admit there are limits to his future."

"Unfortunately, I can't decide for him."

Sandra smiled for the first time. "Thank you for making him see the alternatives. I gather you gave him the usual Mike Constant treatment—with an extra rasp."

For most of that fortnight, hospital routine had kept Mike much too busy for introspection. Melcher (he was sure) had warned his doctors of the need for better procedure—and, save for the fact that the case-history reports had shown no marked improvement, the staff surgeon had found no valid reason to lodge a complaint.

Midway of the first week, when the director announced a meeting in the hospital dining room—a gathering that combined a formal review of the past month's activities with a traditional *Kaffeeklatsch* —Mike was almost reluctant to attend. The revelations of his first night still seemed ominous—but he would have preferred more evidence before discussing them fully.

Ralph Pailey, the secretary for the board, arrived promptly with his ledgers. Perhaps a dozen doctors were seated around the joined tables in the dining room, with Melcher presiding. Among them were Louis Garstein, and most of the members of the New Salem Hospital Corporation. Bradford Keate had sent regrets because of a heavy case load—but appeared at the last moment, his manner wary, his hussar mustache bristling.

After Melcher had introduced him, Mike reminded himself that his contact with these men was still too tentative to permit a forthright criticism of their methods. Rising to address them, he knew it would be wiser to recommend rather than to insist. At the same time, the opportunity to stress much-needed reforms was too valuable to be missed.

"When I was employed by this corporation as staff surgeon," he said, "I assumed you would welcome constructive criticism, based on my own experience in university hospitals in California. In fact, since Dr. Melcher's immediate goal is a seal of approval from the Joint Committee, I assumed this was my primary function."

"You assumed correctly, Dr. Constant," said the director. The ripple of laughter that ran round the table was not precisely an endorsement—but it was an icebreaker of sorts.

"Please bear with me if my remarks seem on the didactic side," said Mike. "I'm stating the obvious when I say your equipment and facilities—compared to a university hospital—are relatively Spartan. That doesn't mean they aren't adequate to the average situation, but I still feel we must be prepared for the unusual. As luck would have it, I faced such a crisis in the first operation I performed here—an emergency splenectomy, with the owner's daughter as my patient."

Keate spoke up promptly; his booming voice matched his manner.

"Do you consider a splenectomy a dangerous operation, Doctor?"

"By no means," said Mike. "Any surgeon should be able to cope with such a situation. I refer to facilities—not to the technique itself. Time is of the essence in dealing with a ruptured spleen. The patient's life can depend on an adequate supply of blood—which we didn't have."

"I've already remedied that lack," said Pailey. "The nearest blood bank has agreed to supply us with stored Type O not more than five days old. Unused flasks will be replaced weekly. I might remind the members of this corporation that my order has doubled our blood costs."

"While also doubling your supply," said Mike.

"Don't look so worried, Ralph," said Melcher. "You'll find ways of passing that cost on to the patients."

The administrator reddened, but Mike saw he was pleased by the backhanded compliment. "I accept the challenge, Larry. It's just a matter of an extra punch on an IBM card." He smiled at Mike—but there was little warmth in that fleeting grimace. "Forgive me, Dr. Constant. I didn't mean to interrupt your indictment."

"The real emergency that first night was cardiac arrest," Mike said. "Granted, not many hospitals of this size would have a pacemaker, or a defibrillator, as part of its equipment. Fortunately, we acquired both instruments the next day, through the generosity of the owner. As it happened we needed the pacemaker immediately—for a case of syncope from heart block."

"When will you need it next, Doctor?" asked Garstein. "Misfortune always travels in threes."

"When I perform pacemaker surgery on Jason West—if he'll permit me."

Keate spoke up from his side of the table. "What technique did you have in mind?"

"The pacemaker is used to control the heart—via a catheter electrode, while the operation is in progress. The actual procedure is to implant electrodes in the heart muscle. The circuit is completed later with a miniature pacemaker—a portable counterpart of the machine we now have, attached to the patient's chest."

"Isn't that rather drastic surgery for New Salem Memorial?"

"I performed the operation a dozen times on the Coast."

"So you've rounded out your equipment inventory, and stocked our blood bank. Does that conclude the catalogue of our sins?"

"The greatest defect in this hospital, Dr. Keate, is not in equipment but in records. Frankly, there must be tremendous improvement in your files before you can hope for accreditation."

"A busy doctor hasn't time for paper work," said the outsize surgeon. His eyes roved round the table, picking up several approving nods.

"It's still essential, if you'll think the problem through. With adequate case histories, and a busy and thriving hospital, every doctor in New Salem will have a chance to upgrade himself in his profession. Our surgeons can aim for fellowships in the American College of Surgeons. Our medical men can hope for membership in the Academy of General Practice, or even the F.A.C.P. Medicine is changing fast, gentlemen. No doctor can afford just to ride the current. Unless you get in and paddle, you'll be left behind. And the place to start is our file room."

Keate's scowl had deepened with the recital of these home truths. As Mike paused, he banged the table with his hand.

"Are you going to take this lying down, Larry?"

"I'm afraid the criticism is long overdue, Brad," said the director. "The inspectors from the Joint Committee called on us just ten months ago. They gave up all thought of approving the hospital, after a visit to our record room."

"Damn it all, Larry, I can't handle this type of paper work and see all my patients." Again, the rising murmur round the table told Mike that Keate had scored a point.

"I think you could manage both, Dr. Keate, if the hospital provided a few short cuts. Mr. Pailey has been reasonable in the matter of the blood bank. Perhaps he'll agree to dictating machines—and an extra secretary to type the records. Dictation of this type can now be done by phone, from your own office, before you send a patient to the hospital. That means a carbon for your files—and the sort of records we'd be willing to show to any examining board."

"How do I pay for this extra help?" asked Pailey.

"While he's dictating, the physician can add the details required for insurance patients—which probably means ninety per cent of his practice. Your department can then perform that service for the doctors, and earn the fee paid by most companies."

"I'd pay to get rid of that chore," one of the general practitioners volunteered. "To say nothing of the arguments over diagnostic procedures."

"One final item, gentlemen," said Mike. "Your hospital, at this moment, is far too crowded."

"Are you saying we should do less business?" Keate asked.

"Not when it needs to be done. I am suggesting that diagnostic studies should be made in your offices, whenever possible. Instead, the patients are being sent into the hospital, so their insurance will cover the bill."

"That's our privilege, since we're corporation members," Keate shot back.

"Not if a New Salem resident dies—because he can't find a bed here."

"What's *your* opinion, Larry?"

To Mike's surprise, Pailey leaped into the breach, before the director could answer.

"Dr. Constant's right, Brad. We've had far too many overnight admissions for diagnosis alone. And the way X rays have been ordered lately, I'll have to put on an extra technician. I want those beds free for the five-day appendix jobs. *They* show a real profit. Besides, we've been getting squawks from the insurance carrier for Zeagler Electronics; these diagnostic admissions are beginning to run up his costs. Suppose he makes his next complaint to the owner? Do you want Zeagler to think we're running a gold mine here?"

"Aren't we?" Keate asked—and joined in the laughter that ran round the table.

"We won't, if Zeagler doesn't renew our lease."

Melcher took back his authority smoothly. "I'd suggest we forget mammon for the moment, and get back to Hippocrates. All of us should think carefully about the suggestions Dr. Constant has made —particularly in reference to the records. I, for one, am grateful he's made them. If there are no more questions, I move we tackle the refreshments."

Over the coffee cups, Mike found it easy to renew his acquaintance with the corporation doctors. It was too soon to wonder if his remarks would bear fruit—but he could not help feeling their logic had sunk home. He was not surprised when Bradford Keate departed immediately, on the plea he could keep his patients waiting no longer. It was obvious that the most glaring offender at New Salem Memorial was now a potential enemy. Here, at least, he was sure that his plea for reform had fallen on barren ground.

On the fifth day of Anna Van Ryn's convalescence, she was transferred to a wheel chair on Mike's orders. That same afternoon, he found her seated in a patch of sunlight that fell through the open window. She had been a sadly docile patient—and her resignation had troubled him even more than her refusal to open her mind on his visits. Today, there was no mistaking her new alertness. Like the quick lift of her head when he entered, and the spots of color in her cheeks, it suggested the liberated captive—still hesitant on the prison doorsill, but conscious for the first time, of his freedom.

"Something about your manner tells me I'm in for a frank discussion," she said. "Can't we postpone it until I'm stronger?"

"In my opinion, you're strong enough now to hear the truth."

"Truth's a big word, Dr. Constant. Are you its sole custodian?"

"Truth number one is obvious. You've decided that recovery is worthwhile."

"I'm giving the idea a trial run, thanks to you."

"Any surgeon could have saved you from the blow you suffered. You owe me no thanks for that."

"I wasn't thinking of your surgery. And it was a *fall,* not a blow."

"It's time to look at the record, Anna—to admit what really happened. You've had five days to think about it."

"I fell on the kitchen stair. Wasn't that enough to damage the spleen?"

"There are faster ways. In the Far East, where the incidence of malaria is high, the spleen is often swollen. Professional assassins can kill a victim with a single blow, just under the rib cage. Death comes from internal hemorrhage. The attacker doesn't leave a trace —except for a bruise that generally goes unnoticed."

"Are you implying I was attacked by an Oriental thug?"

"I've known Paul a long time, Anna. He was middleweight boxing champion at Cornell. His skill came in handy on the football field, when the referee wasn't looking."

"This is New Salem. And I never had malaria."

"You can't go on protecting him forever."

"What you're suggesting is only a guess, Mike. I won't accept it."

"Your three hospital admissions prove it's more than that."

"Those injuries were caused by falls."

"Shall I go to the Duchess—and recommend psychiatric treatment for her son?"

Anna showed no sign of wavering. He had expected none.

"You'll have even less luck with her. We both agree that Paul's art is his life. We'll permit no interference as it develops."

"My advice is still on the record. Do you have any idea why he went to Washington?"

"It's only a guess, but I think someone offered him a commission. He has friends there—in and out of government."

"Isn't it odd that he *always* leaves you—after these so-called accidents?"

"Don't make me tell you to mind your own business, Mike."

"I wouldn't listen, so don't waste your time. I'm an old-fashioned doctor, Anna. When I save a patient's life, I try to follow through on the job."

"Believe me, I appreciate your concern. But I won't accept your estimate of my husband—and I'm standing behind him, so long as he needs me. Once I failed a man who loved me. I can't let it happen again."

Mike shook his head. "Feminine reasoning always defeats me in the end. Nothing I ever studied in medicine prepared me."

Anna laughed. It was the gayest sound he had heard from her. "Don't try, then. Just tell me when I can leave the hospital."

"In a week, if all goes well."

"I'm making arrangements to expand the Zeagler Clinic. And we're reopening the children's playhouse I built in the annex. It's taken doing, but I think both will be going concerns from now on."

The day supervisor had just informed Mike that Anna had

phoned Sandra West that morning. Later, she had spent a half-hour on the floor below, in conversation with Sandra's brother. Mike could understand the purpose of that phone call now—and the visit with a fellow patient. Anna Van Ryn, it seemed, was one of those rare mortals whose only true happiness was service for others. Now that the shadow of her husband was lifted, she had begun to give of herself again, as freely as the sun gives light.

"I've asked Sandra to take charge of patients, when she isn't on cases of her own," Anna continued. "She's promised to reorganize the whole clinic, and train two practical nurses to fill in for her. It will mean a full-time job, until her arm heals."

"And you found work for her brother as well?"

"Jason has promised to rehearse the children, for a production of *Peter Pan.* Wouldn't you say I'd put in a good morning's work?"

"Is that the real reason you thanked me just now?"

"Of course, Mike. Jason has avoided me ever since he returned to the Gate House. Finding him pinned to a hospital bed was a heaven-sent chance. I made the most of it."

"It's sure to cause talk in town—when Sandra starts at the clinic."

Anna colored, but her eyes were steady. "Are you suggesting I should be a jealous wife—simply because Sandra knew Paul, and loved him, before we met?"

"Surely you realize she loves him still."

"Then her love can be a bond between us. Or is that too much for a man to understand?"

"I can understand you're a woman in a million, Anna. How did you persuade Jason to take on the children's theater?"

"Why don't you ask him yourself? You'll be interested in his answer."

Mike found the actor propped in pillows beneath a reading lamp, with an open book on his lap. Three days of bed rest had done wonders for Jason West—smoothing the pain wrinkles from his forehead, and reducing the sparrow pouches beneath his eyes to a fraction of their former size. The spectacles he was wearing, and the air of concentration, gave him an almost professorial air.

"Don't look so amazed, Mike," he said. "You find me perusing the works of Sir James Barrie. That doesn't mean I've taken leave of my senses."

"Were you surprised when Anna visited you this morning?"

"Delighted is a better word. For the past two days, I had been nerving myself to visit *her*—when you doctors let me up."

"I hear she's offered you a job."

"Strictly as a trial run. I've always wanted to direct. We'll call this my first testing. If I fail, my peers need never know. If I succeed, we'll call it a portent."

"Have you ever worked with children?"

"Oddly enough, yes. At an actors' school, on the old Paramount lot. Again, at a community center in Pasadena, when I was still living with my third wife. I was known to my young charges as Uncle Jay, and universally respected—once I convinced them I must be obeyed. Most children are natural mimes, if properly handled. All of them enjoy acting."

"I'm glad the idea appeals to you."

"It's a stopgap, Mike—while I weigh the choices we discussed. I can still say no, if you forbid such exertions."

"Once you leave this hospital, you'll do as you like. I don't expect you to take advice from me. But you'll last much longer, if you admit that your heart needs artificial help."

"As of now, I intend to make do with present equipment."

"You're a fool to crowd your luck, Jay."

"Perhaps I was born a fool, Doctor. A fool of fortune, with . . . *that one talent which is death to hide*. Milton: the sonnet, 'On His Blindness.'"

"As I remember, the next line is *Lodged with me useless*. . . . That just might happen, with another syncope."

"You're learning my trick of quoting much too well. Let's drop the subject, for the present."

"Just one more question. How did Anna persuade you?"

"I've told you I loved her, when we had our brief idyl onstage. I love her still—though I've found her ravaged by a bad marriage. This morning, she charmed me out of thought. Had she asked me to step out that window into space, I'd have done so gladly."

"What if *Peter Pan*'s a failure?"

"*Peter Pan* isn't the sort of play that fails. Not with a professional hand at the helm."

"Anna's theater is part of the Zeagler Clinic. It stands on made land—across the creek from the foundry slums. Most of the children will come from families on relief. Are you sure you can make actors of such material?"

"Children are the same anywhere, Mike. Unspoiled savages, crying for a purpose and a guiding hand. I daresay these will be wilder than others—but I can handle them."

"You've visited the clinic?"

"Only the wing that houses the theater. Sandra took me there, when it was still building. Zeagler spared no expense; many Broadway houses aren't as well equipped. Of course you know he gave Anna both buildings as antidotes for her husband."

"That I can easily understand."

"Anna learned social work the hard way—at a New York youth center. Since she married Paul, she's had just one *raison d'être:* to mold his devil's clay into human shape."

"I've spent the last half-hour trying to convince her that's impossible."

"And failed, I'm sure—because you used logic. My friend, you have to be married a few times before you even begin to understand women. Anna will stay at Rynhook, as long as she feels she's needed there. But it helps, knowing she can escape when she wishes—merely by crossing Bear Creek, and closing the clinic door. My job is to convince her she'll find real fulfillment there. Far more than she'll get from Paul's alleged art."

"It's a tough assignment."

"No tougher than yours. *You'd* like to persuade Sandra to give him up. To find a new life for herself, preferably with you. Between the clinic and the theater, we might accomplish both—providing we're willing to make haste slowly."

"I haven't had time to look the buildings over. Is it a good setup?"

"One of the best. Zeagler built it while this hospital was still under construction. I suppose it was a sop for his conscience—when he was forced to refuse work to old foundry hands who didn't have the skills he needed. The theater was a later addition, when New Salem Heights started using the play center, along with Old Town families. Before Zeagler went abroad, he wrote a check for expansion—whenever Anna was so inclined. Part of it will go into the costumes and scenery for *Peter Pan.*"

"Apparently you told each other a lot."

"Anna did most of the telling. What she did, mainly, was convince me I'm not the utter failure I seem. And I'm sure our little talk brought back a happier time for her—when her life wasn't complicated by a psychopathic husband, and the need to drink after dark."

"Whatever the therapy, it was good for you both."

"I hope I helped Anna. I know she helped me—by reminding me that old actors, unlike old soldiers, don't fade away. Not while there's a playhouse on their doorstep."

Ten minutes later, when he stopped at the lab, Mike was still filled with a sense of achievement he had been careful to conceal from the actor. There was no need for reticence when he repeated the gist of their conversation to Louis Garstein.

"It's enough to restore one's faith in miracles, Louis."

"There's nothing miraculous about it," said the pathologist. "*I'd* call it a routine example of human chemistry in action."

"People don't shed their traumas as easily as a snake drops its winter skin."

"They do sometimes—when they really want to change. Warmth and springtime are usually involved. Or should I say the chance to make a fresh start?"

"I can still hardly believe what I heard, Louis."

"You saw it happen today—in two hospital rooms. Anna has convinced herself she can help a fading star to rise again. Your friend Jason's decided *he's* vital to the success of her clinic. Even with Paul's shadow between them, it's a start on the road back—for them both."

"Why has Paul disappeared?"

"Sight unseen, I'd say my brother-in-law's behind it. That's only a guess, so don't misquote me."

"Zeagler's still in Tel Aviv."

"Aaron could pull wires, if he were based on the moon. Paul's the basic problem, here in New Salem. Anna's climbed out of her glass before, when he's away. For all we know, Sandra may postpone her own plans, where he's concerned. In your place, I'd give some of my free time to the Zeagler Clinic, and see how things are going. Melcher will be delighted. Running full time, it will take the charity load from our doorstep."

Mike shook his head. He could still remember Sandra's cool politeness in the hospital corridor.

"She knows where to find me, if she wants help. So does Anna. I've run across a problem right here that interests me more. A hepatitis flare-up in New Salem Heights."

"We've had that on the books for some time."

"I did a research project on the disease in Los Angeles. It's intrigued me ever since."

"It's intriguing enough to my department," said Garstein. "In fact, it's the damndest enigma you ever saw. But don't you have enough to do—running a surgical service, and remaking lives on the side?"

"The last project is running itself, Louis."

"Never make assumptions where the human animal's concerned," said the pathologist. "They seldom follow the rule book—including the one composed by Sigmund Freud."

SEVEN

One of the things that had troubled Mike from his first day at New Salem Memorial was the unusual number of patients with jaundice, or infectious hepatitis. The disease had always been an unwelcome hospital visitor, since it was difficult to isolate and responded to no known therapy save bed rest, vitamins, and diet. Only that morning, he had noticed that two more severe cases had been admitted for treatment—both of them private patients from the factory's executive rolls.

Melcher had been co-operative when he had asked for a free afternoon to make a preliminary survey.

"I'm delighted at your interest, Mike. What started it?"

"My graduate thesis at Stanford was on diseases of the liver. Hepatitis has always brought out the Sherlock Holmes in me."

"Detect to your heart's content. I hope you'll come up with more results than the County Health Department."

"How far has the epidemiology been checked?"

"Their team has worked both sides of Bear Creek. The score's been virtually zero."

"No source of infection so far?"

Melcher shrugged. "Not to my knowledge. I'm not even sure the Typhoid Mary label applies here."

"At Stanford, we stopped a student epidemic cold when we pinned the infection focus to a diner just off campus. The culprit was a short-order cook, with no visible symptoms of his own."

"We haven't had that sort of luck. Frankly, I'm beginning to worry —and so is Ralph."

"I can understand Pailey's concern," said Mike dryly. "With its bed-rest requirements, hepatitis can raise hell with your turnover rate."

"I know that's a sore point with you, Doctor—but we *do* like to keep our patients moving."

"Even when they're paid for in advance by the County? You have plenty of ward beds—and enough practical nurses on the register to handle routine cases."

"That's just the trouble. Most of these patients are from the Heights. Their hospital insurance runs for around thirty days—with only partial coverage for this type of illness. Which means the IBMs must do extra billing."

"The disease is at home on both sides of the tracks, Larry. I discovered that in my own studies of epidemic patterns."

"Pin down the cause, and you'll have two sets of people grateful—Pailey's bookkeepers, and the salesmen in Zeagler's development."

"Has it begun to frighten off homeowners?"

"No one has moved, so far. But the building committee hesitates to expand, until they can offer a clean bill of health."

"How long has the disease been epidemic?"

"It doesn't have that status yet, thank God. But we're getting close. The trouble started about two months ago. We hoped it would rise to a peak like most flare-ups and then subside, as immunity developed. This one has kept building steadily. I'm not sure how well we'd stand a really acute change."

"I'll look at the records after rounds," Mike said. "Then I'll take a one-man tour of the Heights. Sometimes a new viewpoint helps."

In the record room, he brought out the file of hepatitis admissions. It was already extensive enough to cause alarm, since many cases of this particular ailment were treated at home. He needed almost two hours to jot down the essential statistics.

Most of the patients were young adults or teen-agers—a characteristic he had observed in his California surveys. A majority, as Melcher had remarked, were bunched in New Salem Heights. Using a street map, and tracing paper as an overlay, Mike marked each residential street involved, in both the Old Town and the new. Then, using a series of red dots, he ticked off each house where hepatitis had struck. The pattern was an instructive one. Folding the overlay carefully, he went to his quarters to don street clothes for a visit with Dr. Coxe.

When he drove up to the hospital on Lower Street, his mentor was waiting on the porch. He whistled softly after Mike had spread the tracing and pointed out what he had observed.

"That's an impressive layout. I never realized so many cases were concentrated in one area."

"It isn't just the Heights that have been invaded. Most of these homes are to the north of the Van Ryn dam."

"Are you suggesting the disease moved from the Old Town, to the southern fringe of Zeagler's development?"

"That seems evident from this chart," said Mike. "Three cases out of four are on waterfront adjoining the lake, or directly above it. At first glance, the lake would seem the culprit, but the town water supply doesn't come from it and it's too early yet for much swimming. The next guess would be the dam itself. It's been a footpath ever since I can remember."

"You could be right," said Dr. Art. "Why not go to the public health officer with the idea?"

"Not until I've made a spot check. Can we use your car? Mine isn't too happy on those Old Town grades."

Five minutes later, the two doctors were climbing the grassy slope of the dam, to gain the footpath that linked New Salem proper and the Zeagler housing units on the Heights. When they stood on the high ground above the spillway, Mike found it hard to believe that anything so dangerous as hepatitis could travel this route.

The waters of the artificial lake, extending into the green fold of the hills, made a mirror for the afternoon sunshine, except where a water skier was cutting patterns along the western shoreline. Only to the south, where the better-paid employees of the Van Ryn Foundry had once dwelt, were there signs of decay—boarded house fronts in gardens gone back to scrub, a storm-wrecked dock whose pilings stood in gaunt relief against the sky. At that distance, the turrets of Rynhook were only a dimly sensed presence in their screen of boxwood.

"Are *all* those south-side houses abandoned, Dr. Art?"

"The sheriff moved in on the last one shortly after the foundry closed down."

"People are still living in the tenements. How do *they* make ends meet?"

"Some of the old ironmongers have bottom-rung jobs at Zeagler Electronics: they don't have the know-how to handle the machines. A few others work as gardeners and handy men on the Heights—or hold down jobs like Wilson, your orderly. By and large, our Lower Streeters are working New York State relief for all it's worth. It's easier than joining the fruit tramps, or going south with the birds."

"Most of the foundry people have been here for generations. You can't blame them for staying."

"True, Mike—but even in our day, the pattern was breaking down. Since then a lot of migrant Southerners have moved into those tenements. Most of them are former sharecroppers from the cotton states, too untrained to hold even a good blue-collar job. Their wives find work as domestics. The men just draw relief checks, after they've qualified as residents. In a sense, it's the fault of the state welfare program; the places they came from weren't so generous."

Looking down at the roofs of the ancient tenements below, Mike felt a vague sense of uneasiness. He remembered the smoking chimneys in winter, and the swarms of children playing in the street. Even in prosperous times, this corner of the Old Town had been a slum. Until now, it had kept its self-respect.

"What will become of these people, if Zeagler can't upgrade them?"

"Eventually, they'll drift elsewhere. He's offered to set up a training school for a new factory, if the city authorities will agree—and he can find room to expand. Unfortunately, there's no adequate site except the foundry."

While they talked, a band of school children crossed the footpath on the dam, laughing and pushing as they ran. Dr. Coxe smiled at the group, and called several of the youngsters by name.

"Listen closely, and you'll hear Southern accents," he said.

"They've been climbing the slope of the Overlook after school—just as you once did. If Anna gets her theater going again, they'll have a better playground."

"The reproductive rate hasn't suffered in Lower Street," Mike observed. "If *I* were unemployed, I'd think twice about procreation."

"These Old Towners have a different point of view. Each new child means a bigger welfare check—and more packages at the surplus food depot. It's hard to accept in America, but some of those families have never lived so well before."

"Who provides their medical care?"

"The County—when they ask for it," said Dr. Coxe. "Anna's clinic does its share. I ran a baby clinic of my own on Lower Street, when I could afford it."

A huge cockroach, darting from the tall grass at the dam's edge, scuttled for the footpath and disappeared in the direction of the higher ground to the north. The old doctor eyed the insect with a shrug of distaste. "You might call that a symbol," he said. "Even the roaches would settle for Zeagler, if they could vote. I don't blame them; the pickings are better on that side."

"Maybe that six-legged migrant is more than a symbol," said Mike. "It lives on filth and carries it. On the Coast, we found that infested apartment projects had a high infection rate. Once the buildings were fogged with an agent capable of killing roaches, the case load tailed off."

A second insect had just followed the first, to be joined by a pair in tandem. Dr. Art shook his head in bewilderment—then stared down the slope at the sullen blocks of tenements.

"Got that map tracing with you?"

Mike spread the overlay on a rock at the dam's edge. From this observation point, the living pattern was clear—a half-moon of red dots, centered on the point where the dam entered New Salem Heights.

"The footpath's a logical channel of infection," Mike said. "Why couldn't these specimens of the order Hemiptera be vectors?"

Dr. Coxe was still frowning at the map. "If that's true, the disease should be centered in those tenements. They've swarmed with roaches for a half century."

"When people live under minimal conditions of sanitation, they tend to pick up mild forms of hepatitis. The same was true of polio and other diseases, before adequate vaccines were developed. Infection often hits such people in their infancy, when they've enough hangover immunity from the mother to protect them. The result is a mild case of hepatitis, polio, or whatever—and a clean bill of health thereafter, on the vaccination principle."

"It's true that hepatitis has been striking harder in the Heights," said Dr. Art. "Joe Saunders, our public health man at City Hall, has been working hard on the same case-incidence principle, hoping he'll come up with an infection pattern. *His* map will probably go you one better, Mike. Hepatitis is a reportable disease, so he has a file on every case, in the hospital and out."

"What are his conclusions?"

"He knows the trouble centers in New Salem Heights. Like you, he's bothered by the fact the Old Town seems the logical source of infection—since the Van Ryn dam leads directly to the Zeagler tract. There's just one drawback to your theory. There have been no hepatitis cases in those tenements—mild or otherwise—since it first invaded the Heights."

"What about a carrier? Someone with no visible symptoms, who lives on this side of Bear Creek?"

"Produce him, Mike—and the town will give you a medal."

"He's *got* to be there, Dr. Art. How about lighting a fire under your friend Saunders—while I do a little more prowling on my own?"

"I'll get on it at once. Meanwhile, since you've come this far, you might cross over to Bearclaw Point. Sandra moved back to the Gate House this morning."

"How does that concern me?"

"It's pretty lonely on the Point after dark—and Paul's been away for eight days. This could be the time to advance your own cause."

"I think not, Dr. Art."

"Isn't it worth a try?"

"I'll stop by, just to please you."

"We'll pick up your car on Lower Street. It should take you that far without pushing."

Once he was under the wheel of the Ford, Mike found he was not quite ready to cross the bridge to Bearclaw Point; a return to the hospital seemed advisable, if only to don his best suit and tie. The phone rang as he was about to leave his quarters. It was Garstein—and the pathologist's first words froze him to the receiver.

"Paul's in town. He drove in this afternoon from Washington."

"How do you know?"

"I've *seen* him—from a discreet distance. Like a good husband, he came straight here, to visit his ailing wife. I stationed Wilson outside the door to make sure he behaved—but Paul was in one of his better moods. After he'd gone, I faked a reason for stopping by. I've never seen Anna happier."

"Did you learn where he'd been?"

"She couldn't wait to tell me. I know this is hard to believe, but Paul's been tracking down a job. Two jobs, in fact. The big one's in Munich—a series of murals for the plant Aaron just opened there. He has a second commission at an Army PX outside of town—from the Defense Department in Washington."

"Is that all she could tell you?"

"A genius has come into his own. What more could you ask?"

"I'll go to see her right away."

"I wouldn't, if I were you. Too much interest on your part might make her suspicious."

"Surely Zeagler's on the level?"

Garstein's hoarse chuckle filled the receiver. "The night you operated on Anna, if you'll recall, I suggested my brother-in-law might offer Paul a bribe."

"Is that what you'd call these commissions?"

"Call them what you like. They'll remove him from New Salem."

A light was flooding Mike's brain. Until he adjusted to its meaning, he could not pin down his racing thoughts.

"These jobs are real, Louis. Paul *is* a painter. What if he has talent?"

"If he has, there's no harm done. Aaron gets a return on his investment. If not, he's put an ocean between Paul and Anna—and given her a chance to escape from a doomed marriage. Either way, it's the break I've been praying for."

"I can understand Zeagler signing his son-in-law for a factory mural. You haven't explained the Army contract."

Garstein's chuckle was even deeper. "Aaron owns the construction firm that's building this new Post Exchange. It's on the Frankfurt *autobahn*—so his architects plan to make it something special."

"Zeagler's thorough. I'll have to give him that."

"Two jobs will keep Paul abroad longer than one. The head architect, by the way, is *another* genius, named Werner Von Helm. Paul will work under his orders."

"How does Anna feel about his prospects?"

"She's positive Paul can't miss. That's why I want nothing said that would start her thinking. Anna's no fool, you know."

"In that case, I'll postpone my congratulations until tomorrow."

"This news is a weight off her heart, Mike. Paul has his first real job—and *she* has months of free time ahead, to do as she likes. Keep that in mind when you talk to her."

Mike hung up the phone with lighter spirits. In the doctors' parking lot Wilson's voice stopped him as he was kicking the motor of his car to reluctant life. The orderly had just emerged from the side entrance, with an envelope in his hand.

"This came by messenger, Doctor."

The envelope was addressed in a familiar, spidery hand. Mike could guess the contents, even before he broke the seal.

Dear Michael Constantinos:

I need advice badly. Will you come to Rynhook at once?

Marcella Van Ryn

A full hour of daylight remained when Mike parked on the gravel turnaround at Bearclaw Point. The red Porsche stood under the porte-cochere, but there was no sign of the driver. A shadow took form on the towering granite porch as he crossed the driveway. It was Nellie, the colored maid. Beckoning to him to follow, she led the way down a flagstone path that circled the mansion's north wing. She did not speak until they had threaded a maze of boxwoods, to reach the lawn that faced the Hudson.

"Madame's out by the summerhouse, Doctor. She wants to see you there alone. That's why I waited; I was afraid you'd meet Mr. Paul in the driveway."

"Is he here now?"

"Upstairs—in that big room where he works. He'll be takin' off for the city any minute now."

"Is madame well?"

"This evenin', she's as well as she'll ever be. When she sits out-of-doors—which ain't often—you *know* she's got back her head."

Marcella Van Ryn awaited her caller near the white-latticed gazebo that stood, like a prim Victorian ghost, at the far side of the lawn, where the Van Ryn land sloped to meet the Hudson. Remembering the raddled figure he had encountered in the hall, Mike could hardly believe his eyes when she held out a hand in greeting. This afternoon, she was wearing a pearl-gray skirt that ended at her ankles, a starched shirtwaist, and a straw boater that rode almost gaily on her high-piled pompadour. Once again, there was a feel of costume in the moment—but the fresh river breeze, and the last rays of sunlight in the boxwoods made the costume real.

"You're looking well today, madame."

"You find me at my best, Michael—because I feel my best. I suppose you know the reason."

"If you mean Paul's commission in Germany—?"

"This is the happiest day of my life. My son's talent has been recognized, much sooner than I had dared to hope."

"I just heard the news at the hospital," Mike ventured. He was still feeling his way, certain that a false note would destroy the dream picture the Duchess had created, as a breath collapses a house of cards. "You have every reason to be proud."

"When I saw you last, I was still standing between Paul and reality. Do you remember?"

"Not too well, madame." The thumping lie had come naturally; he was learning his responses fast.

"Reality is something Paul can't always bear, Michael. From the start, I've done my best to protect him from people who couldn't understand—and give him a place where he could create. So, I must say, has Anna." With a commanding gesture, Marcella Van Ryn led the way to the summerhouse, where she settled in a basket chair. "There were times, these past few years, when I feared we must go on sheltering him forever. Do you follow me, so far?"

"I'm doing my best," Mike said carefully. When the Duchess pointed to the hassock at her feet, he hastened to sit there. The position, he told himself, was appropriate. Bit by bit, he was adjusting to the contrast between the crumpled figure he had last encountered in the lower hall of Rynhook and the elegant beldame who faced him now. For all her turn-of-century air, Marcella Van Ryn might have been any normal mother, happy with her son's first triumph. Zeagler, it seemed, had played his cards admirably, and his timing had been perfect.

"Paul's offer came from the last source on earth I expected to give him help," said the Duchess. "At first, I feared it was another of that man's tricks."

"Aaron Zeagler wants to be your friend. This is his way of showing it."

"I will never be his friend. In my opinion, he has no such illusions. This morning, I received his note from abroad. It assured me that there were no strings attached to his commission. It stated that he has accepted Anna's opinions of Paul's skill, and is giving him a free hand."

"Zeagler is a man of his word," Mike said. "If he made those promises, he'll keep them."

"Tell him I will make no concessions. You might add that I thank him for his perception, where my son's concerned."

"I'll convey your message, madame."

The old woman's face was lit with an inner glow, now that he had resolved her last doubt. He no longer felt guilty at the white lies he had told her so glibly. Tonight, he would leave the Duchess of Rynhook a happy woman—regardless of the woes tomorrow might bring to her door.

"Artists down the ages have had rich men for their patrons," she said. "Why shouldn't Zeagler follow their example? Particularly since Paul is his son-in-law?"

Mike did not speak. The queries had already been answered, in the Duchess' own mind. They were part of a decision already made, one he had no intention of changing.

"New Salem has accused me of tying Paul to my apron strings," she said. "I could hardly reveal my true reason for keeping him here. *You* understand it—don't you, Michael?"

"I think I do, madame."

"I couldn't let him go, until he was truly ready. The risk was too great."

"Of course you couldn't."

"He's ready now, thanks to those years of training. Today, he promised me he'd do great things in Munich, and I believed him. I haven't minded his despair, or his black moods. I've forgotten the times when he wasn't—quite himself. Such things are privileges of the artist. Don't you agree, Michael?"

It was another hard question. Hoping it was his final testing, Mike forced himself to answer steadily.

"Artists are a law unto themselves, madame."

"You *do* see why I gave him the tower suite? Why I let Anna live there, once I saw she was good for him? A genius needs his special comforts; he must have his own way. While he was perfecting his art, I kept out unwanted visitors. Now, at least, I can open my doors, and throw away the keys. Have I done right?"

"You had no other choice."

"Thank you again, Michael. Today, I like your answers. I'm glad I sent for you."

When she gave him her hand a second time, Mike needed a definite act of will to avoid lifting the gnarled knuckles to his lips. This afternoon, the Duchess of Rynhook had put on the mantle of the patroons. It had been easy to accept her status.

"I'm glad I could reassure you, madame. I'm sure Paul will make the most of his first real chance."

When she dismissed him—with a last queenly gesture—he was careful to bow from the steps of the gazebo. Only when he took the path through the boxwoods, and heard a rustle of branches, did he realize his visit had had an audience of one. He did not need the glimpse of the face in the leaves, the hot, staring eyes, to know that Paul Van Ryn had wondered, even now, whether the door to his prison was really open.

A step into the boxwoods would have cut off the eavesdropper but Mike did not risk the move. Instead, he paused on the path, pretending to light a cigarette until a faint sound of footsteps told him Paul had gone.

The Duchess knows her son is mad, he told himself, as he walked on to his car. *She's praying he'll outgrow that madness in his work. What's more important, she knows that I know, and she's relying on my silence.*

The Porsche was gone when Mike left Rynhook. He could only conclude that the artist, having made peace among his women, had already departed for New York.

A light was burning in the Gate House parlor. He parked at the curb, breathed deep to steady his racing heart, then marched straight toward the porch—half expecting, even now, that his knock would go unanswered. His spirits lifted when the door swung open. Sandra stood on the threshold—and her smile of welcome was all he had hoped for. So was the gesture inviting him to enter the dusk-dimmed hall.

"Come in, Mike. When I saw you drive in, I hoped you'd call on me. Shall we go into the parlor?"

She led the way to the Gate House living room—a long, wide-windowed apartment whose bookshelves and deep leather chairs reminded Mike that Sandra's father had been a man of letters, as well as a competent estate manager. Taking the chair she offered him, watching her choose a matching chair across the rectangle of

Persian carpet, he could almost believe this was a visit of friend to friend.

"Will you have a cigarette? Or a drink?"

"Neither, thank you. I just stopped by to ask your plans, now that you're out of the hospital."

"For the clinic? Or for Paul?"

"We'll take Paul first. I gather you've already seen him."

"He came straight here from the hospital. Zeagler's commission has made another man of him."

"So his mother tells me."

"It's something you must see to believe, Mike. Even you would be convinced."

It was not the reaction he had hoped for from Sandra West—but he was careful to hide his chagrin.

"Paul has pretended with you before," he said quietly. "This could be a repeat performance."

"He wasn't pretending this time. I'd stake my life on that."

In a sense, you've done that already, he told her silently. It was harder now to keep control—intolerable that he must hide his true thoughts from Sandra, as adroitly as he had concealed them from the Duchess.

"Just what did Paul tell you? Or is that an indiscreet question?"

"Of course not, Mike. He means to paint as he's never painted before—now that he's on the brink of great things."

"Did he mention Anna?"

"He'd just come from the hospital, where he told her the good news."

"Were you hurt that he stopped there first?"

"After all, she's still his wife."

"I suppose he promised to divorce her in your favor—after he earns Zeagler's fee."

Sandra took the thrust without flinching. "I can't blame you for judging him harshly—after what you saw on the Overlook, and what I've told you. You'd understand the new Paul a great deal better, if you'd talked with him this afternoon."

"Perhaps I would," Mike said dryly—remembering the rustle of the Rynhook boxwoods, the white, staring mask he had glimpsed among the leaves. Even had he dared, it was too soon to reveal the secret he shared with Marcella Van Ryn.

"It wasn't a time for promises," said Sandra. "Not with Anna still in the hospital. Paul stopped here to say good-by—and to ask my pardon for the way he'd treated me in the past. To say I'll hear from him again, when he has something real to tell me."

"When does he leave for Germany?"

"On a ten-o'clock flight from Idlewild. I wanted to see him off, but he said I'd better not."

"Apparently, he can't wait to begin those murals."

"Can you blame him?"

"Are you sure this is *all* I should know, Sandra?" It was the first time anger had conquered prudence. He could not regret the flash of temper.

"I've left out my hopes—for us both. Somehow, I didn't think they'd interest you."

"They wouldn't. Do you mind if we discuss the clinic? It's a much safer subject."

"Not at all. I hope you approve of my working there?"

"Isn't it a bit odd—considering the fact that Anna will be your employer?"

"I don't think it's odd at all. For one thing, I have to make a living. For another, she loves Jason, and wants him near her."

"Did Anna tell you this—or did you guess?"

"Call it a little of both," said Sandra. "Anna and Paul were never really suited. She knew it, almost from the start. For awhile, I suppose, she was still in love with the idea of marriage to a Van Ryn. Then she felt she must stick it out—because Paul needed help so desperately."

"So far, we're in complete agreement."

"Try to see things from her viewpoint, Mike. When she met my brother, he was still a great star. Anna was another rich man's daughter, who'd tried to be an actress and failed. When Jason went back to the Coast, she felt she'd failed him, too. Paul was in New York, waiting to be helped—"

"We still agree. Anna's the sort of person who must help *someone*."

"You do understand, Mike—far better than I hoped. She's seen him through a bad time. Six whole years, while he waited for recognition. Now that he's launched on his own, her usefulness is ended. Isn't it natural that she should turn to Jason?"

"Will she give Paul a divorce?"

"I'm sure of it—the moment he's on his own feet in Germany."

"Do you honestly think that life arranges itself that simply, Sandra?"

"Why not—if people know what they want, and have the courage to take it?"

It would have been easy to tell this love-deluded girl that the chimera she was pursuing had never been more unreal—that the knight she had clothed in brand-new armor was still a dragon who could blight his victims with a breath. Once again, Mike reminded himself that the logic of truth would be wasted. Sandra would open her eyes to the real Paul Van Ryn—or risk the fate that Anna had escaped by a hair. There was no middle ground where she could find salvation.

"Even for you, that's quite a vision," he ventured. "Paul's deserted you in the past, and returned, when it suited his whim. Why think he'll *marry* you—on a promise he hasn't made? Can you even be sure he has an outside chance to succeed in Munich?"

"Are you telling me this job abroad is a trick of Zeagler's?"

"The thought's yours, not mine," Mike said quickly. "If I were Anna's father, I'd do anything to separate them."

"Even if it's true, it alters nothing. The commission is genuine. In a month's time—less, if he works fast—Paul will prove his talents to the world."

"With a factory mural? And a decoration in a Post Exchange?"

"Werner Von Helm's a famous architect. When those buildings are opened, they'll be photographed for every paper in Europe. There'll be features in the New York press, and a photomontage in *Life*."

"Are these facts—or did Paul imagine them?"

"They're part of his contract. What better start could an unknown artist hope for? He's sure to get other offers later. There are already enough canvases at Rynhook for a one-man show—"

"Suppose those paintings are explosions of the ego, and nothing more? How long will he last with Von Helm?"

"Do you always have to think the worst of him?"

"Some habits die hard, Sandra." Again, he could not regret a flash of anger.

"Then at least be fair and reserve judgment—until he's shown what he can do."

"Why? Because he's turned on his charm one more time—and you've been foolish enough to believe his promises?"

"I've told you he made no promises."

"But he did ask you to wait, until he was really free?"

"Yes—since you insist. And I told him I'd be *proud* to wait."

Sandra had spoken with her head high. For the last time, he repressed the urge to confound her with the truth—the fact that her lover had almost killed his wife, and might easily try to kill again. Tonight, Sandra West was immune to facts.

"Let's not quarrel any more," he said wearily. "I came here to offer my services to the clinic. I hope you'll accept them."

Darkness had fallen when he left the Gate House, with no clear idea of a destination, no plan save an overriding need to be alone.

It had been a relief to talk no more of Paul—to turn instead to the organization of the Zeagler Clinic, the equipment New Salem Memorial would furnish, the assistants Sandra could recruit among the practical nurses in the County. The clinic would specialize in rehabilitation, since the bulk of New Salem's indigent patients were now routed direct to Indian Hill. Sandra had already found two physiotherapists, who could work part time at the exacting task of training both the long-disabled and the convalescent cripple in new skills. There would be a prescription counter, where those unable to afford much-needed drugs could fill their needs. And part of Zeagler's last donation would go to enlarge the baby clinic and the child-nursery center—two departments whose routine medical needs were so often neglected by parents on relief.

Mike had taken what comfort he could from Sandra's eager questions, from the evident pleasure she felt in planning her new job. Now that the conference was over, he admitted it had been a poor antidote for the fears still gnawing at his brain—fears which had grown even more intense, now that he had measured the extent of her surrender to a hopeless dream. . . . He was still deeply depressed when he took the highway to Indian Hill, changed his mind at the crossroad, and turned into the series of hogback turns leading to the Overlook. Until his torment had eased, he was in no state to face his fellow man.

When he reached the gravel parking space at the tor's edge, he found a dozen other cars already there—and guessed, from the silence enveloping each back seat, that the Overlook was still New Salem's favorite trysting place. His own visit—he admitted wryly—had been only a reflex act, a fumbling effort to recapture the emotion he had felt on his first and only date with Sandra, ten years in the past. Already, it was nearly time to relieve the doctor in charge at New Salem Memorial—to admit, once and for all, that work was now his only solace.

He realized he was being followed, a few seconds after he had eased the Ford into the first steep downgrade—and, dim though the memory was, he had a working image of the car that had just left the parking lot in his wake. He knew it had trailed him from the valley, at a discreet distance; he recalled how cautiously it had parked on the far side of the tor, with its engine idling, while he had held communion with the past. . . . Memory stirred again when his pursuer coasted into the downgrade behind him, with his lights out, and gunned his motor to close the gap between them. That whirring evidence of leashed power was the hallmark of the sports car. He was all but certain this was the brick-red Porsche he had seen at Rynhook—even though Sandra had said Paul was on his way to Idlewild.

Both cars were now on the first hogback. Mike blinked his lights in warning on the turn, cramped his brakes and shifted to low gear. His pursuer answered with a burst of speed that brought them almost bumper to bumper. On the next curve, his lights came alive, a blinding burst that forced Mike to hug the center of the road. Then, with a wild horn blast, the sports car leaped forward to close the gap—and nudged the jalopy's rear bumper, in a deliberate attempt to force it through the guardrail.

The attempt failed, with inches to spare: only a stout guidepost, catching Mike's right hubcap, saved the Ford from plummeting into the void. The sports car backed sharply—and Mike braced himself, for a second thrust. He would never know if he owed his deliverance to the enemy's loss of nerve, or the sudden appearance of a convertible crammed with teen-agers on the road below.

He let out his breath in a belated roar of rage as the still-unseen driver, cutting his lights a second time, whisked round the curve, to roar toward the valley. The Ford's motor panted mightily while Mike backed free of the splintered barrier. Risking his life a dozen times on the last hogbacks, he reached the highway in time to pick up his enemy in the traffic stream—but the other's nimble driving, plus his headstart, were too great a handicap. When Mike reached the clover leaf to the thruway, the sports car had long since merged with the southbound flow.

During that headlong pursuit, he had been too choked with fury to realize how narrowly he had missed death. He would never remember turning into the doctors' lot at Indian Hill, or how he reached his quarters. The inevitable reaction set in when he staggered through his bathroom door. He was still retching over the bowl when he felt a hand at his elbow, and found himself facing Lenora Searles.

"Head under the tap, please," the nurse said crisply.

The water was a tonic—but Mike was still glad of her support. He had been nearer to fainting than he knew.

"Better, Doctor?"

"I'll be all right in a moment."

"Forgive me if I startled you. I was on the terrace when you came in. I saw you needed help."

"I'm the one to apologize," said Mike. He steadied himself on the doorjamb, while he waited for the room, and his visitor, to settle down. "I don't do this often. You can take my word it isn't alcohol."

"Come into the fresh air. Your head will clear faster."

On the terrace, Lee Searles led him to a canvas chaise. "We share this space with Miss Ford," she said. "Why haven't you used it?"

"I'm afraid I've been too busy."

"Dr. Brett is covering for you until eleven. I'm on O.R. call—and was resting here. Would a drink help?"

"A drink is just what I need, at the moment."

The nurse vanished into her own living room, to return with a tall glass. Mike tried to sit up, only to find his vision had not quite steadied. When Lee sat beside him on the chaise, it seemed quite natural to rest against her, while he drank down a potent mixture of brandy and water. The contact, at another time, would have stirred his pulses; tonight, it was more comforting than erotic. While the sensation lasted, he was glad to accept this unexpected solace in a whirling world, to let his senses drift. . . .

"Don't pass out entirely, Doctor." Even in his half drowse, he knew the voice belonged to the paragon of the operating room. "Would you like Will to put you to bed? Or do you need Dr. Brett?"

Mike sat upright in the chair. "I can manage, thank you."

"Want to tell me what happened?"

"Call it a belated reaction. No one has tried to kill me for quite awhile." The words had escaped without his volition; the need to confide in someone, to seek some human warmth after Sandra's rejection, had been beyond his control.

"Did you say *kill*, Doctor?"

Lee Searles sat quietly while he told of his visit to the tor, and its near-fatal aftermath.

"Could you identify the driver—or the car?"

"He was careful to keep out of sight. The car was a foreign make. One of the smaller models."

"A Jaguar? Or a Porsche?"

Mike glanced at her sharply. "I'm no authority in that field. I'd better not guess."

"Shouldn't you call the police?"

"I doubt if they'd be much help, when I can tell them so little."

"Didn't you get the license number?"

"I was too busy saving my life to try, while we were still on the tor. When we reached the valley, I never had a chance to catch him." Mike finished the brandy, and got up slowly from the chair. The contact had served its purpose, he told himself; he had no right to prolong it.

"You must have some idea who it was."

"I can't help you there, either."

"Can't—or won't?"

"Let's leave it at won't. It's probably wiser."

"It was Paul Van Ryn, wasn't it?"

"Why do you think that?"

"The New Salem grapevine's efficient. So is the extension on Indian Hill."

"Why should Paul want me dead?"

"Both of us could think of several reasons."

"Are you a detective in your spare time?"

"Hardly. I had a few dates with him, when I first came here. It didn't take me long to see behind his façade. I've nursed enough psychos on the wards. For my money, they can stay there."

"You realize, of course, that all we've said tonight stays between us."

"Perfectly—since you insist on being noble."

Mike started toward the door of his suite, then turned back. "There's one thing more—and it's still off the record. With your training and ability, why did you come to a hot-bed hospital?"

"For the best of motives," said Lee Searles. "I fell in love with someone who happens to be married, and must stay married. He's the medical director of New Salem Memorial."

"Larry Melcher's a lucky man."

"I'll accept the compliment. Good night, Doctor."

She was gone before Mike could frame a reply. He stood alone on the terrace—watching the glass doors close behind her, letting his mind settle into the groove of the everyday. Now that Paul was gone, he knew he should be happy that he still lived and breathed. His deliverance seemed a small thing when his mind veered back to Sandra West—and the awakening in store for her.

EIGHT

Aaron Zeagler leaned forward at his desk to study the man in the visitor's chair. So far, his interview with Mike Constant had proceeded cautiously—on both sides.

"When we first met in this office, Doctor, I had planned a second talk in two weeks. Affairs abroad delayed me. I hope I'm forgiven my tardiness."

"You're a busy man, sir. Why apologize?"

"Since my daughter's welfare was at stake, I can hardly do otherwise. The problem of her husband should have been faced long ago. I won't say I've solved it by sending him to work with Werner Von Helm. At least his absence has relieved the pressure in New Salem."

"There's no doubt that it speeded Anna's recovery."

"Sooner or later she must divorce a man who's unfit for marriage, regardless of his talents. I've been careful to hold my tongue on the subject. Naturally, I felt encouraged when she came straight from the hospital to Mohawk Knoll."

"I'm glad you didn't broach the subject, Mr. Zeagler. If there's to be a divorce, she must work it out her own way."

"Would it help, if *you* advised her?"

"I'm her doctor, not a family counselor."

"You are also her friend—in the best sense of the word. Surely that gives you special privileges."

"Not to change people's destinies."

"You've seen her at work in the clinic this past week; you've watched her in the children's theater. She's now a happy woman, Doctor—but she'll lose her happiness tomorrow, if *he* comes back. What are we going to do about that?"

"She's happy at the clinic, because she's helping others there—in ways she could never help Paul Van Ryn. I think she'll break free of him, when she feels she's done all she can to advance his career. Six years at Rynhook is enough for any woman."

The industrialist pondered the answer, as he studied Mike Constant for the first time during the interview. It was true that he had improvised two jobs for Paul Van Ryn, with the offhand ease of a magician producing rabbits from a hat. Today, he could tell himself that those commissions had been an inspired blending of means and ends. He had just received a cable from his German architect, praising the artist assigned to his factory lobby. He had meant to keep that cable to himself, until Von Helm's opinions were more definite. Now that his thoughts had meshed with Mike Constant's, it seemed unfair to hold back.

"Paul is settling into his job, Doctor. Von Helm is delighted with his sketches for the murals. He tells me they show real aptitude."

"Have *you* seen a sample of his work?"

"Only the painting that now hangs at Rynhook. Anna brought it here to show me, before she had it framed. It moved me deeply—but I don't pretend to grasp its meaning."

"Nor do I. Most of all, it reminded me of Van Gogh. I won't push the comparison too far."

The industrialist leaned back in his chair and closed his eyes. The visitor's last remark had raised an unwelcome echo in his brain. Until it subsided, he could not trust himself to speak. The hammering of his pulses, and the ringing in his ears, were warning enough.

"Doesn't a touch of lunacy often go with genius, Dr. Constant?"

"So I'm told, sir. The subject's outside my field."

"It is another world from mine. *My* speciality is measuring a laser beam, and adapting it to my purpose. I can build a linear accelerator on order; I can make sure our first moon missile will be on target. *You* can save a woman's life with cold steel. It's a bit harder to look into Paul's brain, and decide how it functions."

"The effort's beyond me, sir."

"In that event, I'd suggest we give him the benefit of the doubt.

Providing, of course, that Anna has the good sense to divorce him—and he puts no obstacles in her way."

"Your forebearance does you credit, sir. I'll do my best to share your optimism."

"Optimism has its uses, Doctor. May I ask whether it applies to my hospital?"

"You've had my initial report, Mr. Zeagler. Much has been accomplished since I came there. Much remains to be done."

Zeagler nodded soberly, and drank deep from the water carafe at his elbow. The hammer blows of his pulse had subsided, but the need for caution remained.

"I don't suppose it's news to you that tempers are rising among the medical shareholders."

"I expected as much when I took the job."

"So did I. Sometimes there's nothing like a battle royal to clear the air. I trust you'll call on me, if you need help."

"This is a doctors' war, sir. We'll settle it with our own weapons."

Zeagler smiled. "I hoped for that reaction—and I'll respect it. Now that you're established on Indian Hill, I'll give odds on the outcome."

"Don't bet your money too soon. The problems in the hospital are far from settled. The hepatitis flare-up, to name just one. I'm sure Dr. Melcher's briefed you on that."

"My real-estate salesmen were ahead of him. Melcher says you have a theory about the disease."

"Nothing too definite, I'm afraid. We'll get nowhere until we pin down a definite source."

"What about the next visit of the Joint Committee? Will New Salem Memorial get its blessing?"

"We've a fair chance—if we upgrade our records, and keep the staff in line."

The industrialist rose from his desk and extended his hand. "At least you'll permit me to wish you well?"

"As things stand now, I'll need all the luck I can get."

"You're quite right to insist I stay clear. Either my hospital functions properly without interference, or I'll disown it. *Your* future's another story. After what you've done for Anna, I must find some way to reward you."

"If she puts her life in order, I'll ask for nothing more."

The two men walked to the office door together. Zeagler paused there, as he had done after the first interview, to put a paternal hand on Mike Constant's shoulder.

"What about your own life, Doctor? Can I help you to a better job—if this one's shot out from under you? May I be a friend in court, where Miss West's concerned?"

"The answer's no—on both counts. Thanks just the same."

"The rebuke is deserved," said Zeagler. "Miss West must work out her salvation alone. So, of course, must you."

"I'm afraid it's the only solution that has meaning."

Driving toward Bear Creek, Mike was glad he had ended his visit on a note of independence. As before, Zeagler had lifted him from his usual self with the sheer magic of his presence; it had been hard to control his own enthusiasm while the man's mind had raced on, leaping every obstacle in its haste to reach its target.

He had expected a candid avowal when Paul's name had entered the discussion; he was sure that Zeagler had sensed, if he had not defined, the torment Paul had sown through all their lives, erring only in his estimate of Paul himself. From Zeagler's viewpoint, it had been natural to assume that Paul's failings were those of the creative personality—that the artist could be separated from Anna with the offer of a ready-made showcase for his talents. He could hardly guess that Paul (obeying none of the rules of God or man) had accepted the commissions as his due. Or that he might return to Rynhook at any moment, to leave a fresh path of destruction in his wake.

Approaching New Salem from the Heights, Mike turned left into the now-familiar side road that led toward Bear Creek Crossing, and the Zeagler Clinic. It had been mandatory to talk around the threat of Paul Van Ryn, without giving that threat its real name. Now that his interview with Zeagler was over, he could regret that he had not stressed his own problems at the hospital—even though he could not accept help in that quarter.

His undeclared war with the stockholder staff was still a thing of thrust and parry—but it was inevitable that it would change to head-on collision at any moment. When the clash came, the final decision would be Melcher's: either the director must accept his recommendations for reform, or his usefulness—at an institution where profit was the watchword—would be ended. . . . The realization was unsettling—and he felt badly in need of a sympathetic ear when he left his car behind the Zeagler Clinic, and entered the building by a side door.

A lamp still glowed in the room he had fitted out as a laboratory, with Sandra's aid. Ever since Jason had begun evening rehearsals at the children's theater, it had been her custom to recheck the notes that had piled up during the day—immunization records, referral slips on communicable diseases which would be forwarded to Public Health, the data that crowds the files of every dispensary whose patients are largely the submerged poor. . . . Tonight, Mike paused for a moment in the darkened hall to watch her at work, saw that her concentration was deep, and passed on.

It had been two days since he had sat beside her at that table, helping to process the long file of patients waiting outside the door. The tasks he knew, had been handled perfectly in his absence: Sandra West was a born nurse, and her training was more than equal to any emergency she might encounter here. He was happy that she had found this outlet for her abundant energies—and thankful for the camaraderie they had established in those work hours, though he dared not ask for more. . . . Tonight he hoped she would finish her work in time to watch the finale of the rehearsal.

The children's theater was connected to the clinic proper by a glass loggia. It was a relief to slip into the last row of seats in the darkened auditorium and surrender to the now-familiar magic Jason West was creating on the stage. Tonight, the cast was in costume for the first time. Mike had arrived halfway through the opening scene in the nursery: a charming setting, featuring animal wallpaper and a wide-open casement to facilitate the dramatic arrival of Peter Pan. It was the first climactic moment of the play—when Peter, rising triumphant above the ties that bind mortals to earth, was proving that his ability to zoom into space was no idle boast.

Once again—though he knew most of the play by heart, thanks to these off-duty visits—Mike found his attention held instantly. It was hard to remember that these youthful Thespians were not professionals, now that tonight's rehearsal was assuming the shape and the tempo of a performance. Here, Mike told himself, was living proof that the actor-director had transferred his image to others, as naturally as Peter had just soared into the beyond, leaving the problems of the earthbound far behind.

Jason West might never perform again; his stubborn refusal to submit to remedial surgery could cut him down tomorrow. Tonight, at least, he had remade these children of the destitute, infusing each of them with his own divine spark—as artfully as he had once held whole audiences in his palm.

Now that Mike's eyes had adjusted to the dark, he could pick out the director's gaunt silhouette, in a seat on the side aisle, just outside the footlights' glow. Jason sat proudly erect, letting the scene go forward without a single interruption. Apparently, he had looked upon his work and found it good.

Anna was in the seat behind. A cloak was tossed about her shoulders, giving her the air of an acolyte awaiting orders from the altar. As the scene ended, and Jason's hand lifted to signal the fall of the curtain, she bent forward to whisper in his ear, before she rose to tiptoe from the theater. Mike had only a fleeting glimpse of her face as she passed down the aisle. It was enough to remind him that the light in Anna's eyes these days was only another outward proof of her transformation.

"Do you believe me now, Mike?"

Sandra's whisper brought him back to reality: she had slipped into the seat beside him, without distracting his attention from the business onstage. He did not reply at once—while the director ordered the curtain raised, and began to develop, in loving detail, the entrance of the infamous Captain Hook.

"You were a first-class prophet, Sandra."

"And *you're* directly responsible for what's happened. In your place, I'd be very proud."

"If anyone's responsible for this change in Jason, it's Anna herself."

"Neither of them would be alive today, if you hadn't saved them. Don't tell me it was part of your job—and nothing more. You talked Jason into wanting to live. He's played back that talk to me, word for word."

"It's Anna who made him feel needed again. What will he do when these rehearsals are over?"

"He's going back to New York—to take the first work he can find."

"Did you warn him he'd be signing his death warrant, without a pacemaker?"

"At this moment, it's impossible to tell Jason anything. He's always like this when he's in rehearsal. It makes no difference whether it's a picture spectacular, or a cast of small fry."

"He has to come back to earth eventually. When does this production open?"

"A week from Saturday."

"Then you still have time to persuade him."

"He's beyond my persuasion, Mike. I've asked him to look at Anna, to see how love has transformed her. He simply closes his mind—as though he slammed down a shutter."

"*I'm* familiar with that technique, too," Mike said—but she chose to ignore the thrust.

"He's convinced himself that a heart cripple has no right to think of marriage. He reminds me that Anna has made one bad choice, and mustn't risk another—"

"Perhaps Jason's the one who's avoiding risks."

"If he were a whole man, he'd propose to her in a moment. I'm sure he's been spinning out these rehearsals deliberately—making this show a perfect thing, as a thank offering to her."

"Swan song might be a better word."

Sandra put her hand on Mike's arm in a pleading gesture. "You saved him from the Van Ryn dam. You've made him function again in the theater. Can't you convince him that *real* life is worthwhile? Even when it's a shade less perfect than the parts he's played?"

Again, they fell silent—while Jason, with easy competence, restaged the meeting of Captain Hook and the crocodile. . . . It was the supreme irony, Mike reflected, that Sandra should plead her brother's cause and Anna's—when Anna's freedom from bondage would doom her to the same fate.

"I'm waiting for my answer, Mike."

"I discharged Jay two weeks ago. So long as he refuses my advice, there's nothing more I can do."

"I didn't know you ever discharged a patient until he was well."

"In my opinion, we've interfered enough. Why not trust Anna to cure him, from now on?"

"Anna may need help as much as Jason. Have you thought of that?"

"Many times. Can you tell me what *her* plans are, at present?"

"You know I can't, Mike. I've no right to question her, when I have a stake in her decision."

"So have I."

"I'm not asking for myself alone. You must see that."

Mike had already risen from his seat. "You're right, of course. Your brother's still my patient. So is Anna. I'll do what I can to see them through their illness. Let's hope this is the final stage."

"Then you *do* have a plan?"

"Not yet. Let's say I'm feeling my way."

He left the theater quickly, without giving her time to question him again. For the second time that day, he was glad he had spoken his mind—even though he had not dared to open his heart as well.

Lenora Searles emerged from her quarters with two gin and tonics on a tray. Accepting a glass, Mike relaxed in one of the terrace chairs and let his eyelids drop in frank surrender to weariness. Since his brush with Paul on the Overlook, these midnight encounters had become almost a ritual. He had begun to look forward to them, as islands of peace in the driving pace of the hospital day.

"How was Aaron Zeagler?" the nurse asked.

"Still full of plans—and still betting on the staying power of *homo sapiens.*" It was a luxury to speak his mind without editing, to know his hopes and fears would go no further.

"Including his son-in-law?"

"He's giving Paul every chance to prove himself. No one could be fairer."

"Did you suggest it was money down the drain?"

"You know better than to ask. Nothing annoys a philanthropist more than a suggestion that his philanthropy's wasted. Besides, it may not be true of Paul the artist. If we can believe the great Werner Von Helm, he'll deliver the goods."

"Does Zeagler suspect Paul's off his rocker? Or does he think he's just another king-size ego in search of an outlet?"

"So far, he's drawn no firm conclusions. You might say he's given us our heads, and hopes for the best."

"Did he discuss your chances at the hospital?"

"He offered to back me in a showdown. Naturally, I declined his help."

"You're in your second month here, Mike. Everybody's making book on how much longer you'll last."

"I suspected that."

"The first of the month is a milestone in a proprietary hospital. Particularly if the black-ink entries aren't quite so impressive as the month before. A lot of people have been studying the admission records besides Ralph Pailey."

"I'd be glad to show him the clinical histories."

"Ralph's too fast on his feet for lectures," said Lee. "He'll bring charges and make you defend yourself."

"I've evidence to show he's a gouger. Item one: ten grains of aspirin costs maybe a cent at the drugstore. Pailey punches another IBM card, and gets fifty cents for 'medication ordered' on the chart—"

"That's standard practice, in the cashier's cage."

"Item two: a normal appendix removed from a girl whose whole trouble was colon spasm, because of bad school grades. Item three: a County patient, kept in bed after a slight stroke, when he could have gone to the Zeagler Clinic for rehabilitation training. I'm not mentioning a couple of routine D and Cs—" Mike broke off his recital. "I hope you didn't scrub for either of them."

"No, Mike. But I can assure you they were both quite legal."

"Both girls were barely eighteen."

"It's the age of consent. Two physicians certified both as necessary abortions."

"How do you explain the way the tissue was flushed down the drain—before Dr. Garstein could make a section and diagnose normal pregnancy?"

"You don't miss much, do you?"

"I probably miss a lot. After all, Pailey's had three years to perfect the art of dodging."

Lee Searles put down her glass. "Has it occurred to you to ease off a bit?"

"I was hired to improve our standards. Larry's still behind me."

"He can't fight his partners, if a majority gangs up against you."

"With Bradford Keate the ringleader?"

"I'm surprised you haven't locked horns with him by now."

"I've been warned to keep out of his path. So far, I've managed. Fortunately, we've had no reason to consult."

"Consultation isn't Dr. Keate's way of practicing medicine. He's the kind who loves to operate—and loves to keep his patient load moving. That's why he's been steaming over the slowdown on admissions. You're bound to hear from him soon."

"You operate with him constantly. Is he a good technician?"

"As good as they come—providing the surgery's routine. He'll always earn his keep."

"So long as there are dissatisfied women—ready to part with a uterus they no longer plan to use?"

"You've summed him up, Mike."

"Maybe I'm asking too many direct questions. I know you're here because of Larry, but I never quite understood why *he* settled for New Salem."

"You must have heard about Mary."

"Only that he has a wife."

"She's the reason he accepted Zeagler's offer to lease the hospital. He needed cash—and it was easier to care for her here, without the pressures of big-city practice. Now that we're a going concern, it's become his way of life. Or, if you like, his success symbol to atone for his failure at home."

"Why doesn't he ask for a divorce?"

"Mary was his childhood sweetheart. They grew up together in Baltimore—and married while he was a resident at Hopkins. You know how hard that sort of test can be for the average girl. Mary just didn't have the patience to put up with the demands of a doctor's life. She began to open bottles to cheat her loneliness; she was a confirmed alcoholic before Larry could start his own practice. Not a compulsive drinker, mind you—like Anna Van Ryn. Mary was the kind who can't stop, once they smell a cork."

"Surely that was grounds for divorce."

"Not if you're both Catholic—and not if you feel partly responsible, as Larry did. A community like New Salem seemed the quickest answer. For a while, he thought he had the problem solved. Then he found she'd developed diabetes, as a side effect of alcoholism. The Lahey Clinic in Boston did its best for her—but she kept forgetting her insulin or her diet, and he couldn't be with her every moment."

"No wonder the marriage isn't mentioned at the hospital."

"I haven't told you the whole story. A year ago, he was tied up with an all-night cardiac emergency. When he came home, he found Mary in convulsions. She'd sent the maid away and taken her insulin, when she was too drunk to measure accurately. Apparently she'd injected two or three times the normal dose; on top of that, she drank some more, and forgot to eat. They pumped glucose into her until her blood sugar came up, but they couldn't revive her brain. She's been a vegetable ever since, with nurses round the clock. All she can do is swallow—when food is put on the back of her tongue."

Mike knew the picture, in all its horror. He had seen it before, when the brain was damaged by drugs, or by a simple lack of oxygen—a fate Jason West had escaped with minutes to spare. For the first time, he felt he could understand Larry Melcher. Especially the man's need for money, his even greater need to keep busy each moment of the day.

"Were there any children?"

"Larry wanted them, but Mary felt she wasn't ready. Now, of course, it's too late. The only happiness he has is with me. I'm not ashamed to give him that, no matter what people say."

"You shouldn't be, if you love him."

"I love him with every cell in my body. He'd like to love me the same way, I'm sure of that. It hasn't been easy, for either of us. Fundamentally, Larry is extremely moral. He worries about what people think of us; he tells me he's making no real sacrifice, that he's taking what he can't give."

"Larry's a first-rate person, Lee. Everything you've said tonight proves it."

"Don't let me enjoy my self-pity any longer. Talk about *your* love life for a change."

"At the moment, I haven't any."

"You know what I mean, Mike. You're carrying a torch for Sandra West, and getting nowhere."

"Would you advise me to put it out?"

"How can I, in my position?"

Mike smiled as he got to his feet. As always, this exchange of confidences had cheered him greatly.

"I've a confession to make. I envy Larry Melcher."

"I'll say as much for Sandra. Shall we conclude our visit on that note of mutual admiration?"

Next morning, waking with the memory of the strange dialogue on his mind, Mike was glad to learn that Melcher had driven to Albany to address a medical convention. Several hours later, after a routine morning on the wards, and a routine acute appendix that had called him away from his exhaustive checking in the files, he received a call from Kathi Sturdevant, the director's personal secretary.

"I know it's another busy day, Doctor—but could you visit Mrs. Melcher professionally?"

"Of course. What's the trouble?"

"You may not know this, but she's permanently—well, disabled." Miss Sturdevant's hesitation suggested she was leaving a great deal unsaid. "Her day nurse is with her now. Mrs. Melcher can't speak, but she can indicate discomfort. Apparently she's suffering from abdominal cramps, and they're growing more severe."

"I'll go to the house at once."

The director's home, a modest split-level above the dam, was only a short drive from the hospital. Mike had passed it a score of times on his way to the Zeagler Clinic; he had never before remarked the shuttered downstairs windows—and the other, less tangible signs of an invalid's abode. Mary Melcher's nurse, an elderly woman who had done fill-in work in the wards, answered the doorbell promptly.

"I'm glad you came, Dr. Constant. Her temperature was a hundred and two an hour ago, but it's gone up since. And she's having a lot of pain."

"Is she conscious?"

"As much as she'll ever be."

The day nurse led the way to the sickroom. Mike noted that it was charmingly furnished; only the hospital bed facing the picture window betrayed its function. Mary Melcher was a still-handsome woman who seemed no more than thirty-five. Her hair had been freshly waved, and the nightgown and bed jacket she was wearing could have come from Paris. Larry Melcher, Mike reflected, had done his best to keep the illusion of marriage intact.

"Will she respond if I speak to her?"

"No, Doctor. All she can do is show the spot that hurts."

The patient's hands, slender and lily pale, had just fluttered over the counterpane, to touch her upper abdomen. The motion was swift and tentative. When it subsided, there was no obvious sign of life from the bed, save for the woman's somewhat rapid breathing.

"She's dropped off again," said the nurse. "I can rouse her, if you wish."

"That won't be necessary. When did this trouble start?"

"The night nurse said she began to get restless toward morning. She had a slight temperature when I came on duty. We weren't too concerned, since it's happened before."

Mike opened his medical bag and turned back the covers of the bed. There was no tenderness in the patient's lower abdomen. When his palpating fingers touched her right side, he met the first sign of resistance, a distinct enlargement of the liver, lowering its edge more than an inch from its normal position. Though he searched with care, he found no further evidence of abnormality until he turned back one of the lower eyelids to expose the yellow-hued sclera.

"It's jaundice, isn't it, Doctor?"

"A rather severe attack, I'm afraid."

"There's a lot of it around these days."

"Any cases in this part of the Heights?"

"Not a single one. Most of the sickness is at the lower end of the dam."

"Has there been any hepatitis in your family?"

"No, Doctor. You don't think we could—?"

"People can be carriers without having the disease. I'm told both you and the night nurse have been on duty here for some time."

"We've had this case for over a year."

"That probably rules you out. What about the servants?"

"There's only the cook. She's been with the Melchers since they moved here."

"Have either of you been on vacation recently?"

"Mrs. Bancroft took a week, back in March. A girl named Ellen Stanley filled in for her. You can check on her through the nurses' register."

"I'll phone from the hospital. All we can do for Mrs. Melcher now is ease her discomfort. Can you get her to take oral medication?"

"She swallows anything we put in her mouth."

"Give her ten grains of aspirin in water. Follow it with fluids and carbohydrates at regular intervals. This is a disease that must run its course. No medication is of real value, except in a supportive way."

Back on Indian Hill, Mike needed only a phone call to solve the mystery of the contact. Ellen Stanley lived on Lower Street. A week after her service at the Melcher residence, she had come down with a mild case of jaundice—almost the only reported example of the disease that had turned up in the Old Town—had recovered easily, and gone to Florida to recuperate. A second phone call, to New Salem Heights, confirmed Mike's hope that the patient was resting well. He left a report with Miss Sturdevant and returned to his rounds with a lighter heart.

One of the staff surgeon's collateral duties was to cover Louis Garstein. The anesthesiologist had assisted him during his morning's operation, he had just left for Albany to speak at the afternoon session of the conference Melcher was attending. Since he had had considerable training in anesthesia during his years on the Coast, Mike had been glad of the increased experience, though his services were seldom needed in these slack hours of the surgeon's calendar. . . . That afternoon, he had returned to the still-skimpy hospital records when the day supervisor summoned him to the chartroom phone. The switchboard's note of urgency alerted him at once. So did the domineering voice that rumbled over the connection.

"Bradford Keate here, Doctor. Where's Garstein?"

"Reading a paper in Albany. I'm covering."

"One of my patients is coming in for an emergency. The banker's wife, Mrs. Vincent Schneider. I've ordered the O.R. set up for a gall bladder, at three o'clock."

"Do we have her history?"

"You'll find the details on my report. Will you order the pre-op medication?"

"Of course, Doctor."

"You've had some training in anesthesia, I suppose."

"Six months on that service."

"I'll be ready to scrub in an hour." Keate's tone was still bellicose, and more than a little hurried—the bark of the drill sergeant, addressing a backward private.

"You'll find your patient ready, Doctor." Mike hung up the phone with a grimace. Bradford Keate had been reasonably civil during his first weeks on Indian Hill—but Mike had noted recently that the man's natural itch for combat was gaining the upper hand. He had already wondered if Keate's bullying manner was a result of his demand for more complete records—or a still-tentative ruling that all postoperative tissue be cleared with pathology before the case history was filed with a final diagnosis.

The patient had just been admitted when Mike reached the private wing—and the banker was waiting outside his wife's door. Vincent Schneider was one of the best-liked men in New Salem. Mike would never forget how his bank had accepted his three-hundred-dollar note to clear up first-year expenses at Cornell—and how cheerfully Schneider had waited for its repayment.

"She's in real pain, Mike. I'm glad you're here to look out for her."

"We'll see she's made comfortable, Mr. Schneider."

"Is this operation a bad one?"

"Dr. Keate must have told you it's routine."

The attending surgeon's history of the case, which a nurse had just brought to the chartroom, was even briefer than usual; as he scanned it, Mike could be almost sure it was a personal challenge to his authority. That noon, the patient had complained of severe discomfort in her lower right chest or upper abdomen—the report was vague on the exact location. When the ache had grown worse, Keate had been summoned for a house visit and diagnosed an acutely inflamed gall bladder, with immediate surgery indicated.

Mike dutifully transferred these curt notations to the chart, along with the information on the patient's medical history, before he began his examination. It was a routine he had insisted on from the first, and he was careful to set down Keate's cablese verbatim. Mrs. Schneider was propped in bed when he returned to her room. She summoned a wan smile for his arrival, and indicated the focal point of her pain, a spot on the right side, just under the rib.

Mike made no immediate attempt to examine the abdomen, since he intended to make the usual complete evaluation, with particular attention to the heart and lungs, as a necessary prelude to anesthesia. He noted at once that the patient's breathing was somewhat rapid—interrupted at frequent intervals by a hacking cough. The picture could be explained by an inflamed organ lying just beneath the diaphragm, as did the liver and the gall bladder; he did not question it until his stethoscope touched the lower right side of the chest. Here, it picked up an unexpected finding, a faint but distinct rubbing sound, as though two pieces of leather were chafing under the chest wall.

Alerted now, and troubled by a premonition he had not yet defined clearly, Mike percussed both sides of the chest with extreme care. He was positive that the note on the right side was lower in pitch, an almost-flat sound that had none of the resonance of a normal lung.

"Will you read back Dr. Keate's diagnosis, Miss Bolton?" he asked the nurse who was helping him.

"Cholecystitis, Doctor. Acute and fulminating."

There had been no error in the transcription. He had asked the question for the record—and to establish an echo in Miss Bolton's memory.

"I want an immediate chest X ray."

When the nurse had left the room, he covered the suspicious area with the stethoscope another time, to make doubly sure of the pleural rub. The patient coughed again while he listened; the instrument picked up a spattering sound, like a rain of bird shot against glass. The *râles,* as the sounds were termed medically, gave an added warning of infection within the lung itself.

In another moment, the stethoscope had outlined the entire area of inflammation. At least half the lower lobe of the right lung was already consolidated. The diagnosis, which he was virtually sure the X ray would confirm, was pneumonia.

A final check remained—and Mike made it reluctantly, knowing in advance what he would fail to find. There was some minor rigidity in the upper abdomen, a logical side effect of the basal lung infection he had already outlined. But only the hastiest of examinations would have suggested the gall bladder as its primary cause.

"We're going to take you to the X-ray room, Mrs. Schneider."

"Is something else wrong, Doctor?"

"I can't be positive, without a film. It's nothing too serious to cure."

At this hour, there was no technician on duty in the darkroom, but Mike was familiar with the machine and its settings. He was giving the film its last washing when he heard a familiar bellow in the hall.

"Get this patient to the O.R., Miss Bolton! I didn't order X rays!"

Bradford Keate loomed in the darkroom door as he spoke. He was wearing a green operating suit, and his jowly face was suffused with rage. Mike faced the man calmly. He had crossed swords with the likes of Keate in California, and learned to enjoy the encounter.

"I think this X ray will interest you, Doctor."

Mike lifted the film from the tank, and held it against the ruby-red lamp that was the darkroom's only illumination. As he had expected, the lower lobe of the right lung was thick with milk-white shadow. It was the final confirmation of his diagnosis, a silhouette that spelled pneumonia to any doctor's eyes—though the man who faced him was still too angry to notice it.

"For your information, Constant, I don't expect help with my diagnoses."

"I made this discovery—as the hospital anesthesiologist. It's my duty to tell you that surgery's contraindicated."

"Have I asked your opinion?"

"You need it, to save you from a suit for malpractice."

Again, Mike held up the film for Keate's inspection. The surgeon, whose eyes had now adjusted to the darkroom, stared at the evidence with ominously narrowed lids. For an instant, Mike expected him to wrench the picture from the frame and destroy it.

"Well, Dr. Keate? Can you diagnose pneumonia from an X ray?"

The big man turned, and left the room with a resounding oath. Mike hesitated before he placed the film in the drying rack. Eager though he was to reassure Mrs. Schneider and her husband, he knew that protocol required him to keep clear. Now that Keate had been taught an overdue lesson, it was his privilege to select an internist—who would prescribe the treatment the patient should have received from the beginning.

Our war's in the open now, Mike thought.

In a way, he welcomed the knowledge.

Two days later, just before the regular monthly meeting of the staff, Mike stopped in the pathology lab, to find Louis Garstein hunched over his table as usual, in the act of transferring a culture from a Petri dish to a tube of broth. When he had sterilized the platinum loop he had used to lift the living bacteria, flamed the cotton plug and reinserted it, he faced the surgeon with his familiar crooked grin.

"Is it time for our *Kaffeeklatsch*?"

"We've got a moment to spare, I stopped here to try on my armor."

"Did you look in on Mrs. Schneider today?"

"I didn't think it necessary, Louis. After all, she's Dr. Melcher's patient now."

Massive doses of penicillin had already worked their magic with the pneumococci that had invaded Mrs. Schneider's lung. Mike had glanced at her chart on his afternoon rounds, and found both temperature and respiration close to normal. Fearing she might ask questions he could not answer honestly, he had been careful to avoid her room.

"I should have thanked you sooner for covering me two days ago," said Garstein. "You probably saved me from killing the banker's wife."

"You'd have discovered the pneumonia."

"Maybe. Keate's such an overpowering bastard that it's simpler to give his cases a lick and a promise. I might have missed it."

"It was his job to consider pneumonia, as part of the differential diagnosis. In cases of this sort, it's mandatory."

"They still get missed sometimes, Mike. Then, of course, they're called postoperative pneumonia, or maybe atelectasis."

"The grapevine's warned me to be prepared for what the French call *guerre à outrance* at today's huddle," Mike said. "Was it as accurate as usual?"

"That depends on Keate. What are you going to bear down on first—record keeping?"

"I can hardly avoid it, the way the files have been tailing off lately."

"If you do, he'll start swinging from the floor. Keate likes things the way they were, before you started reforming us. He expects you to back down this afternoon, now he's bared his fangs."

"Does he think I'll overlook the blunder he made on Tuesday?"

"Yes, Mike—if you want the truth. Make it a live issue, and you could find yourself fired on the spot. Keate and Pailey own fifty-five per cent of the corporation's stock. That gives them control, even though they're supposed to accept Melcher's rulings on policy."

"I'm sure Larry will endorse the reforms I've asked for. How else can New Salem Memorial be accredited?"

"That isn't the major consideration to some members of this club. Profits were down last month, because you vetoed corner cutting. Keate has been moaning ever since, and so has Pailey."

"They still need accreditation desperately. This afternoon, I'm going to demand up-to-date records. If Keate hits me, I'll hit back. *Next* time, I'll go all out for an active tissue committee. Will you back me?"

"Of course—if there *is* a next time, where you're concerned." Garstein covered his microscope, and picked up his aluminum arm rests. "I suggested a crackdown on tissue procedure, the day I came here as a pathologist. The committee was appointed—with Keate as chairman. It hasn't met since. He's been too busy operating to spare the time."

"What about a review committee—to check mortality rates?"

"Larry proposed that. He was voted down." Garstein stumped toward the door. "Arguments in the lab will get you nowhere, Doctor. Present them on the floor. I hope you keep your scalp when the fighting's over."

The meeting was held in the hospital dining room, and featured the inevitable coffee urn, the chef's best sandwiches—and an air of good fellowship that seemed genuine enough when Mike and Gar-stein entered. All of the eight-man staff were present, except Keate and Pailey. Mike nodded to Gideon Bliss, who specialized in obstetrics and gynecology; to Hugo Brett, a surgeon whose family name was one of the oldest in the valley; and to Crosby Pendergast, a New Salem internist whose practice was second only to Melcher's.

The three doctors returned his greetings cordially enough. The director, who was arranging chairs at the conference table, indicated that Mike should sit on his right, and welcomed him with a smile.

"We're waiting for Brad," he said. "He phoned he'd be late. This is a big day at his office."

Mike spread his notes. It was like Bradford Keate, he thought, to stress the extensive practice he enjoyed. Glancing at the faces around the table, he read a mixture of feelings there. Evidently this was not the first time his enemy had used an ancient gambit to build up his entrance.

Pailey came in a little later, staggering under the load of ledgers he carried, and followed by a secretary with an identical burden. Keate appeared while they were settling in their places—a glass of fashion in a pearl-gray suit, his brows knitted into a solid scowl as his eyes met Mike's. His response to Melcher's welcome was more growl than greeting. Mike just escaped smiling when Pailey leaped to his feet to hold out a chair.

Melcher took charge smoothly. There was no sign of an impending storm during the reading of the minutes, a debate on future expenditures, and a review of last month's admissions and discharges. The news that at least a dozen cases had required extended hospital care, and the fact that the ward beds were now crowded with County cases (including a heavy load of hepatitis admissions) were received in a silence that held no hint of strain. Only Keate's taurine breathing, and the lift of his pointed mustaches with each exhalation, suggested that the principal stockholder was biding his time.

"We will now hear from Dr. Constant, gentlemen—on the conclusions he has drawn from six weeks' tenure."

Mike rose from his seat and balanced with both palms resting on his notes, while he waited for an uneasy stir to die down. Keate's scowl, he noted, had changed to a naked glower. Hesitating to touch a match to the powderkeg, he found himself speaking mildly.

"Our primary purpose, as stated at our last meeting, is to gain a certificate of accreditation from the Joint Committee. As you know, I've spent much of my time studying our records, as well as our physical layout. The latter, I am glad to repeat, remains adequate, with a noticeable upgrading in surgical supplies. Once again, let me congratulate you on the caliber of your operating-room staff. In its present state, that department would be accredited tomorrow."

"Tell us something we don't know, man!"

Keate had almost snarled the words. The look he fastened on Mike was black with hate. The older surgeon, he realized, meant to force the issue with no waste motion.

"At our last meeting, Dr. Keate, I stressed the importance of adequate records. Meticulous paper work is essential, if we're to survive the next visit of the committee. I was promised improvement. Most of you have complied. Others have fallen by the wayside, after a promising beginning. *You,* Doctor, have shown no change whatever."

The murmur that ran round the room, led by Louis Garstein's cackle, was too startled to be called mirth. At the table's head, Melcher sat with his face a patient mask. Keate was on his feet instantly, and his voice was just under a shout.

"Can you prove this ridiculous assertion?"

"In your own words," said Mike. "It doesn't stop with operative records. Your clinical histories are much too sparse. Progress notes and discharge summaries are practically nonexistent. You aren't the only offender, Dr. Keate—you're merely the most outstanding."

"Stick to the point, Constant. What do you object to in my operative descriptions?"

Mike slid a sheet of paper from his files. "Here's one such entry, in toto. *Anterior and posterior perineal repair performed, usual technique. Supravaginal hysterectomy. Closure with chromic catgut, and silk for skin.* I submit it as grossly inadequate. There are a dozen others in this folder. Shall I read them too?"

This time, there was no mistaking the laughter that filled the room. Keate looked at his colleagues in sullen amazement. He seemed unable to believe that he, and not Mike, was the cause of the mirth.

"If this is the extent of your indictment, I can't take it too seriously," he said. "My record of postoperative recovery will stand unchallenged."

"It's still a fact that such reports would never be accepted by the College of Surgeons. Nor can we hope for an acceptable rating while they're standard practice here. On top of that, the pathological reports on your cases still show an amazing amount of normal tissue removal. Especially in appendices and uteri."

"I defy you to back that charge."

Mike opened the folder, to take out the hysterectomy report. "This is a prime example. Why did you make an abdominal approach to a uterus that showed only one fibroid tumor, no more than two centimeters in size?"

"Are you instructing me in surgery, Constant?"

"Not at all, Doctor. But you'll find—from even a cursory study of the literature—that vaginal hysterectomy has long since been favored in such cases. The technique is simpler—and it has the added advantage of removing the entire uterus without leaving the cervix. As you surely know, that organ can develop its own malignancy later."

So far, Mike's counterpunching had been routine. As he finished, he glanced again at Melcher—but could read neither reproof nor encouragement in his poker face.

"Dr. Brett is the only other general surgeon present," said the director. "Do you concur with Dr. Constant's views, Hugo?"

"Yes, Larry. I've meant to keep more complete files for a long time. I'm sure I could improve, with the proper help."

"What does our gynecologist say?"

Gideon Bliss spoke in a tired, old-man's voice. "For my money, Larry, paper work is poison. So long as our mortality rate stays down, I vote for the status quo—and to hell with the Joint Committee."

"Dr. Pendergast and I aren't qualified to discuss operative techniques," said Melcher. "Especially the advantages of vaginal hysterectomy over abdominal. I still agree with Dr. Constant, when it comes to the records. They've always been the weakest department in this hospital. The Joint Committee came to a similar conclusion—and I can't dismiss that august body as lightly as Gideon. In fact, I must warn you all that its approval is essential to our future well-being. I move that we take firm steps toward reform, under Dr. Constant's guidance. Do I hear a second?"

The motion was carried by a five-to-two vote, with Bliss and Keate recording the only nays. Mike noted that Pailey had abstained; the administrator was racing through his files at top speed, as though in search of a missing document.

"Are there any suggestions from the floor?" asked Melcher.

Pailey spoke without raising his eyes from his search. "Larry, I think it's up to Dr. Constant to set the example in this new regime. All of you gentlemen have bigger practices than you can handle. *He's* in residence here, as a staff surgeon, with time on his hands—"

"As of now," said Mike, "I don't have time to sleep."

"You can make the time," said Pailey. "I'd suggest you take charge of this record keeping—and write up each admission, from the data available, as you wish it done. I believe that's the usual procedure, in a hospital of this size."

The suggestion was grotesquely unfair; Melcher's objection was automatic.

"Ralph, you *know* that's impossible—"

Keate cut in; his tone was almost jocular. "Dr. Constant has been extremely free with his criticism. He feels our reports are inadequate. Let him correct these lacks, with his own hand. Perhaps we can learn from his example—though I doubt it. I'm a surgeon, not a composer of medical literature."

Mike kept his temper. His opponents' teamwork had been flawless—but he refused to be goaded into resigning.

"Does Mr. Pailey have a copy of my contract in those files?" he asked. "Perhaps he'll refresh my memory on my duties."

The secretary, Mike observed, had discovered the missing document at last. She handed it to the administrator, who glanced at it briefly before he passed it across the table.

"Here are the paragraphs that concern you, Dr. Constant. It's quite true you're employed as chief surgeon—with the right to oversee activities in all departments, and offer suggestions for their improvement. It does not include the right to make unfounded accusations against members of the corporation—"

"*Unfounded,* Mr. Pailey?"

"It's also stated clearly that you must undertake any work we assign to you. Will you begin the revision of our files—and write up each admitting-doctor's report in future?"

"Of course not," said Mike. "I'd be snowed under, and you know it." The crudity of the attack had registered by now; he could see that several doctors at the table had recognized it fully. "The write-up of full case histories is a collateral duty of attending physicians—and a routine one. Your director has just asked each member of this group to discharge it efficiently. I'll help all I can, of course. I can't perform that function for them."

Keate cut in again. His voice was cold with purpose. When he smiled, his resemblance to an overweight bull was more pronounced than ever.

"How long does this man's contract run, Ralph?"

"For a year. It's renewable by agreement."

"You can terminate it, as of today." The surgeon glanced at Melcher, who had risen in his chair at the threat to his authority.

"A procedure for personnel improvement is under discussion, Brad. I ask you not to interrupt it."

"If Constant won't take orders, his usefulness here is ended. Don't ask me to put *that* opinion to a vote: it isn't necessary. I own forty per cent of our corporation stock. Ralph owns fifteen, and he's given me his proxy. We came to this meeting, determined to fire your protégé, if he proved difficult." Keate turned toward Mike, with an effort at irony that would have seemed comic at another time. "I'm sorry you forced the issue, Constant. Perhaps you'll decide in future that you'll get nowhere by attacking your betters. You'll find a month's salary waiting at the office."

Melcher spoke quietly, but his tone was scalpel sharp. "You've played the fool at these meetings before, Brad. Today you're being a damned fool as well. I'm asking you to withdraw this demand."

"It's already in the minutes, Larry."

"Do you want a breach-of-contract suit?"

"We'll risk that."

"Will you risk letting the whole county hear the story of Dora Schneider's admission? We all know you planned gall-bladder surgery, when any first-year intern would have diagnosed pneumonia—and only Dr. Constant saved us a costly damage suit. Don't forget our lease comes up for renewal next month—with Vincent Schneider the financial agent for Zeagler Electronics."

"Is this a threat, Larry?"

"It's a promise—if that motion isn't erased from the minutes."

The silence that descended on the room was all the answer Mike needed. Regardless of his reasons, the director was committed; it was evident he had won before Pailey spoke. His voice was shaky, and his eyes were on the open ledger before him.

"I withdraw my proxy, Larry. I'll have no part in breaking Dr. Constant's contract."

Keate's face had gone from red to purple; for an instant, it seemed he might succumb to a stroke. Steadying himself with a hand on a chair back, he fixed Pailey with a final glare and left the table without a word. At the door, he paused, and turned to meet Mike's eyes; it was an open avowal of enmity, and the younger surgeon accepted it, as coolly as he could.

Melcher had already resumed his seat. "Shall we proceed with the matter at hand, gentlemen? With your permission, I'll outline some thoughts of my own on record keeping."

For ten minutes, the director discussed the suggestions made at the last meeting—which had been agreed on in principle. To Mike's surprise, all of them had since been implemented, on Melcher's order. Standard record forms were now in the mail, for the use of office nurses; the copying machine would make duplicates for the hospital files—and dictaphones were soon to be installed on each floor, to permit the attending physicians to fill in details. . . . Pailey interrupted just once to protest the expense, and was firmly overruled.

Hugo Brett rose at the end of Melcher's report to propose a vote of thanks for the director. It was carried by acclaim—and Mike could tell himself that the immediate threat had subsided. When the meeting ended, and both Pendergast and Brett approached to congratulate him on his stand, he knew he had taken the only possible course. New Salem Memorial was still far from its primary objective, but the ground had been broken.

"I'd like to see Brad's face when he opens his mail tomorrow," said Brett. "Don't let him upset you with his politicking, Dr. Constant. He's one of those fellows who has to be top dog in his back yard, or die of distemper. He'll make proper reports in future, when he realizes it's a matter of survival."

"I'm afraid there are others who enjoy things as they are, Dr. Brett."

"Bliss, to name just one? Gideon has to sound off for the record too. He always does. He'll be a good boy tomorrow. Just let him simmer down."

Melcher had been careful to avoid direct contact with Mike at the coffee hour; the surgeon, in turn, had kept clear of the dissidents. At the moment, the director's endorsement was all he could hope for, thanks to the feuding within the corporation. It was too much to expect him to cut all contact with his majority stockholder, and declare himself on the side of the angels.

Mike's final encouragement came hours later, from Lenora Searles, when they met in the supply room for the weekly inventory.

"You haven't asked about the battle," he said. "Are you a woman without curiosity?"

"Ralph Pailey's secretary kept a transcript of the whole meeting—including the fireworks. She gave me a rundown at supper."

"Was I too heavy-handed as the reformer?"

"You were in good form, Mike. But you also have a talent for making enemies."

"It's a price you always pay for change."

"That's precisely what I said to Larry, when we discussed the subject this morning."

"Were *you* the secret agent who saved me?"

"I wasn't that heroic," said the nurse. "I *did* tell Larry I'd never speak to him again, if he threw you to the wolves."

"Thanks, Lee. As it turned out, I needed all the backing I could find."

"New Salem Memorial can't go on much longer, unless we clean house. Larry will help you all he can. Just remember he's walking a tightrope with the others."

"I'll remember," said Mike gratefully. "One battle doesn't win a war."

"Keate will be back with more ammunition—you can count on that. What's important is that Larry really took his measure today. I've warned him that Brad's only a barroom bully. From now on, he'll believe me."

NINE

Three nights after the stormy staff meeting, the Jason West production of *Peter Pan* opened at the clinic theater. The audience packed the playhouse to the rafters. After the final curtain, a surf of applause called cast and director before the footlights for a dozen bows.

The performance was repeated five times, all the run Jason would allow his youthful charges. Practice for their next production, a modern version of Thackeray's *The Rose and the Ring,* had begun with a junior director from the New York Actors' Workshop in charge. The substitution had been arranged by Jason himself—after his *Peter Pan* had received glowing coverage in both the New York papers and the national magazines, and fellow actors and producers, hearing he was active again, had trooped up the thruway to pay him homage.

Already he had been offered a dozen chances to act. After some pretended reluctance, and conferences with Anna, he had decided to appear as Hamlet and Lear, at the next Shakespeare Festival—at Stratford-on-Housatonic in Connecticut. In Jason's view, the roles would be a supreme testing—proving to himself, and his peers, that he could function as ably as before, and opening the way to Broadway and Hollywood.

Mike had attended the children's premiere—sitting between Sandra and Anna, and enjoying their pride as the wizardry of Jason's direction swept the audience off its feet. The afternoon before the final performance, he was not too surprised to receive a visit from Anna at the hospital.

"The contracts are being drawn for Stratford," she said. "Rehearsals begin in two weeks."

"One push from you was all Jason needed. He was born to act or die."

"Don't you mean act *and* die?"

"He's chosen to run that risk."

"Can't you persuade him to wait a while longer?"

"Waiting won't help. The risk will always be there."

"Tell him it's madness, then."

"I've painted the picture in the darkest colors—but Jason won't even look at it. Not while his eyes are on another goal."

"To die in harness?"

"You can't expect a performer of his stature to remain here forever, Anna."

"I don't. He has every right to return to his world, now that he's made his contribution to mine. But I can't bear to think of those parts he'll be rehearsing—and what they'll take out of him."

"It's natural for him to turn to Shakespeare. Hamlet and Lear are his greatest roles."

"His heart *can't* stand the strain, unless he lets you operate. You can still convince him of that."

"I'll do my best, if you'll help me."

"What did you have in mind?"

"Don't ask me yet," said Mike. "Above all, don't say another word to Jay. Just promise you'll back me when I call on you."

"I'll do anything you ask me."

"Remember that promise when I see you again. I'll want to rehearse you beforehand."

"Did you say *rehearse?*"

"The man you love isn't the only actor in the world."

"Can't you tell me more?"

"Not another word—until it's time to play your scene. I'll have your lines ready before the week's over."

Mike had planned to attend the children's final performance, but an emergency forestalled him. It was ten o'clock before Hugo Brett relieved him at the hospital—and he put down the urge to hurry to the theater for the final curtain. . . . Instead, he went to his quarters, to review the strategy he had now perfected. The phone call he had awaited came just before midnight. It was Sandra, speaking in a whisper, as though she feared she might be overheard.

"Are you on call tonight, Mike?"

"I'm free until the morning shift."

"I need your help. Jason is taking a morning train to New York; he's already packed his bags. I think he plans to leave without seeing you."

"I expected that, Sandra. Didn't you?"

"In his prime, he lost five pounds each time he played Hamlet. He won't live through the summer, if he signs that Stratford contract."

"I couldn't agree more."

"You *said* you'd help, when the time came."

"I'll do what I can. Expect me in fifteen minutes."

When he hung up, Mike reached into his desk for a closely typed page of notes. While he scanned them, he dialed the number of Aaron Zeagler's home on Mohawk Knoll. *A hard-working surgeon has no business turning playwright,* he told himself dourly. *In this case, it's your last resort. When an actor's life is at stake, the pen may be mightier than the scalpel.*

The hill that Zeagler had chosen for his New Salem estate was at the northern edge of the Heights. When the guard had passed him through the massive iron grille that barred unwanted visitors, Mike noted with approval that Anna was already waiting in the doorway, muffled in a cloak. His instructions on the phone had been specific: he had been sure she would follow them to the letter.

"Do both of us have to go to the Gate House, Mike?"

"It's now or never. Jason's taking the morning train."

"Watkins can drive us there, if you like," she said, with a doubtful glance at the Ford.

"This is no time to arrive by limousine. Tonight, you're playing Cinderella after the ball."

"I wish you'd be more definite."

"Not until we reach our destination."

She did not speak while they drove through the Heights, skirted the looming mass of Zeagler Electronics, and took the road to New Salem proper. It was only after they had crossed Bear Creek, and parked on the elm-shaded street before the Rynhook gatehouse, that she voiced her next doubt.

"I still don't see why *I'm* needed here."

"You will in a few moments, if things turn out well. I'm going inside now, to argue with Jason. You stay here—until I send him out."

"What makes you think he'll come?"

"If I know Jason, he'll come running. Before I go, let's review your last talk with him."

"I told him a pacemaker was his only hope, if he meant to resume acting. I said he was a stubborn mule—refusing a precaution that would save his life."

"In other words, you bore down on his welfare, without mentioning your own."

"He's the artist, Mike—not I."

"You said that when you sent Paul to Munich, remember? Beginning tonight, you're to stop fretting over other people, and concentrate on *your* future."

"Jason West is my future."

"Has he replaced your husband?"

"Paul's only a bad dream. I'm in love with Jason, all over again."

"Because he needs you, and Paul no longer does?"

"That was part of the reason, at first. Now it goes much deeper. I love Jason as a man—not as the matinee idol I once worshipped. If he dies at Stratford, I'll want to die too."

Mike thought swiftly. Jason had declared his love for Anna, in almost the same terms, at the bar on Division Street. He could hardly quote those words now.

"Did it ever occur to you to tell him that?"

"It's his survival that's important," said Anna. "I'm not thinking of my happiness."

"Then it's time you did. How can you possibly help Jason—if *you* aren't happy too?"

"He must live his own life. I've no right to interfere."

"That's the first thing we're changing. Starting tonight, we're giving Jason West an interest outside his own ego. Something he's never really had before, when he isn't acting. In other words, you."

"I can't play this sort of game," said Anna.

"You promised to follow orders. Of course, if you insist, I'll take you back to Mohawk Knoll. Or would you prefer to return to Rynhook, and wait for Paul?"

"What do you expect of me, Mike?"

"Something that should come naturally. I'm going to remind Jason that only he can save you from slipping back to drink—and a second try with a psychotic husband. Once that fact has sunk home, I'll send him to you for the *coup de grâce*."

"I won't tamper with his emotions at a time like this. It isn't fair."

"Who said anything about being fair? This is a game women have played—and won—since the Stone Age."

"I'd be trapping him."

"Of course you would. At the same time, you'd be appealing to his deepest need—to *give* love, not just to receive it, just as he gives himself to an audience onstage. You've watched him with those kids, day after day. You must realize it's the wellspring of his being."

"I'd still be tricking him into marriage."

"Listen carefully, Anna. Just one thing has kept Jason off my operating table—the fear that he'll end as a cripple you'd care for out of pity. Convince him none of that matters. Swear you'll die, if *he* refuses to go on living. You'll find that his love won't let you go."

Anna Van Ryn took a deep breath and turned away. When she faced Mike again, her eyes were shining.

"I'll follow orders, Doctor."

"Remember he's saving *you* tonight. Bear down on that. The rest will come naturally."

The door of the Gate House was unlocked. Mike stepped inside without announcing his presence, as Sandra emerged from the living room, with a finger on her lips.

"He's upstairs now," she whispered. "For the past hour, he's been rehearsing his favorite part."

"I expected that."

They fell silent, as a well-remembered voice boomed down the stairwell.

'Tis now the very witching time of night
When churchyards yawn, and hell itself breathes out
Contagion to this world! Now could I drink hot blood
And do such bitter business as the day
Would quake to look on. . . .

"I've tried to slow him down," said Sandra. "He insists on both words and business. Shall I tell him you're here?"

"I'll do that myself. Anna's in my car."

"Why didn't you say so, Mike? Ask her in."

"I'll do nothing of the sort. It's part of the pattern for her to wait in the dark, with a few tears on her cheek."

"What on earth are you talking about?"

"I'm about to ask your brother to play his greatest role. In ten minutes—if my plan works—he'll come down those stairs, ready to speak his first line."

"You haven't been drinking. I'm sure of that."

"Not a drop. Tonight, you must keep offstage entirely. So will I, once I've played the herald's part."

"Since when have you turned actor, Mike?"

"Since I had the bad luck to draw an actor as a patient."

He left her quickly, waving her back to the darkened parlor as she made a last, futile effort to detain him. On the landing, he realized that Jason had reached a climactic moment in Shakespeare's masterpiece—the closet scene where Hamlet corners Polonius and runs him through. The actor was pacing his bedroom carpet; a copy of the play was in his left hand, the Malacca cane in his right. As Mike entered, he was in the act of charging the window curtain, jabbing his impromptu rapier through the folds. It was a fine, taut gesture, worthy of a gymnast.

"How now! a rat? Dead, for a ducat, dead!"

The cane was lowered abruptly, when the actor realized he was not alone. In a flash, he was Jason West again—the anguished, slightly flabby silhouette of departed glory Mike recalled so vividly from their first encounter.

"Sandra confessed that she'd phoned you, Mike. There was no need to come here now. I'd much rather look forward to a backstage reunion at Stratford."

"I'll be there too—if you're still breathing. At the moment, it seems highly unlikely."

"I'm already glib in both parts. I can coast at rehearsals."

"As you were coasting just now?"

Jason shrugged. "Tonight, I'm tuned to concert pitch and ready to sing again. Don't try to cross me with wires and a battery. I'd sound tinny as a barker on a circus midway."

It was time for the first attack of the scene. Mike crossed the room in three long strides, and seized the actor by his shirtfront. "We'll dispense with poses tonight, Jay. To quote the Bard again, you're about to drown—in a sea of troubles. I'm sure you realize that fact, as vividly as I."

Jason freed himself from Mike's grip. "I'm quite resigned to the risk."

"Do you think Anna's resigned?"

"I'm truly sorry for Anna. And profoundly grateful for her faith in me. Because of it, I'm once again the man I was—save for an unimportant footnote. I'm living on borrowed time, Doctor, and I'm reveling in each stolen moment. Does it matter when I go?"

"It matters to her."

"What more can I give her? The clinic is operating full time. I've made her children's theater a model of its kind. Don Trevor will assure its success—"

"Did you ever consider giving her something of yourself?"

"Look at me, Mike. Forget the strutting player, and sympathize with the man. Anna and I have had our small interlude of happiness. It would be folly to ask for more."

"It's you who needs to forget the strutting player," said Mike. "You're a man in love, and you're loved in return. How long will Anna last, if you abandon her?"

"What do you suggest? That I go on staging children's plays, when

I can create a new Hamlet? I'd only be cadging on her bounty. She'd end by despising me—and rightly."

"No one expects you to cadge. Are you afraid to be cured? Afraid of what love might do to you, if you *gave* it for a change?"

Jason West turned quickly, and buried his face in the window drape. There was nothing actorlike in the gesture.

"Believe me, Mike, I love her with all my heart. I can't bear to be near her any longer—unless I can have her, all the way."

"And you're still selfish enough to want all or nothing?"

"I must return to my acting. There's no other way I can function."

"I'll guarantee you can act again—*after* the operation. Anna is willing to divorce Paul and marry you. What more can you ask for?"

"I won't be a half husband."

Mike played his trump. He had been saving it for a final appeal to the actor's ego.

"Did you ever stop to think that millions of women would take half of Jason West—and count themselves lucky?"

"Do you include Anna in the herd?"

"She's a woman in love. Don't rule out her one chance for happiness—and send her back to Paul."

"She won't return to that madman. I've saved her from him, at least."

"Don't be too sure. Only tonight, she told me he was all she had left, if you deserted her."

He saw the other man stiffen, as the import of that solemn lie struck home. "Why did Anna send you with this message? She could have come to me herself."

"How could she, after you snatch at the first chance to leave her?"

Jason West raised clenched fists to heaven. Mike was sure it was his gesture of surrender, but he did not dare ease the pressure.

"I won't call you a coward twice," he said. "If there's a man beneath that shell, you'll prove it by going to her now."

Jason's hand closed on the window drape, so violently that the material ripped from the rod. Even in capitulation, he managed to strike an attitude. With the white monk's cloth draped at one shoulder, he resembled an ancient Roman, his toga only slightly rumpled, his spirit invulnerable.

"I'll see her in the morning—and tell her how selfish I've been. Will that do?"

"There's no time like now, Jay."

"It's after one o'clock."

"Anna's outside—in my car."

Jason flung his false toga aside. "You're a tyrant, Mike. Won't you ever let up?"

"Not until you take my advice—as a doctor. You can't deny her that."

"It's a promise," said the actor—and started down the stairway. Mike waited until the sound of his footsteps had died, then moved to the window. When he heard his car door open, he knew he had won.

The pacemaker operation Mike had planned, though it would have seemed risky to the layman, was now an accepted feature of heart surgery, requiring co-ordinated action—but no more than the usual nerve on the surgeon's part. He had posted it two mornings after Jason's readmission to the hospital. Aware that its comparative novelty would arouse interest among his colleagues, he had yielded to Melcher's urging and permitted a few observers—an unusual favor in the compact operating theaters of New Salem Memorial. . . . It was fitting, he told himself, that the actor should have an audience, even though he was unaware of its presence.

Intratracheal anesthesia was a vital part of the procedure he had planned: it would require deep sedation before the tube could be passed through the larynx into the windpipe. A small balloon surrounded its lower end, an ingenious device that insured a snug fit. Louis Garstein would thus be able to inflate and deflate the lungs at will, to counteract their inevitable collapse when the chest was opened to expose the heart.

Another far more radical technique was needed to bypass an accidental stoppage of the heartbeat, a common hazard in cardiac surgery. While the operation was in progress, the contact electrodes of the hospital pacemaker could not be placed in their usual position on the chest—yet the stimulus of its electric pulse was essential. Before the operating room was quite ready—and before the anesthesiologist had begun his work—the already-drugged patient was wheeled to the X-ray room, where Lee Searles waited with an instrument tray. Here, Mike injected Novocain over one of the large veins of the arm, tied off the vessel, opened a small slit in its wall, and inserted a flexible catheter.

The instrument was fitted with a wire core and a metal tip. Using the fluoroscope as a guide, he began the cautious process of threading it up the arm. His first goal was the superior *vena cava,* the large vein that collected blood from the upper half of the body. Once this was reached, the catheter was deflected downward into the right side of the heart itself. The technique was a simple one, requiring only an exact knowledge of anatomy and the help of the fluoroscope, which gave the surgeon an absolute diagnostic approach as he studied the catheter's ever extending shadow.

When he had inched it to the point of contact, the pacemaker could be attached to the wire, permitting him to stimulate the heart from within its own cavity. The precise spot he had chosen for electrical contact was the septum, the area separating the two muscular chambers of the heart, the twin pumps that sent blood coursing to the lungs—and, via the aorta, to the rest of the body. A final, feather-light touch of his fingers, and a last check on the fluoroscope, assured Mike that his preliminary surgery had served its purpose. After the tiny arm wound was dressed, the patient was ready for the table.

Dr. Brett, who had volunteered to assist, was waiting in the operating room, and the hunched figure of Louis Garstein could be seen behind his wire-framed hood. A half-dozen observers were grouped on the far side of the room. Earlier that morning, Wilson had built a special temporary platform, permitting them a clear view without hampering the operating team. . . . Mike smiled warmly at Dr. Artemus Coxe, there at his special invitation; he exchanged nods with Gideon Bliss and Melcher, and accepted the icy stare of Bradford Keate with composure. He had been sure that Keate would fight a losing battle with his curiosity.

When Mike had connected the hospital pacemaker to the emergency wire, he changed to a fresh gown and gloves. Garstein had already proceeded with the induction of anesthesia and the placement of the intratracheal tube—and Lee Searles had begun to paint the operative area with antiseptic, according to the surgeon's instructions. As he approached the table, a second nurse handed him the first of several towels; Lee, her task finished, assisted him in the precise draping of the chest.

It was time to begin—but Mike turned from his patient for a moment, to face his small but attentive audience.

"The purpose of this operation is to introduce two permanent electrodes into the heart muscle," he said. "These will be connected to a small antenna coil—to be implanted just beneath the skin at the front of the chest. When the whole apparatus is in place, the heart can be stimulated as needed, via radio-wave impulses, originating from a power source which the patient will wear on his chest wall."

As he spoke, Mike took a scalpel and scratched a transverse incision across the chest to demonstrate his approach. The incision itself was made over the fourth rib, extending the wound to bone level—and exposing both the rib and the section of whitish cartilage connecting it with the sternum, or breastbone. The knife cut through the outer lining of the bone for a distance of four inches, leaving the cartilage intact. Then, using a periosteal elevator—a scraperlike instrument designed to fit neatly round the rib—Mike rocked the steel gently, until the outer bone lining had separated from the rib itself.

When the separation was complete, he cut the bone free with heavy forceps. Through the bed of the rib he could now see the lung moving beneath its pleural lining—as well as the heart inside its own sac, the pericardium, thrusting strongly toward the chest wall with each beat.

"We are now ready to open the chest," he said. "The coil antenna —as you will soon observe—will pick up radio-frequency waves from its externally-worn generator, a device no larger than a package of cigarettes. The antenna itself is of platinum iridium, encased in a hard-rubber substance called Silastex; it can be implanted in the chest wall easily, without inflaming the tissue. Actual contact with the heart muscle will be made with two leads, shaped like springs to absorb the whiplash action of the average heartbeat. The design of the whole apparatus will hold the danger of breakage to a minimum."

"Does the coil act like a radio receiver?" Melcher asked.

"Exactly, Doctor. Except that, in this case, the broadcasting station is less than an inch away."

Mike picked up the antenna from the instrument table—a roundish disc in a plastic-rubber bed, with rubber-coated leads extending from its center. Each lead ended in a tiny rectangular plate, from which protruded a metal spring.

"When the attachment is complete," he explained, "the apparatus creates what is known, in the language of electronics, as a parallel-resistant circuit." He turned to a clipboard propped upon a stand and read the instructions he had placed there before the operation began. "For the record, it is noted here that the disc in my hand contains a ceramic capacitator, connected in parallel. One of the leads includes a silicon diode in series. The diode is needed to rectify the radio-frequency wave into a single directional impulse. If the impulse alternated, the heart might be stimulated into fibrillation—which could, of course, be fatal."

"Is this the only method used?" asked Gideon Bliss.

"Other techniques have been successful, Doctor. Some surgeons prefer to install battery units under the skin beneath the lower ribs, where the tissues are relatively loose. In this case, I've chosen an external source for the current. In my opinion, the approach is simpler, in case the generator needs attention." Mike turned to Garstein, who was busy with the complex routine of positive-pressure anesthesia necessary to keep the lung from collapsing.

"I'm ready to open the pleura, Louis."

"Go right ahead. I already have him on a closed system."

"We'll enter the pericardium through the bed of the fourth rib." Mike used his forceps to pick up the outer of the two membranes—

pericardium and epicardium—enclosing the heart. Across the table, Hugo Brett matched the move. With the membrane safely tented, Mike made a small opening in the sac, enlarging it in either direction until an adequately sized portion of the heart muscle was exposed. When the technique was completed, he stepped back to give the observers a clear view of the heart, pulsating steadily under its own power. So far, the added stimulus of the pacemaker had functioned only as a safety factor.

"Clinical experience has shown that the leads should be placed high on the ventricular wall. I'm choosing the area between the two coronary arteries." He indicated the two vessels that provided blood for the heart muscle itself: they were plainly visible now, a branching, treelike pattern against the darker muscular wall. "The coronaries seem healthy. Let's hope the infarct involves only a small part of the septum."

"Then the prognosis is favorable, so far?" Bliss asked.

"As of now, the operative pattern's ideal. Thanks to the catheter, I'm almost positive we can keep things under control."

Using a scalpel with a narrow-pointed tip, Mike made a small wound in the heart muscle—a precise stab that did no more than nick the epicardium, the second lining of the organ. Lee Searles passed the pacemaker disc across the patient's body, holding it in both hands while the surgeon took one of the small electrode terminals and pushed its tip into the tiny incision, pressing the rubberized plate from which it projected snugly against the heart itself. Silk sutures were used to anchor the plate to the epicardium. He repeated the maneuver with the second electrode, planting it no more than an inch away from the first. Finally, he sutured a small square of plastic-foam sponge over each of the plates.

"The sponges serve as insulation between epicardium and pericardium," he said. "Since plastic foam is essentially inert, there should be no adverse reaction in the surrounding tissue—and the heart can move as freely as ever in its sac."

With the ticklish portion of his job behind him, Mike permitted himself a long-drawn breath before he took the suture needle Lee Searles held ready. "We will close the pericardium with silk. As you see, our whole procedure has been relatively simple, including the mechanical contact I've just established with the heart muscle."

"What about the portable pacemaker?" Dr. Art asked. "How do you anticipate a dead battery?"

"There are two circuits inside it, Doctor. One delivers the stimulating current. The other controls its rate. The battery in the second circuit has a shorter life than the first. Even if it fails without warning, the patient will recognize the slowdown, and can get help in time."

While he spoke, Mike had been closing the pericardium. Dr. Brett had brought the leads through the inner angle of the opening; the somewhat larger circular antenna was now positioned carefully in front of the sternum, in the slight concavity at its lower end. The entire connection was now established, ready to receive the external stimulator. When in place, it would fit beneath the wearer's clothing with no apparent bulge. . . . Surveying his handiwork, Mike still found it hard to believe the connections had been made—as casually as a journeyman electrician might install a telephone circuit.

The remainder of the operation was routine. There was no need for additional surgery on the small portion of the rib that had been excised. Thanks to the preservation of the periosteal lining, the bone would regenerate completely. With the antenna receiver several inches from the break, there would be no interruption in wound healing—and actual stimulation, via the just-established circuit, could begin whenever the doctor ordered.

With the last external stitch applied and the dressing in place, Mike stepped away from the table. The wall clock showed that the whole operation had lasted less than an hour. Its effect on the patient would be negligible.

"The battery pacemaker will be connected tomorrow, or the day after," he told his audience. "In this type of heart surgery, we prefer to wait until the patient has recovered from the anesthesia." He picked up the black-coated battery pack from the tray, and consulted the notes on the clipboard. "Let me read a few more facts—in case any of you are electronic buffs. This portable lifesaver consists of a mercury battery, with a current output varying from zero to thirty volts. It has an output impedance of about two hundred ohms, to cut down the danger of overstimulation. The actual impulse lasts for no more than one two-thousandth of a second, just long enough to stir the heart to a normal contraction. As you'll observe, it has control knobs, as simple as the dials on your television set. The patient can vary both current and rate at will—or shut it off entirely, if the heart behaves naturally without its help."

"Is there an optimum time for beginning stimulation?" Melcher asked.

"We can answer that tomorrow, when we take an EKG. Until then, we'll continue with our hospital pacemaker, using the catheter wire I've installed in the vein. It's a usual precaution to leave the catheter in place for another twenty-four hours, even after the portable instrument takes over." The surgeon stood aside, as Lee Searles came forward at his nod. In another moment, the patient had been moved to a wheeled stretcher and taken to the recovery room.

"Are there any more questions, gentlemen?"

"Just one, Dr. Constant," said Artemus Coxe. "How does it feel to pass a miracle?"

"You can address that query to the man who invented the Silastex disc," said Mike. "*I'm* the mechanic who installed it. The directions are printed on the label."

Forty-eight hours later, in the private room where Jason was completing his convalescence, Mike placed the bell of a stethoscope against the patient's chest, listened carefully for a pleural rub that would have warned of infection—but heard none. With Miss Ford's help, he adjusted the hospital bed at several levels, while he checked the steady rhythm of the heart. The bedside chart had been normal since the actor had left the recovery room; since midday, the battery nestled against his sternum had been in constant operation. Already, it was apparent that the tune-in with the heart was complete.

"How does it feel, Jay?"

"You won't believe me, but I've already forgotten it's there. I never knew it was *this* easy to live with a built-in transistor."

"When I remove the catheter tomorrow, you may have a little discomfort in the arm. The stitches in your chest can come out in a few more days. After that, you'll be as good as new."

"How long do I stay here?"

"You can begin rehearsing in two weeks, if you take it easy."

"There's been a switch in the repertory they offered me. They now plan to do *The Tempest* and *Romeo and Juliet*. Prospero never appealed to me as an acting vehicle—and I'm a bit too old for the balcony scene."

"It's well you didn't sign a contract last week, then."

"It is indeed, Mike; you've been my guardian angel, all down the line. I might have broken my heart at Stratford-on-Housatonic, in more ways than one."

"Do you have another part in prospect?"

"Fortune has smiled on me again, in that respect. Next month, I'll begin rehearsing *The Demon Lover*. It's an English import, a symbolic melodrama I've wanted to do for years. The title, of course, derives from Coleridge's *Kubla Khan*."

"I'm waiting for the quotation," said Mike resignedly.

"I'm through with quotations—and with tragic gestures."

"Does Anna know?"

"Not yet. The offer came by phone this morning. I'm going to tell her, the moment you'll let me have visitors."

"She's waiting now, in the reception room."

"Don't send her in just yet. Before I enjoy my own happiness, I would like a few vital statistics on yours."

"If you refer to Sandra, there's nothing I can tell you."

"No change in that quarter?"

"Only for the worse. From your sister's viewpoint, the last obstacle to her life wish has now been removed."

"Is she still foolish enough to believe Paul will marry her?"

"More than ever, Jay. He's the dream prince."

"It isn't like you to accept that illusion so tamely."

"She's loved him all her life," Mike said slowly. Aware of the bitterness in his tone, he was controlling himself as best he could. "What right had I to hope she'd change?"

The actor considered the pronouncement gravely. "Odd, isn't it, the strange tastes some women have in men? By and large, we call them a civilized sex. If I may echo Coleridge after all, there's still a savage place in every female heart, where desire is king—"

"I thought you were through with quotations?"

"Forgive the lapse, Mike. Like you, I prayed that Paul's long absence would restore her sanity. Unfortunately, it's had a reverse effect."

"Has he written often?"

"By each airmail. You might say he's been working overtime to build up that dream prince you spoke of."

"Don't tell me Sandra reads you his letters."

"I've seen their effect on her—that's more than enough. God knows what he's been promising her, but I'm sure she believes him. When he comes back, he means to pick up where they left off. There *must* be a way to stop him, Mike."

"Not short of murder, I'm afraid."

"Would it help, if Sandra learned the whole truth about her idol?"

"The *whole* truth?"

"There's no need to hold back with me," said Jason. "Anna's mentioned his fatal flaw."

"I've made up my mind to tell her that story, the next time I see her."

"Why have you held it back so long?"

"Because I'm convinced she won't believe me. I'm speaking up for just one reason—to ease my own conscience. I can't keep the facts from her any longer."

"If you like, Anna will tell her the same story."

"Let me do the talking, Jason. If Anna intervened now, Sandra would think it was a conspiracy to undermine her."

"Why don't you have Paul locked up? After all, he nearly killed Anna—and it wasn't the first time."

"I've explored that angle too. It's a blind alley. If Anna had brought charges after her last injury, she might have made them stick. The chance has gone glimmering, now that she's divorcing Paul."

"Won't the Duchess help? She knows the score, where her son's concerned. If you caught her in the proper mood—"

"In her way, Madame Van Ryn is more deluded than Sandra. She's still prepared to forgive Paul everything—providing he succeeds as an artist."

Jason shook his fist at an invisible enemy. "I'll shoot him, the minute I leave this bed. My hand is steady now; I'll promise not to miss."

"I can't permit that—when you have a new play waiting. Don't fight my problems for me, Jay. I'll learn to live with them."

"Promise me you'll have a straight talk with Sandra."

"I promise—but it will be the shortest talk on record. Your sister's immune to the truth."

The encounter Mike had dreaded came unheralded—less than twenty-four hours after his visit with Jason.

He had just left the operating room, after checking next day's postings with Lee Searles, to go to the office Pailey had assigned him on the ground floor of the hospital. During the past month, he had built up a small but respectable private practice in the free time his routine allowed him. This afternoon, with no patient scheduled, he had looked forward to a rough first-drafting of an article on pacemaker surgery, which he would submit later to one of the medical journals. . . . Pausing to chat with the receptionist in the lobby, he was humming a tune that found no echo in his heart, when he turned the knob of the office door and found himself face to face with Sandra West.

She was seated on the couch beneath the window, turning the leaves of a magazine with a nonchalance that did not mislead him for a moment. Today, she had put aside her clinic uniform for a smart summer frock and gay costume jewelry; high-heeled pumps that did the most for her slim, tanned legs when she rose to offer him her hand. . . . He could not help wondering if her attire, like her too-bright smile, was deliberate—a reminder that she now stood ready to begin an existence he could never share.

"I swore Miss Jenks to secrecy, Mike," she said. "We decided to surprise you, since you've no patients this afternoon."

"Have you seen your brother?"

"I just came from his room. The miracle is registering—slowly."

"Don't look at *me* when you say that." Mike sat down behind his desk, grateful, for once, that there was now a barrier between them. "Jason is a beneficiary of the electronic age. My contribution was negligible."

"I'm here to thank you for what you did at the Gate House. That was the true miracle."

Mike found he could smile, despite his inner tumult. "Were you listening downstairs?"

"I admit it, Mike—without shame. You gave an inspired performance."

"As I told you, I was a herald that night—not an actor. All I really did was give Jason a much-needed cue. It was his scene, from then on."

"You lifted him outside himself, for the first time in his life: you changed him from an actor to a man. I've no way to thank you for that service."

"Don't try, Sandra. His happiness, and Anna's, are quite enough."

"Look at me, Mike. Can't you wish *me* a little happiness while you're about it?"

"Not if I have to include Paul Van Ryn."

"Won't you admit he's changing for the better too—now that he has something real to live for?"

"People like Paul never change inside."

"Then we're back to the old argument."

"I've no intention of arguing. Jay tells me you've been in constant touch. Did you tell Paul that Anna's planning a divorce?"

"Of course not. They'll settle the divorce as they see fit. When he's free, I expect him to come to me, of his own accord. Meanwhile, I'm quite willing to wait."

"Has he spoken of returning to the States?"

"He expects to get back next month—perhaps even sooner. His

work in Munich is going splendidly. Werner Von Helm is most impressed."

"Is that a direct quote?"

"From Von Helm—not Paul. Do you refuse to believe that?"

"Did he promise to break his bondage to the Duchess, and the Zeagler money? Is he planning to earn his living with his brush—once he's arranged a New York show, and picked up a few more commissions?"

"It's exactly what he plans. Until the plan's a reality, he said he had no right to speak to me of love. *Now* do you see how wrong you've been about him?"

"I can understand those promises well enough. What I can't accept is the way you believe them."

"You can't deny Paul his success, Mike. Or my right to hope it's only a beginning."

"I'm denying Paul nothing. For all I know, he may be as great a genius as his namesake, *Rembrandt* Van Ryn. I'm asking you to look at him—in the clear light of day. And I'm saying these promises have no meaning whatever. People like Paul have no moral sense, no concept of right or wrong. His one yardstick is his own self-interest. At the moment, it amuses him to play with your affections—"

"No human being could have so low an opinion of another, Mike Constant!"

"I'll answer that by telling you Paul isn't human. If you resume your liaison, he'll discard you the moment you cease to please him. My only hope is that you'll escape undamaged."

"Say it all, please." Sandra's voice had risen to an icy pitch of fury. "Don't hint at things you're afraid to put into words."

Mike breathed deep, then took the plunge. "I'll accept the dare. The man you love is hopelessly insane. Eight weeks ago, he nearly killed his wife. Take her place, and you'll run the same risk—"

"That's quite enough, Mike. I know you're eaten up with jealousy. As a doctor, you've no right to tell an outright lie—"

He felt suddenly drained of emotion, now he had spoken the truth and heard her rejection. "I didn't expect you to take in a word of this, Sandra. But I'm sure you'll remember my warning, before you're too much older. When you do, I pray that your wisdom doesn't come too late."

Sandra's hand lifted, and he made no effort to ward off the blow he expected; he would have welcomed it, if only as a sign he had reached her at last. Instead, she turned on her heel and left the office. Watching the door close behind her, he felt himself sway under the burden of his loss. He could not regret the instinct that had forced him to unburden his mind—even though he had known the effort would be futile.

Mike was still standing at his desk when the office phone rang. He found the receiver in his hand, though he had no memory of lifting it.

"Dr. Constant here."

"Can you come straight to the lab, Mike?" Garstein's voice was taut with concern. "We've had eight more hepatitis admissions since noon."

"I saw the roster. We can handle them."

"Art Coxe has taken as many more on Lower Street. His last bed is gone. And Saunders just called from the Health Department. If the case load doesn't slack off by the weekend, the State Board at Albany will call it an epidemic."

TEN

In the six weeks that followed—after the hepatitis epidemic had assumed official status—the disease developed in a classic pattern. An infection whose reason for spreading was as elusive as its cure, it continued to strike at will, in both the Old Town and the Heights—though the majority of cases were reported from New Salem's most affluent suburb.

On the whole, the community accepted its affliction well. As usual, there were few fatalities—since the initial mortality rate in this type of liver infection was always low. Dr. Saunders and his Health Department teams combed the area constantly, to remind each householder of proper precautions. Every effort was made to induce new victims to accept home treatment, but most of the well-salaried workers at Zeagler Electronics, accustomed to take full advantage of their hospital insurance, preferred to descend on Indian Hill.

In the second week, the medical ward of the hospital was jammed. In the third, the tide of patients threatened to invade the surgical beds as well—until Mike insisted that most of these facilities be kept open for emergency admissions. While the crisis lasted, elective surgery was kept to a minimum—and there were several near battles with Dr. Bradford Keate, and other staff members who continued to post cases which could have been deferred. The situation was saved, in a stopgap fashion, by New Salem's gradual reluctance to go under the knife in a hospital crowded with victims of a mysterious affliction that had struck so many friends and neighbors.

The decline of surgical admissions produced a fresh tempest in accounting. But Mike had learned by now to brush aside Pailey's complaints, confident that the director—who was working round the clock with Dr. Saunders—would back his decision. He knew he would be facing a fresh crisis when the situation returned to normal and his two chief enemies—still licking their wounds after the head-on collision at the staff meeting—recovered their second wind. While the emergency lasted, he felt it was safe to ignore them.

By the fourth week, every nursing home in the county had been drafted into service. Dr. Coxe's establishment on Lower Street had commandeered two vacant buildings across the way, before it was forced to refuse patients for the second time. As a final resort, the Zeagler Clinic was outfitted with a score of beds—and a team of practical nurses was pressed into service on clinic funds, to fill the breach. Rehearsals at the children's theater were suspended, and the space utilized by the clinic—to the consternation of the young New York director, until he, too, was stricken, and forced to take a bed onstage.

The most baffling thing about the flare-up was that no apparent source existed. Generally speaking, the disease ran its course—burning itself out after the number of patients susceptible to its inroads were whittled down by the immunity pattern of those who had recovered. Mike could only assume that the sudden recurrence was caused by the June heat waves. His study of the disease had suggested that warm weather was its most dangerous ally.

Anna had insisted on doing her share of nursing at the clinic, and Sandra had set up a bed in the office to be available day and night. The actual duties involved were taxing rather than dramatic—the endless preparation of special diet trays to tempt appetites dulled by the virus, meticulous attention to sanitary facilities, and alcohol rubs to reduce the ravages of fever.

Mike managed a daily visit to the clinic, between his own expanded shifts at the hospital. There had been no mention of the bitter encounter in his office, no reference to Paul. If Sandra had had further news from Munich, she gave no sign of it. If Anna Van Ryn had noted the tension between doctor and nurse, she was too deep in her personal nirvana to interfere.

Forty days after Albany had given epidemic status to New Salem, the ominous label was recalled, as the incidence of cases slackened at last. Three days later, when no new infection had been reported, Mike received a phone call from Dr. Coxe.

"It's time we put our heads together," said the old doctor. "You need updating in several departments, and so do I. How's your heart patient?"

"We sent him to New York to complete his convalescence—because we needed the bed."

"That must have been quite a while ago. I see by the paper he's rehearsing in a new play."

"I gave him the green light for ordinary activities a month ago, Dr. Art. Anna's starting action for her divorce. They plan to be married after his show opens in New York."

"That proves how far I am behind the times. How is Sandra holding up?"

"She's been a tower of strength at the clinic this past month."

"Have you visited Rynhook lately?"

"I've had no time to visit anywhere. With all this sickness about, I was afraid we'd have the Duchess as a patient—but I hear she's been sound as a dollar."

"Her mind's been clear for nearly six weeks. I've stopped by twice to be sure."

Something in Dr. Art's voice alerted Mike at once.

"What's the purpose of this conclave? Are we going to discuss the hepatitis case load, my personal history, or Marcella Van Ryn?"

"I'd like to review them all. How soon can you get here?"

"I'll be off duty in another hour if things are in control downstairs."

Mike found Dr. Coxe in his office—his feet on the desk, his bald head wreathed in cigar smoke. The older man seemed dog-tired —but his eyes held a light that warned the visitor this was no routine meeting.

"I can breathe again, Mike," he said. "Can you?"

"If you refer to the jaundiced-colored cloud above New Salem, I'm beginning to see daylight at the edges."

"Let's skip medicine for the present. Have you settled your quarrel with Sandra?"

"Who told you we'd quarreled?"

"People usually do when they're in love—and one of them is too blind to realize it."

"Sandra happens to be in love with Paul. It's a topic I'd prefer to leave unmentioned."

"I suppose rope is a word one doesn't use in the hangman's house?"

"This is no time for Greek proverbs."

"Why not—if they clear the air? I've got a great deal to say about Paul this afternoon. And I'm afraid you'll have to listen, because I need your advice badly. Things came to a head last week, when Omar Dean paid me a visit—"

Blocked by his own grim thoughts, Mike's mind had only half absorbed the older doctor's remarks. The mention of Omar Dean snapped him to attention. As senior member of the firm of Dean and Irving, Omar was the town's best-known lawyer—a man whose opinions were ex cathedra in the valley.

"If he's about to sue the hospital, I'll take to the woods."

"This doesn't concern Indian Hill. Dean and Irving have just accepted Paul Van Ryn as a client. His mother has willed him her estate at her death. He wants to take title now."

"Even Paul must know that's impossible."

"Not if he can get two doctors to certify the Duchess as incompetent. Omar asked me if I'd join Hugo Brett in signing commitment papers. He's thought the matter over carefully, since he read Paul's letters. All things considered, he came to the conclusion it would be good for New Salem."

"Can you picture Paul as the squire of Rynhook?"

"Paul has no intention of keeping Rynhook, Mike. If he can get control, he'll sell the estate at once—castle, factory sites, and tenements. Providing, of course, that Zeagler Electronics meets his price."

"What comes afterwards?"

"He promised Omar to provide Marcella with private-sanitarium care. Paul himself is ready to move to New York—where he'll lead the life a gentleman-artist deserves. Omar's convinced he'll do just that, if he has his way in court."

"Did you mention Paul's failings? Or suggest *he's* the one who deserves commitment?"

"It seemed unwise to bear down on that angle. I could hardly deny Paul has a case—if you concentrate on the mother, and forget the son. Look at the facts, as Omar sees them. The Van Ryns have been doomed—ever since Paul turned out to be the last rotten apple in the barrel. From the town's viewpoint, a commitment—*and* a quick sale—could wipe the slate clean. Paul would be just a bad memory; Marcella would live out her days in comfort in a nursing home, and everyone could find work in the new Zeagler plant."

"What sort of answer did you give Omar?"

"I promised to brood on the problem. After he left my office, I made the first of two visits to Bearclaw Point."

"To break the news to the Duchess?"

"Far from it. That visit was strategic, to see if she would move faster than her son—in her own interest. I advised her to sell out at Zeagler's best figure, give Paul enough to prove he's America's answer to Van Gogh—then take off on a world cruise. Imagine my surprise, when Marcella admitted she'd been thinking along the same lines—"

"When I saw her last month, she swore she'd never sell Rynhook."

"Circumstances can alter cases, Mike. They can even change an iron-clad mind. The Duchess is a tyrant—but Paul's welfare has always been her first concern. In his playboy years, when his painting seemed only a diversion, she was right to keep him on a short halter. It was another story, when Paul's talent was recognized. Now he's poised on the verge of fame, she seemed ready to make his liberation permanent. She even spoke of financing his first one-man show from a property sale."

"I take it you didn't mention your talk with Omar Dean."

"I knew she'd hear that story soon enough," said Dr. Art. "It seemed safer to leave her on an upbeat, as it were. Four days later, Anna stopped at Rynhook to say good-by. She and the Duchess had a lengthy huddle. I gather the daughter-in-law pulled no punches—

including Paul's habit of beating up his women. For the first time, Marcella had the true story of the marriage, and why Anna was leaving him. On top of that, she learned that Paul is preparing to bring a suit for her commitment. Naturally, she was fit to be tied when I went there the second time."

"I can't believe much of what Anna told her was news. They've lived under the same roof for six years. The Duchess must have seen her son in action."

"She knew of his tantrums, of course," said Dr. Art. "In her heart, she realizes he's living on the brink of madness. What she couldn't take was the fact that Anna was leaving him. It meant that Paul has now lost one of the two anchors he can depend on. Rynhook is the other. When he returns, she'll insist that he go back to the tower studio, until he's *really* proved himself to the world. The one-man show is out, of course—unless he wants to hold it in New Salem."

"What about his scheme for committing her?"

"Marcella laughed in my face when I mentioned it—as though it were an example of her son's naughtiness, and nothing more. In that respect, she's completely divorced from reality. Now she's made up her mind to dig in, she plans to hold the fort forever."

"Meaning, of course, that fireworks are in the offing."

"A Roman-candle circus," said Dr. Art.

"Will she have a prayer—when Paul tries to lock her up?"

"I'd have given her odds a year ago, if Omar Dean weren't on the son's side. Judges are usually old enough to throw their weight toward the past. With Dean and Irving representing the plaintiff, you can count on a heavy turnout. Especially when the town smells new money, and jobs for everyone."

"Don't tell me *you're* tossing in the sponge."

"I haven't told you the whole story, Mike. Marcella had one of her spells, before we finished that second talk. It wasn't too bad—but it took a shot of paraldehyde to quiet her. After I put her under, I made Nellie give me a real tour of the castle. The basement's water-logged. It's been a cockroach haven for years."

"Which brings us back to the epidemic."

"Doubled in spades," said Dr. Art.

"Do you think *Bearclaw Point's* the focus of the infection?"

"It's a logical assumption—though I'm still without proof. You know it's almost impossible to culture the hepatitis virus successfully. It's even harder to nail down migrants from that basement as vectors."

"Besides the fact that nobody at Rynhook had hepatitis."

"I reached the same conclusion when I departed. An hour later, I started kicking myself for being a half-blind old man."

"You've lost me somewhere, Dr. Art."

"Just before his death, I treated Nicholas Van Ryn for hepatitis. A little later, Marcella had a light attack."

"That doesn't make her a carrier—with no discernible jaundice."

"The pattern makes sense, though. Practically the same thing happened in your California apartment project; I looked it up in the literature. After they fogged the buildings and wiped out the vermin, the disease practically vanished. Doesn't that prove the cockroaches were being infected by carriers—and transmitting the virus to others?"

"The theory's ingenious," Mike admitted. "And the facts seem to support it all the way. But you still have no solid evidence, since you can't really culture the virus. Until you do, you'll never pin a Typhoid Mary label on the Duchess."

"We needn't go that far," said Dr. Art. "Joe Saunders went up to Albany yesterday, and presented the story to the State Health Board. This town is pretty jittery, after six weeks of epidemic status. The State House can spot a good chance to improve public relations, when they hold all the trumps. They're buying my theory, even though I can't prove it."

"Where do they plan to start?"

"First off, Joe is going to lay down a barrier of California-type insecticide at the dam—enough to keep new six-legged visitors from improving their social bracket. Next, he'll bring in a special crew, to treat every house on the Heights. The epidemic is definitely on the wane. If my theory's valid, wiping out the vermin population will give it the quietus."

"You forget the focus at Rynhook."

"*That* part I wish I could forget, Mike. Joe insists the castle must get the same treatment. If the Duchess balks—and she's bound to—she's had her day in New Salem."

Mike nodded soberly. The picture was clear now. Every medical instinct he possessed insisted that Dr. Art's reasoning was sound. If there was another flare-up of hepatitis, after Marcella Van Ryn had refused admission to a Public Health team, Omar Dean could win his case in a walk.

"Where does this put us? Behind the eight ball?"

"Not quite. I've convinced Joe he can leave Rynhook alone for the present; he'll have his hands full for the next few days. If the Duchess recovers in the meantime, I'll do my best to persuade her to sell. Zeagler will tear down the castle to make room for his plant. She'd get a top price—and there'd be no need for condemnation. With that kind of money, she could hire an even better lawyer than Omar to hit back at Paul."

"How long do we have?"

"Joe has agreed to hold off until next Monday."

"How does all this involve me, Dr. Art?"

"If Marcella will listen, I'll want you to add your voice to mine. Nellie has orders to call me as soon as she seems rational. We can save the day, if she'll face the facts."

"What if she still won't sell?"

"Then we'll have to remember we're doctors, and support Omar Dean. The situation will be made to order for Paul—another dotty beldame, refusing to leave her rat's nest after it's been branded as a menace to health."

"Do you mind if I talk this over with Larry?"

"Do, by all means. It's your duty, and his, to decide where the hospital will stand."

"Monday's four days off. It doesn't leave much time."

"We may have less—if Paul decides to push hard for an immediate court decision. I'm sure he's had a rundown on his chances."

Melcher was in his office when Mike returned to the hospital;

he had just flown back from Baltimore, where he had gone to attend his wife's funeral. Mary Melcher had been one of the last hepatitis victims on the Heights—and her will had specified that she be buried among her own people.

Busy with the crisis at New Salem Memorial, Mike had had no real chance to offer his sympathy. He was relieved to find Melcher in reasonably good spirits, though he was still numbed by his loss.

"Please thank the staff in my name, Mike. I know you did all you could for her."

The two men shook hands in the darkened office. There was no need to discuss the case. The patient had seemed to fight the virus at first—but the damaged liver had been unequal to the strain. Once she had begun to fail, the terminal phase of her illness had been brief.

"I won't say this is a blessing in disguise, Larry."

"It was for Mary, God knows—but I still can't believe she's gone. For years, I've thought of her as dead. Now I find myself turning back to the start of our marriage—when I could at least pretend she was happy."

"No one will reproach you for anything you've done. You'll realize that in time."

"I suppose I will, if I'm patient enough. Man's an irrational animal at best, Mike. When I thought deliverance would never come, I could pray for her death in my heart, even though my religion wouldn't let me pray openly. I promised myself I'd marry Lee as soon as I was able—"

"You can keep that promise now."

"Lee has a plan we hope will save us both. You might call it a kind of mutual atonement." Melcher rose to lift the window blinds, flooding the office with light. "She's been wanting a postgrad year at Hopkins to pick up the latest improvements in her speciality. Yesterday she signed for her first class at summer school. When her year's over, we'll marry quietly—and do our best to forget what came before."

"Surely you needn't wait that long."

The director turned from the window. His shoulders had squared with the move; Mike knew that his self-reproach was behind him.

"A year's the shortest probation this town will allow us."

"Or you'll allow yourselves?"

"I'll need that much time to make sure of my tenure here. Zeagler could dissolve our enterprise tomorrow, if he got a wrong report on the hepatitis flare-up."

"I've news on that angle, at least."

Melcher listened attentively while Mike repeated the gist of his talk with Artemus Coxe, and the strategy the older doctor proposed.

"He's completely right, of course. Your only chance is to persuade the Duchess to sell out. The property's ripe for some kind of legal action, in any event. Vincent Schneider's bank has a whopping mortgage on all of Bearclaw Point, and he won't hold off forever."

"Even so, she'll probably refuse to budge. I hate to see her go to the wall—no matter who does the pushing. Will you back me when I go to Rynhook?"

"All the way," said Melcher. "Nothing would please me more than to see Paul beaten at his own game."

At seven that evening, a light still glowed behind the doors of Louis Garstein's basement domain when Mike finished his rounds. At his knock, the glass doors were opened by the pathologist himself. Garstein was in street clothes. His heavy brows were knotted in the sort of frown Mike had long since associated with disaster.

"Great minds, Dr. Constant. I was on my way to find *you*."

"How about a drink on my terrace?"

"I won't deny I need one, but I can't spare the time. Walk with me to my car. What I'm about to say will sound better outside the hospital."

The pathologist's car—a ten-year-old Buick with special levers permitting him to drive with his arms alone—stood at the far end of the parking lot, in the shade of a dogwood that had just burst into flower. Garstein scowled at the canopy of blossoms as he eased himself under the wheel. In the sunset light flooding Indian Hill, he seemed strangely careworn.

"Art Coxe tells me you talked things over."

"We can see daylight in the epidemic, Louis. It's something to be thankful for—even though I've no notion how things will end at Rynhook."

"In your place, I'd be realistic—and admit that Rynhook has always been beyond your control. It's another story at New Salem Memorial."

"Don't tell me *you've* been nursing a bomb all afternoon."

"Only since I talked to my esteemed brother-in-law."

"Zeagler's in Rome—if I can believe today's paper."

"There's always the transatlantic phone," said the pathologist. "Aaron has some of his best thoughts there."

"I hope you told him the hepatitis scare's behind us."

"He'd already had word on that from Schneider. You know, of course, that your friend the banker is Zeagler's deputy in his absence. With full authority to carry out his wishes—including a power of attorney."

"Larry stressed that point at our last staff meeting."

"You're to call Schneider at once—and make an appointment for tomorrow. He'll explain a decision Aaron's just made."

"What sort of decision?"

"A rather drastic one. Zeagler Electronics won't be renewing its lease with the hospital corporation."

Once the news was in the open, Mike realized he was more shocked than surprised. He could even wonder why the blow had not fallen sooner. It was appropriate, in a way, that Zeagler had chosen to inform him in this fashion, without so much as a hint to Larry Melcher.

"What prompted this decision? Our trouble with hepatitis?"

"I don't think the epidemic entered the picture," said Garstein. "Aaron could hardly blame its spread on us. In fact, he said he was damned glad the threat is ending. It was causing a lot of personnel trouble at the plant."

"He must have given you some reason."

"Only that he'd been considering canceling the lease for quite awhile. Schneider has definite orders. He'll give you a complete rundown when you see him tomorrow."

"Why can't I see him now?"

"I wouldn't, Mike. When Aaron's playing God, it isn't wise to disturb his timetable." Garstein put his car in gear, and backed slowly from his parking space. "One thing more—and this is important too. Larry's to be kept in the dark, until you've seen Schneider. He'll get the news in the morning, by overnight cable."

"Is this all you can tell me, Louis?"

"I don't like mysteries, any more than you," said the pathologist. "They happen to be routine with Aaron." He drove off with a last angry snort—leaving Mike standing in the shade of the dogwood, and a bewilderment that seemed to grow blacker as he shook off his daze and re-entered the hospital.

The phone was ringing when he entered his quarters, but he hesitated to lift the receiver. All the day's news had been bad; he was convinced that the bell was yet another warning that affairs in New Salem were rushing toward a climax he was powerless to control. When he heard Sandra's voice on the wire, he knew the premonition was justified. The pattern that had begun to take shape in Dr. Art's office was now complete.

"I've called to say good-by, Mike."

"You're leaving New Salem?"

"Paul is flying back tonight. I'm meeting his plane at Idlewild. It seemed only fair to let you know."

"You can't, Sandra—!"

He would never know if he had shouted the futile command at a dead phone. Perhaps the words were only an echo in his brain. For a while longer, he sat with the receiver in his hand before replacing it in its cradle. Now that he was off duty, he told himself numbly, it was time for the sunset drink he often shared with Lee Searles.

Only when he stood in the doorway and stared out at the empty terrace did he remember that even Lee had deserted him. Tonight, if he meant to drink, he would drink alone.

ELEVEN

New Salem's bank, the Fidelity Title and Trust Company, occupied the lower floor of the Schneider Building, a venerable brick-and-sandstone pile that stood at the juncture of Lower Street and River Road. Nine o'clock was striking from City Hall when Mike drove through that major intersection, swung into the parking lot, and left his Ford in the slot next to the whitewashed rectangle reserved for the president's Packard. It was part of the banker's legend that he had always driven himself to work. He had continued to do so, long after he had plowed back his second million into the valley. It was appropriate that he should use a car that had vanished from the market—and service it (at wholesale rates) in the Hudson Garage, an establishment the Schneider family had owned before the century's turn, when it had been the town's one livery stable.

This morning, the empty parking slot told its own story. Citizens of New Salem en route to their jobs could set their watches by the banker's arrival at the Fidelity. The fact that he was still absent at its opening meant great events were afoot—or, more precisely, that the telephone had detained him at his home.

Mike's head still throbbed with the aftermath of a largely sleepless night when he walked through the lobby and presented himself at the railed enclosure of the trust department. The desks of the two vice presidents were still empty, but Schneider's personal secretary was already typing busily in her corner.

"Am I too early, Miss Barnes?"

"Go right into his office, Dr. Constant. He's on his way."

The banker's lair was on the modest side. The desk where he worked, at the plate-glass window commanding a view of River

Road and the anchorage below it, was no larger than its counterparts outside. The office itself was almost surgically bare, save for its leaded-glass bookshelves, and the Morris chair where Schneider napped after lunch, in full view of all New Salem. . . . Mike was still pacing the bare parquet, and cursing the weights on his eyelids, when he heard the step outside the open door.

The president of New Salem Fidelity carried a well-filled briefcase briskly to his desk. This morning, he seemed the epitome of rubicund health and humor. It was impossible to picture him in the role of Machiavelli.

"Thanks for being prompt, Mike. *I'm* never late by more than a minute. This morning, unfortunately, I was trapped by my telephone. At least, it means the decks are cleared for action."

"I hope you're ready to explain the mystery, sir."

"No mystery's involved in *this* decision of Aaron Zeagler's." Schneider was busily emptying his briefcase—with the precise motions of an executive to whom stamped paper is more precious than meat or drink. "Transatlantic phone bills are the least of his worries. This morning, he wanted to review the whole picture before I talked with you."

Mike managed a tentative grin. It was unlike the banker to evade the point at issue.

"I'm beginning to understand why you're late."

"Aaron has his own way of doing business. Sometimes, it seems to bypass the human element, but it usually gets results. There was also a call from Larry Melcher. The leasing group is meeting in an hour to review the situation—and decide what action, if any, should be taken. Do you plan to join them?"

"I'm afraid I must, Mr. Schneider. I can hardly deny Keate and Pailey the pleasure of firing me."

"Why should they take so drastic a step?"

"Obviously, they'll assume I'm behind this move."

The banker was still busily shuffling documents. "In that case, we'll get down to business with no more delay. That assumption of your enemies is quite accurate. You've had a great deal to do with Aaron's refusal to renew their lease. Here's a copy of the cable he sent to Dr. Melcher."

Mike scanned the terse message the banker tossed across the desk. His heart sank as its meaning struck home. Larry Melcher, as president of the New Salem Memorial Hospital Corporation, had been given just six weeks to vacate Indian Hill. No reason was offered for the abrupt ending of the lease, and there was no hint of Zeagler's plans for the future.

"No wonder Larry's in a state of shock. This is on the curt side, even for a tycoon."

"We'll go into Aaron's motives in a moment," said the banker. "Meanwhile, I want your answer to the big question. How much will you need to take over?"

"If you mean the hospital—?"

"Why else do you think Aaron is throwing out the corporation? I'm offering you the job of director, with his full approval. The Fidelity is prepared to finance the transfer—including the take-over of all equipment owned by the present leasing group. Just name a tentative figure, so I'll have something to work on."

"I'm only a surgeon, Mr. Schneider. What makes you think I'm competent to run a hospital?"

"You've been on Indian Hill for three months, Mike. In that time, you've streamlined procedure, all down the line. With the jaundice scare under control, the hospital should begin to make money again. Perhaps you'll never match the twenty per cent Ralph Pailey counted on, but you're sure to do well. Add your own fees to your share of the take, and you can be a man of means in ten years' time. Maybe sooner, if New Salem keeps growing according to Zeagler's blueprint."

"The answer's no. You must see why I can't consider such an offer."

"Will you give me your reason?"

"You know that too. For my money, hospitals aren't run for profit. They're run to heal the sick, help the dying across the river, and bring new life into the world. That's profit enough."

Vincent Schneider put down the paper in his hand, and smiled across the desk. "Thanks, Mike. You passed that test with top marks. Now we'll discuss the *real* plan Aaron has in mind."

"Suppose I tell you I've had enough of Zeagler's planning? That I'm going to bow out with Larry—whether or not I'm fired?"

"If you do, I won't blame you. You've had a hard three months at New Salem Memorial. If the hospital can't be reformed, now's the time to say so."

"Last night, I was ready to pack my jalopy and head back to the Coast," said Mike. "I've a standing offer to teach surgery at Stanford, and practice on the side. As of midnight, a job where medicine came first and politics second seemed damned attractive. My second thought was obvious—I'd need a new car. Mine will never climb the Donner Pass a second time."

"You can have that loan now, if you really want it," said the banker. "Your signature will be enough."

Mike put out his hand, and shook the older man's firmly. "Thanks, Mr. Schneider. That was *my* way of testing. Let's forget Zeagler Electronics for a moment, and talk like friends."

"Nothing would please me more, Mike. I assume that last night was a time of soul searching?"

"At four this morning, I gave up all thought of sleep, and went to my terrace to wait for the dawn. When the sun burned the mist away, I found myself looking at New Salem head on, for the first time since I returned. All I needed was that one long look. It told me why I'd come back—and why I can't leave. This town is part of me; I'll never be a complete human being elsewhere."

Mike got up from his chair, and moved to the plate-glass window, to look down at the traffic on River Road. "Last night, I did my damndest to run away, to put the continent between me and a girl I love, but can't have. The coward part of me was looking for a fast exit—but I turned my back on it before the sun topped the Overlook. I'm going to do all I can to give New Salem a future that will match its past."

"With Aaron Zeagler's help?"

"If he's part of the future, I'll gladly listen to his plans."

"I'm from New Salem too," said the banker. "Is there any reason why a Dutchman, a Greek, and a Jew can't do business?"

"Not if we agree on fundamentals. Patients for profit will be ruled out at the new hospital, if I'm to be connected with it."

"Aaron saw where such an approach could lead, when he almost lost his daughter. I saw the light when a butcher named Keate tried to cure my wife's pneumonia with a scalpel."

"Does Zeagler realize you can't run New Salem Memorial and a factory by the same rules?"

"He realizes his fundamental mistake was putting Ralph Pailey in charge of over-all planning. Ralph's a brilliant bookkeeper—he simply doesn't understand what makes a hospital function."

"Proper management is all we really need, Mr. Schneider. We already have the personnel. In the last three months, Melcher's assembled most of the equipment that was lacking. But I'm not trained to run an entire hospital, any more than Pailey. I'm a surgeon, not a front-office man. New Salem Memorial will need both if it's to stay in business."

"That's good horse sense. How do we fill the gap?"

"With a chain of command that really functions. I can tell you what's vital to my department—but my main usefulness ends at the door of the recovery room. Larry Melcher can do as much on the medical side. What we really need, above all else, is management that pulls its weight—and a total lack of pressure when our books show red-ink entries, as they're bound to do."

"Then you're asking for a board of trustees," said the banker.

"The sort of trustees whose interests are above the market place. If you want names, I'll put yours at the head of the list. With Aaron Zeagler second, in charge of fund raising."

"You'll need doctors as well."

"Art Coxe will serve full time, now that he's retiring."

"Plus you and Larry Melcher."

"That should be enough for now," Mike said. "With doctors on the board, you'll have a balance wheel for the lay members' decisions. It's the easiest way to smooth out friction before it develops. To say nothing of a built-in personnel bureau for the hospital itself."

"How many doctors would serve as attending physicians, if you're losing money?"

"The hospital's financial affairs needn't concern them," Mike said quickly. "Not if our services are first-class. One of the new board's jobs will be to make sure our losses are balanced—at least, at the year's end—by outside help. New Salem will loosen the purse strings, once people realize the medical care they're receiving is second to none. The same applies to doctors in this area who hesitated to send patients here, because of our hot-bed reputation."

"Zeagler owns the physical plant—except for the equipment Pailey has installed. You've turned down his offer of a direct lease, made out to you alone. Shouldn't this brand-new group incorporate—and sign with him, after it's granted a charter?"

"I think we've gone beyond leases, sir. How much would it cost Zeagler to donate New Salem Memorial to the community?"

"With his tax pattern, probably less than ten cents on the dollar."

"Will you tell him it's the easiest way out, when you talk again?"

The banker smiled. "I already have, Mike. He'll go along—but only if you serve as our principal advisor, and continue as chief surgeon."

"You realize, of course, that the attending staff can't be new in the strict sense? Most of the available doctors are already members of the profit group."

"Surely you can work harmoniously with the men we choose."

"You've forgotten one vital point, Mr. Schneider. The hospital lease, as it now stands, has six weeks of grace before it expires. The group Melcher now heads will be in full control for that period, and they'll have my head in the next hour. Some of the members—perhaps even a majority—will argue that Zeagler may give them a second chance, if they promise token improvements."

"They couldn't be more wrong, Mike."

"If they stand firm, it's quite possible they can stampede the others. Doctors are individualists; they have to be, to succeed in their profession. They're always prickly, when things are forced upon them. In this case, their big sticking point would be their refusal to take dictation from their landlord—when it means closing the one up-to-date medical center in New Salem. It could turn into a powerful pressure group. The one thing Zeagler won't buy here is bad publicity."

"Can they present a united front?"

"Keate's a good man with a bellow. Gideon Bliss, and some of the others, will second almost any motion he proposes."

"How do you rate Melcher?"

"Larry's still broken up by his wife's death. Normally I'd expect him to back me. Today, I'm not so sure."

"Suppose I call him now, and lay the alternatives on the line?"

"I'd rather you didn't, sir. First, I think I should go to the staff meeting, and permit myself to be fired. Once I've faced the group, I'll know what people we can count on—and who'll go on fighting for a fast dollar."

"Shall I come with you?"

"Only as far as my quarters in the hospital. Give me fifteen minutes in the lion's den before you rescue me. It's only fair to my enemies to let them have their moment of glory."

At Mike's suggestion, the banker followed at a slight distance during the drive to the hospital—lest a simultaneous entrance destroy the surprise element that was to be their secret weapon. He needed no orientation to locate the meeting; the roar of voices that shook the library door was advertisement enough. An hour ago, the sound would have filled him with foreboding. Now that his battle plan was formed, he approached the reception desk with confidence.

"I'm expecting a call, Miss Jenks. Will you put it through in there?"

"Dr. Melcher said no calls would be taken during the meeting—"

"I'm sure he'll take this one."

As he spoke, Mike rapped sharply on the library door, then opened it before the argument inside could quite die down. The eight doctors who made up the corporation were gathered at the oval table. Melcher, as president of the group, sat at its head. There was a vacant seat beside him, and Mike moved toward it deliberately, ignoring the stony silence. Keate and Pailey, he observed, were in their familiar tandem position. The administrator, who was serving as secretary today, avoided his eyes. The beefy surgeon stared back with insolent triumph.

"I won't ask whether I'm welcome, gentlemen," said Mike. "I know you'll want to hear my report."

"You have the right to speak, Dr. Constant," said Melcher coldly. "I won't deny you that—"

Keate had already bounced from his chair. "Larry, I rise to a point of order—"

Melcher lifted his gavel to still a new babble of tongues. Already, Mike could see that Keate's need to dominate had rasped nerve ends.

"Yes, Brad?"

"A motion is before this meeting. I move we record a vote."

Hugo Brett cut in quickly. "Now that Mike's here, why not listen to his side?"

"Constant is not a member of this body. I won't let him interrupt proceedings."

"Damn you, Brad, do you *always* have to act like a steam roller?"

Several minutes were wasted in a procedural wrangle, with Keate's voice riding down all opposition. When Ralph Pailey was at last permitted to read the motion, Mike was glad to note his hands were shaking.

"Dr. Keate has moved that the employment of Dr. Michael Constant be terminated—because of activities prejudicial to this corporation. Do I hear a second?"

"What activities?" Brett demanded. "Proved by whom?"

"By Zeagler's cable, which you've just heard read!" Keate roared.

"Let him defend himself before we vote. It's only common justice."

"To hell with that, Hugo. Constant's knifed us. What else can we do but boot him out? I'm voting my own stock—and Ralph's. A fifty-five per cent majority. Motion moved, seconded, carried. Are there dissenters—for the record?"

Another murmur spread through the room, but there was no direct defiance. Observing the eight set stares, Mike read every emotion from truculence to fear—but no sign of willingness to take his side. By a somewhat liberal interpretation of parliamentary rules, Keate's vote had been in order; his victory snort was the capstone to a stratagem common in boardrooms the world over.

"You're fired, Constant, as of now," he said. "Your attempt to destroy this group has backfired, to your cost. New Salem Memorial will be ready with a blackball when you apply for your next job–"

"May I defend myself now, Mr. Chairman?"

"You have the floor, Dr. Constant."

Mike rose to face the group, letting the hostile silence build before he broke it.

"I'll begin by reminding Dr. Keate that his threat of a blackball, as he calls it, is without meaning. This hospital has yet to be accredited. Therefore, its censure, or its recommendation, have no standing."

Keate leaped up to protest, but Melcher gaveled him into silence. "You've passed your motion, Brad. Let the other side speak."

"I'm asking you all to bear one central fact in mind," said Mike. "This hospital will never be accredited while Dr. Keate and the cash register dictate its policy. As you know, I hold a certificate from the American Board of Surgery, the highest qualification in my field. Because of my status, and my training, I was hired three months ago to overhaul procedure here and restore the practice of medicine as your primary function. Now, it seems, I'm to be dismissed without a hearing, on an unproved charge. The real reason for my dismissal is my refusal to condone dollar chasing. If I protest to the State Medical Association–and lay the facts before them–I assure you the blackball will go the other way."

Once again, the room was filled with a clash of tongues as Mike paused. He spoke quickly, above the pounding of the gavel.

"Gentlemen, I can sympathize with your anger. It's a bitter snub to all of you that Zeagler Electronics has refused to renew your lease. Obviously, you intend to take this cavalier action before the public, hoping you can force him to change his mind. Perhaps you feel he's in a bind, that his workers will have nowhere else to turn for medical assistance. Let me warn you that steps have already been taken to assure continued operation here. You can take my word they'll succeed."

"What's *your* word worth in New Salem today?" Keate asked.

Mike ignored the question—and glanced at his watch. "In another moment, you'll have proof that Mr. Zeagler's decision was none of my doing. You will also learn just how you can save this hospital." The phone rang at last, and he turned to it with relief. "I'm sure you'll welcome the man who is about to appeal to you as citizens—not just as doctors."

Melcher had already pounced on the phone. His voice all but reached the lobby.

"We're not to be disturbed, Miss Jenks!"

"It's Mr. Schneider, Doctor." The girl's voice carried clearly in the room. Mike smiled as several heads craned forward. "He says he has a message—for all of you."

Melcher covered the receiver with his palm. "Schneider's outside—with a new report from Zeagler. Shall we see him now or later?"

"Don't let him get away, Larry." Hugo Brett's voice was a stage whisper. When a ripple of laughter spread round the table, Mike felt, for the first time, that a human element had been restored to the gathering.

"Show Mr. Schneider in, please."

Keate rose, with a howl that shook the pendants on the chandelier. "This is a trick of Constant's. Why didn't you tell Schneider he's been fired?"

"Shut up, Brad! Have you forgotten who holds our mortgage?"

Keate sat down with a muttered obscenity. Mike could not suppress a chuckle when he saw the interruption had barely registered. Every eye in the room was fastened on the door that had just opened to admit the banker and his briefcase.

Jason West in his heyday, thought Mike, could not have made a more urbane entrance. Schneider accepted the chair Hugo Brett hastened to bring forward. His manner was as relaxed as his smile.

"Forgive my rather abrupt appearance, gentlemen. In cases like yours, it's customary for Mohammed to come to the mountain. Today, it seemed logical to reverse the approach."

"If you've come to argue us out of firing Constant," said Keate, "it's already been done."

The banker glanced down the table. "Our timing's a bit off, Mike. You said they'd need fifteen minutes to give you the ax. I had no idea Dr. Keate was so efficient. Perhaps it's his surgical training."

Keate had recovered his poise by now—and his arrogance. "What kind of collusion is this, Mr. Schneider?"

"For your own sake, Doctor, I'd choose my words more carefully." The banker had opened his briefcase. Now, he extracted a sheet of stationery and handed it to the director. "Here, Dr. Melcher, is a letter, terminating the lease of the New Salem Hospital Corporation on this building, six weeks from date. As your chief creditor, I'm also serving formal notice that the mortgage covering your equipment will be foreclosed at the same time. You will remember we agreed it would be renewed each year, at the bank's discretion—which would be governed, in turn, by the hospital's rating."

The statement was received in silence. Mike glanced at Pailey. The administrator's lips had parted on a protest—which he choked down with a convulsive swallow. Melcher's face was composed, a marked contrast to the hectic flush of Bradford Keate.

"What can Zeagler do with an empty hospital?" the surgeon demanded. "What excuse will he give the community for shutting us out?"

"No doctor in New Salem who is qualified to practice medicine will be shut out," said the banker. "We welcome anyone who's prepared to abide by our rules."

"What does *we* mean?"

"I refer to the New Salem Memorial Hospital Association—a nonprofit trustee group that will take over here. At the moment, I'm its presiding officer."

"You and who else?"

The banker smiled blandly at Keate's insolence. "A three-man board was assembled this morning. Myself, Aaron Zeagler, and Dr. Constant."

"We just fired Constant!"

"He tells me he still intends to practice here. As president of the trustees, I have accepted his application to use this hospital for his private patients. I've also asked him to resume his post as chief surgeon, when the present leasing period ends."

The director spoke quietly, from the table's head. "When was all this accomplished?"

"An hour ago, in my office."

"At whose suggestion?"

"Mr. Zeagler gave me a free hand to work out any arrangement that would save the hospital."

Keate's fist struck the table. "You see, Larry? Constant *did* go behind our backs to make a deal."

"Your business acumen is even worse than your medical judgments, Doctor." Schneider's smile was bleak now; his eyes snapped with fury. "For three years, as your colleagues know you've been cock of the walk here. You've indulged your *furor operativus*—a failing that put my wife in mortal danger. Time and again, you've spoiled the hospital's chances for accreditation. Now, with no proof, whatever, you accuse Dr. Constant of collusion. Believe me, gentlemen, Mike is blameless in this affair. When he came to the bank this morning, he was completely ignorant of our plans."

Even now, Keate refused to yield. Despite his dislike, Mike could almost admire the man's defense of a position he had long since lost.

"You can't deny that Zeagler offered to lease him the hospital. It's right here in the cable he sent Larry from Rome."

"It's quite true he made such an offer, Dr. Keate."

"And Constant couldn't swing the deal. So you cooked up this nonprofit dodge between you."

"Dr. Constant could have swung the deal easily. My bank was prepared to back him."

"Until you heard we were kicking him out?"

"On the contrary. Your enmity for Dr. Constant was the highest recommendation he could receive. As it happened, we both concluded that a voluntary hospital was better for New Salem."

"Spare me the welfare bromides. How can a so-called citizens' group buy and operate New Salem Memorial—when one of its members isn't even solvent?"

"Dr. Constant has a credit rating worth more than all your collateral—integrity."

"Is that an answer to my question?"

"I think so, Doctor. However, since your checkbook is your bible, I'll use words you can understand. Zeagler Electronics is donating this building outright—to the new association. As soon as my own board of directors can act, my bank will donate the equipment covered by our mortgage."

Keate's jowls were still working mightily, but no words escaped him. When Mike's eyes ran round the table, he read the answer he had awaited. Hugo Brett was smiling broadly; Crosby Pendergast's nod was an outright endorsement. Even the sigh that escaped the puritan-thin lips of Gideon Bliss was resignation to the inevitable. When Melcher spoke, his voice had all its old resonance.

"As practicing physicans, we're naturally concerned with the professional standards you'll maintain here. Have you given thought to that?"

"So far, the association has only one physician member," said the banker. "He'll be our consultant on all matters relating to surgery. Since you occupy an identical position on the medical side, I'm happy to offer you a similar position as chief of that service."

Melcher did not hesitate. "I'll be glad to co-operate—for the good of New Salem."

"We can discuss other appointments later. Our trustees will include several of your number." The banker paused, as Keate stormed out with a resounding door slam—then began to close his briefcase. "One vital post remains unfilled. I'm hoping Mr. Pailey will take over as administrator, under the conditions I've outlined."

Pailey reddened painfully. "I accept the post, Mr. Schneider—and the responsibility."

"Are there any more questions, gentlemen? I hope not, since it's my lunch hour—and I'm a slave to my habits." Schneider turned toward the door, and paused there with a hand on the knob. "The problems of the change-over seem covered—with one exception. In the interests of continuity, I'd suggest you rescind Dr. Constant's dismissal."

"I so move," said Hugo Brett.

Gideon Bliss spoke through taut lips. "I second the motion."

There was no need for a roll call. Every man at the table had already pressed forward to shake Mike's hand.

TWELVE

After the stunning reversal in the library, Mike had expected the day to be heavy with anticlimax—and heavier still with black images of Sandra, in Paul's arms at Idlewild. Instead, the demands of hospital routine claimed him before he could finish lunch, when a multiple crash on the thruway filled the accident room and sent a half-dozen patients to the operating theaters. Lost in the task of repairing broken bones and flesh, he had no time to dwell on personal dilemmas. Even after he had finished in surgery, a sudden hemorrhage in one of the hepatitis cases brought a hurry call for flasks of the Type O blood now stored against just such an emergency.

Late afternoon checks on the injured—and the jaundice cases that still filled the medical wards—made him late for supper. It was dusk before he could take time to look back on the day and its events. He was showering in his quarters when the busy phone rang once again.

"You have a visitor downstairs, Doctor."

Mike's heart gave a great bound. Had Sandra reconsidered?

"Who is it?"

"Mrs. Paul Van Ryn. She's waiting in your office."

Anna was pacing the carpet when Mike came downstairs. She was wearing a traveling suit of dark linen, with a raincoat tossed over her shoulders.

"I thought you'd left for Reno, Anna."

"I postponed the trip to see Jason's tryout."

"Did he get my wire in New Haven?"

"I took it to his dressing room myself, Mike."

"The morning paper says both he and the play were a sensation."

"He's never given a better performance." Anna's voice had a curious flatness, as though she was conserving her breath for some supreme effort.

"What's bothering you? Is it Paul again?"

"Isn't it always Paul, just when we think the road is clear?"

Anna's hands were icy when he took them in his own to lead her to a chair—but the look she gave him was steadfast.

"What has he done this time?"

"It isn't what he's done. It's what he's planning. He flew in from Germany this morning—"

"Sandra told me he was coming."

"If you're worried about *her,* I can tell you this much." Anna's voice was filled with purpose now. "He hadn't seen her when we talked this morning."

"Where was that?"

"At my lawyer's New York office. We'd met to go over the details of my divorce. I expected an uproar, but he signed every paper they put before him. Apparently he's written me off to experience—now he realizes he can't hurt me any more."

"I'm glad of that much, Anna."

"It's what he said afterwards that terrifies me. Paul is convinced he can put his mother in a mental hospital."

"With the smartest law firm in New Salem behind him, he may be right."

"Once she's been declared incompetent, and he has legal control of her estate, he plans to sell out here and move to a New York studio—with Sandra as his mistress."

"He told you *that?*"

"In those very words. As calmly as though we were discussing a routine business deal."

"Sandra expects him to marry her."

"The Paul Van Ryns of this world only marry for their own gain, Mike."

"Try explaining that to Sandra. I've given up long ago."

"You mustn't do that. You wouldn't with a patient. We both know Paul's insane. He should be put where he belongs."

"If you'd spoken up after your splenectomy, you'd have had a chance to commit him. Ever since then, he's behaved like a perfect husband—including today's visit with your lawyers. That cuts the ground from under you."

"Then his mother must do the committing. Dr. Coxe would sign the papers, wouldn't he?"

"Of course—but the Duchess would never agree."

"She may, when she sees the evidence I've brought back to New Salem."

Mike had not noticed the folded sheet in Anna's raincoat pocket. He saw now that it was an early edition of a New York evening paper.

"I bought this as I was leaving," she said. "I didn't even see the story until I stopped for gas."

The newspaper was opened to its second page, a two-column spread, with the photograph of a painting. The picture seemed to leap from the newsprint as Mike took the paper from Anna. Even without the caption, he would have recognized Paul's work at once. The tortured writhings of the mind that had created it were evident in each brush stroke; the headline and the story below it were almost needless.

DEAN OF GERMAN CRITICS
CALLS AMERICAN ARTIST "MADMAN."

Professor Heinrich Bultmann, veteran art critic for the Illustrierte Zeitung *of Munich, and head of the art department at the University of Tubingen, today handed down a startling verdict on the much-discussed mural recently completed by the American artist, Paul Van Ryn.*

"This is not art," said Prof. Bultmann. "It is obviously the work of a madman, and can only be labeled as such."

The opinion was shared by a psychiatrist at the same University, who refused to give his name. Mr. Van Ryn's painting had been scheduled for the foyer of a new United

States Army Post Exchange. The artist is the son-in-law of industrialist Aaron Zeagler. He could not be reached for comment.

Mike put down the paper, hardly able to believe that what he had read was anything but a mirage.

"Has Paul seen this?"

"He couldn't. He left New York hours before it was on the street."

"You're quite right, Anna. This could be just the push his mother needs." Mike had picked up the desk phone; he was dialing as he spoke.

"What are you going to do?"

"First, I'm calling Dr. Coxe, and asking him to meet us, with commitment papers. It's an opportunity we may never have again. The Duchess let Paul go abroad—hoping against hope he wasn't the paranoic she already knew him to be. With this evidence, she can't delude herself any longer." Mike spoke briefly on the phone, then hung up. "Dr. Art is out on a case—but Mrs. Bramwell thinks she can reach him. She'll ask him to call me here."

"Shouldn't we go straight to Rynhook, Mike?"

"I don't think we should scatter our shot. With Dr. Art's help, we may be able to settle matters at once."

"Not if Paul's read the story, and told his mother it isn't true."

"Pray he's still in the dark then. It's our one big chance."

Anna shivered, and drew the raincoat about her shoulders. "I'm afraid, Mike. Paul was far too agreeable this morning in New York. When he's behaved like that before, it's meant he was planning to hurt someone."

"At least he can't trouble you any longer."

"He can still hurt Sandra."

Mike tapped the newspaper in his hand. "I'm hoping this will convince her too." The phone rang, and he picked it up. Expecting to hear Dr. Art's voice, he was startled to recognize the soft, slurring accent of Nellie, the Van Ryn maid.

"Can you come here right away, Dr. Constant?"

"What's the trouble?" He had recognized the terror in her tone, and kept his own voice calm with an effort.

"I don't know—but Madame's mighty low."

"Did you try Dr. Coxe?"

"Yes sir. He ain't there. His nurse say I should call you."

"I'll be at Rynhook in ten minutes."

When Mike had hung up, he dialed Dr. Coxe's number a second time. "I'm on my way, Mrs. Bramwell," he said. "I couldn't get much out of Nellie, but I'm afraid Madame Van Ryn is worse. When you reach Dr. Coxe, ask him to meet me at Rynhook. And tell him to bring commitment papers." He hung up, and looked grimly across the desk at Anna. "Let's hope she's lucid when Dr. Art joins me."

"I'm coming too, Mike," said Anna. "I'll feel safer with you."

"I'll get my medical bag, and meet you in the parking lot. We'll take your car."

The wheels of Anna's hardtop convertible rattled the planks of Bear Creek bridge just as full night was descending on New Salem. At that hour, Rynhook should have been a dark fortress bulk against the stars. To Mike's amazement, every downstairs window glowed with light. Even from the gateway, he could hear the roar of the television, as Beethoven's "Emperor Concerto" poured from a wide-open audio.

"At least she must be conscious," Anna observed.

"I doubt the Duchess is listening. She likes the *screen* on television, not the sound." Mike drove past the Gate House, urged on by a conviction that all was not right in the castle. Part of his mind noted that the Cadillac was in the carport, but he did not pause to ponder its presence there.

When he drove into the porte-cochere, the door swung open before he could get out and lift the knocker. Nellie stood waiting in the hall, her face a patient mask.

"How is Madame now?"

"She ain't stirred from her bed, Doctor. Not since—"

Paul Van Ryn's voice boomed above the thunder of the New York

Philharmonic. "Come in, Mike Constant! Don't pump the maid behind my back."

"He *made* me call you, Doctor," Nellie whispered. "The minute he got here—and found her out of her head—"

Mike turned to Anna, who had joined him in the doorframe. "Let me go in first. If there's trouble, you can call the police." He moved to the double doors, without giving her time to protest. Nellie had already vanished through the matching doors at the far end of the parlor.

Paul sat in his mother's Queen Anne chair, before the blaring television. Save for the glare he had fastened on the doorway, he seemed entirely at ease. Mike had seen the same light in the eyes of addicts—but he doubted that Paul took drugs; at a time like this, the fires that raged through his brain were stimulus enough. Aware, even now, of the strategy that had brought him here—and the motives behind it—Mike was glad to note that both of Nicholas Van Ryn's hunting rifles were resting in their wall brackets.

"I asked you to come in, Mike," said Paul. "Don't stand on ceremony."

It was time for the first testing, and the slightest hesitation could be fatal. Bracing his shoulders, Mike strode across the room and cut off the television.

"Your mother's ill. You know she doesn't like the sound."

Paul smiled thinly; the ominous narrowing of his eyes warned Mike of the risk he had just taken.

"What my mother likes or doesn't like can't matter much longer," Paul said, in the same flat tone. "Did you bring Anna with you? I planned it that way, when I drove past the hospital, and saw her car was parked there."

Anna stepped through the door from the hallway, with her head high. She was pale, but Mike could see no sign of trembling when she stood beside him.

"I came back to see your mother, Paul. You must have known I would."

"It was most thoughtful of you, my dear. Otherwise, I might have had trouble arranging this—shall we say—this three-way tête-à-tête?"

"What do you mean?" Mike knew that Anna had spoken automatically to gain time. It was too late to hope for a rational answer.

"As you both know, I'm preparing to declare the Duchess incompetent. Omar Dean assures me I'll have no legal difficulties—and New Salem is just avaricious enough to fall in with my wishes."

Mike took a step toward the chair—and paused, as Paul lifted a warning hand. "Be careful, Mike. It would be a great mistake to try to rush me. Mother's always kept those rifles loaded, for fear of prowlers."

"Why did you come back at this time?"

"I finished the first section of the mural. Von Helm is arranging its critical reception. While I waited, it seemed an excellent idea to check up on things back home—especially you."

Anna started to speak, but a warning look from Mike cut her short, as Paul's voice rode serenely on. "There's no real need to tell you this; I'm sure we understand each other perfectly. For years, I've watched my mother's mind come apart—just as Rynhook itself is crumbling. All those years, I've made a virtue of patience. I've told myself she couldn't rule me forever—with that iron will, and an iron hand on her checkbook. At long last, my patience has been rewarded."

"Where is your mother now?"

Paul nodded toward the far end of the parlor. "In her bedroom. You'll find her drooling as usual."

Mike crossed the parlor to look through the matching double doors, which stood half ajar. Nellie sat at the foot of the huge four-poster. The Duchess lay there, propped in pillows—as though the bed were the bier it resembled. The shutters of the room were drawn, but a night light cast a sepulchral beam across the counterpane. In that almost lunar glow, Marcella Van Ryn's face was parchment yellow, her eyes closed. From where Mike stood, she hardly seemed to breathe—and yet, for no reason he could name, he felt that her apparent coma was not so deep as it seemed.

"Not beyond the doorsill, please," said Paul.

When Mike turned back to the parlor, Paul had settled deeper in his mother's chair. His eyes were fixed on Anna, and his tight-lipped smile had expanded to a grin that warned Mike to proceed warily.

"You've done your duty as a doctor, Mike. I'm sure your observation of my mother's condition bears me out."

"Being only a surgeon, I'd want a confirming opinion." Again, Mike had spoken automatically. He was still sparring for time—with no clear idea just how he would use it.

"Two of New York's top psychiatrists are coming here in the morning," said Paul. "They'll certify the Duchess as incompetent —and Omar Dean will take over from there. Of course I'll be too overcome by my personal tragedy to take any part in the proceedings."

"What personal tragedy?"

"The deaths of my wife and my former classmate."

"Is that why you brought us here?"

"Could I have a more valid reason?" Paul asked gently. "I can't let Anna live, after she publicly spurned me for a broken-down actor like Jason West. And I've always felt the world could do without your personal brand of nobility. Fortunately I could count on it to bring you here tonight—and let me, if you'll pardon the cliché, kill two birds with one stone."

"You'll never get away with murder."

"Murder is justified, under the unwritten law. In another moment, the three of us will take the lift to my tower suite. When the police come, after it's over, I'll tell them I returned here suddenly, and found you in *flagrante*—"

Anna cut in at last—and Mike was glad to note that she was in complete control.

"*You're* the one who's insane Paul—not your mother."

Paul shrugged. "You could be right, my dear. But the burden of proof is on you—if you hope to consign me to a padded cell. In my mother's case, the evidence is at hand."

Mike took a cautious step nearer the chair. Now, he realized—with a sudden surge of excitement—was the time to play the trump he had almost forgotten he possessed.

"You're wrong, Paul!" Unconsciously, his voice had risen almost to a shout. "Since noon today, the whole world has known you're mad."

"What are you saying?"

"Do you know a German critic named Heinrich Bultmann?"

"Of course."

Mike took the paper from his pocket. "Here's a statement he made today in Munich—after he saw your mural. He says it isn't art, but the work of an obvious madman."

Paul did not move to seize the newspaper, as Mike had hoped. Instead he rose from the chair and stood beside it—with his left hand resting on one of the rifles.

"Don't move," he said. "Just toss me that paper."

Mike threw the paper into the chair Paul had just vacated—and watched warily as he shook it open to study the reproduction of his painting and the comment below it. Then, with a convulsive motion, he ripped the page from the newspaper, crumpled it in his fist, and pressed his fist against his forehead. When the hand dropped, his whole body was shaking with a rage he made no attempt to control. The shell of urbanity that had armored him had cracked at last—and the break was beyond repair.

"The swine! The filthy Prussian swine!"

The words were a near scream. As he uttered them, Paul flung the crumpled sheet on the floor and ground it beneath his heel. The maniacal outburst was brief. It ended, as abruptly as it had begun, when the doors at the parlor's end swung wide, and a voice spoke from the shadowed bedroom.

"That's quite enough, Paul. I've warned you before about these tantrums. You've been bad—so you'll have to be punished."

It was the Duchess, in a brocaded housecoat, and her manner was as commanding as her words as she crossed the room to join the group around the Queen Anne chair. Mike saw at once that his hope had been realized. The Duchess, with Nellie's aid, had risen from her coma, in time to hear the last exchange in the parlor. For the moment, at least, she was rational again.

At the sound of his mother's voice, Paul had cowered in the chair, his arms crossed before his face like a child expecting to be slapped.

Mike had observed such regressions before, in the locked wards of a city hospital. After an outburst of violence, they were familiar phenomena in the hopelessly deranged.

After the rebuke, the Duchess of Rynhook paid no more attention to her son. Instead, she turned toward Mike and Anna, with a weary shrug.

"Is it true, Michael—what you said about the German critic?"

Mike could not quite meet her eyes. More than anything in the world, he would have preferred not to hurt this regal old woman, who was facing the final collapse of all she had hoped for in her son, and in her name.

"I'm afraid he was right, madame."

"So am I, after what I've just heard."

"Dr. Coxe is on his way here—with commitment papers. Will you sign them too?"

"Of course, Michael." Marcella Van Ryn turned to her daughter-in-law. "Forgive me for misjudging you, Anna. I don't expect to live much longer—and money will be needed, to provide for Paul. We must make some arrangement with your father to take over my property."

"Don't let it worry you, Mother." Mike was sure that Anna had spoken the last word unconsciously. The answering light in the other woman's eyes filled his throat; for the moment, he knew that speech was beyond him. . . . Bemused as he was by the warmth of that understanding, he needed Anna's quick gasp of warning to swing his glance back to Paul, who had just plunged behind the chair to lift one of the rifles from its rack.

For a moment, no one stirred in the room, while Paul—moving with a hunter's soft-footed tread to get clear of the chair—snapped off the rifle's safety catch, and raised the barrel until the sights were dead on Mike's chest.

"You first, Doctor—if the ladies will pardon me," he said—and his voice had all its old bite, the burst of childlike anger gone as though it had never been. "They don't electrocute madmen for murder—remember?"

Mike lifted an arm to push Anna behind him. Marcella Van Ryn spoke calmly, before he could set himself to rush Paul.

"Put that rifle down," she said—and again, it was as if she were addressing a child. "Dr. Coxe had Nellie remove the bullets months ago. They were afraid I'd hurt myself in one of my spells."

Paul's eyes dropped to the gun bolt and his right hand snapped it back to reveal the empty chamber. Mike had already started to move. He heard Paul's curse, saw his fists close on the barrel as he raised the rifle like a bludgeon. It was too late to break his headlong charge. All he could do was lift both arms to ward off the worst of the blow. Like a man in a self-propelled nightmare, he had reached for Paul's midriff at the start of his football tackle, just as the Duchess flung her body between him and the rifle butt.

The heavy gunstock, sweeping downward with all the maniac's strength behind it, struck Marcella Van Ryn's shoulder, spun her off balance, then sent her crashing against the tall wing chair. The feeling of nightmare deepened when Mike saw her chin hook over the wide-curved arm, just as her body was completing its headlong fall. There was a sharp crack—which, to his medically trained mind, could mean only that the vertebral column had been snapped by the sudden overextension produced by her weight. In another moment, with her head twisted at a grotesque angle, she had slumped to the floor.

The diversion had given Mike time to brace for a second tackle. This time, his headlong rush swept the rifle from Paul's trembling hands and sent his adversary tumbling to the floor. Mike made no further effort to follow up his advantage. Leaving Paul where he had fallen, he moved to the wing chair, to kneel above the Duchess. Nellie was already at her side, her body shaken by sobs. There was no need to explain the strange limpness of the figure in the brocaded robe.

Complete stillness filled the room while Mike took up the Duchess' wrist in a futile effort to find a pulse. Already he knew that her neck had been broken by the whiplash of her fall.

Across the parquet, he heard a child's whimper, and realized the sound had come from Paul Van Ryn's throat. The second regression was even briefer than the first. Mike did not even turn as the scramble of footsteps told him Paul had lunged from the room. In another moment, the roar of a powerful motor outside completed the tragic pattern. There was no need to move to the parlor window to know that the Porsche had just roared from its hiding place in the boxwoods. Once again, Paul had chosen the madman's flight from reality—this time, the death of his mother at his own hands.

"Has he gone, Mike?"

The new voice had come from the door that led to the kitchen. Turning slowly toward the sound, Mike was not too startled to find Sandra West on the threshold. It seemed only natural to hold out his arms to her as she rushed into them and burst into a storm of tears.

"Will someone call the police?"

Sandra spoke, with her face buried in his shoulder: her voice was oddly resolute, despite that burst of weeping.

"I called them—a few minutes ago. On the kitchen phone."

"Are you all right, Sandra?"

"I think so." She had turned toward the Duchess—but he took her elbow and led her to the window seat, where Anna had settled in frozen terror.

"How much did you hear?"

"Enough, Mike. *More* than enough. Madame Van Ryn's dead, isn't she?"

"Yes—from a broken neck. It was instantaneous."

"Thank God for that."

Across the dam, a siren whined insistently. By the time Mike reached the driveway, with Sandra close beside him, Chief Wharton, a bulky man in suntans, was stepping from the police car.

"We met Paul on the bridge, Doctor. He was in that red Porsche, and moving fast. What's wrong here?"

"I'm afraid he's finally cracked."

The officer nodded slowly. "I'd been expecting that to happen, for quite a while. What pushed him over the edge? That business in Germany?"

"How did you know?"

"It was on the last news break. One of the local stations picked it up. I knew there'd be hell to pay, as soon as Paul heard it. Anything else happen over here?"

"Mrs. Van Ryn is dead—from a broken neck, in a fall."

From the base of the tor came the scream of tires on asphalt. Chief Wharton nodded toward the dark face of the cliff.

"That's Paul now," he said. "I figured he'd take the Lookout Road." He watched the crazy zoom of the sports-car's headlights, on the first of the hogback bends. "Wonder if he can stay on course at that speed?"

"He'll stay on," Mike replied grimly. He was remembering the night the Porsche had hunted him on that same sheer hillside.

The police chief lifted his dashboard microphone and spoke into it tersely. While he talked, the headlights followed the next hairpin turn—to race upward, in an opposite direction, on the new incline.

"Looks like he'll hold the road, Doctor. He's still got to come down on the far side. We'll have state troopers waiting when he hits the thruway. They'll stop him cold."

"If something else doesn't stop him first," said Mike. "On a night like this, kids will be parked all across the Overlook. Paul can't see their cars until he rounds the last turn. Then he'll be right among them."

"Good God!" Chief Wharton reached for the microphone a second time, then dropped his hand. No power he could summon would stop Paul Van Ryn from gaining the crest of the tor.

Mike felt Sandra's hand slip into his as they watched the car climb the zigzag inclines. He could not be sure if his imagination was playing tricks, but Paul seemed to be moving even faster as he burst from the last curve and vanished over the summit. He could picture that brick-red projectile perfectly, rocketing from the road to burst upon the cars parked haphazard along the cliff's edge.

"He made it, Doctor!" Chief Wharton's voice was hoarse with relief as the twin beams winked into view again, at the far side of the Overlook. Almost immediately, they vanished from view a second time—a sure sign that Paul had reached the downward slopes. Then, on the cliff's face, they caught the same dance of the headlights, tracing a pattern against the sky—a wild parabola that somehow reminded Mike of the brush work in one of Paul's canvases.

"*Someone's* gone over, after all—"

"Is it Paul, or another car?"

"This far away, you can't be sure." As the police chief spoke, the mad dance of the headlights ended in a burst of fire, just below the cliff's edge. "That's the gas tank exploding—when he hit the first ledge. The next outcrop's a hundred feet below."

As though guided by Chief Wharton's words, the fireball was plummeting now—hanging for a few seconds on the lower outcrop, then streaking like a doomed meteor for the valley floor.

"We'd best go up there, Doctor."

The officer's voice jarred Mike from the trance that had claimed his senses. Releasing Sandra's hand, he turned toward the police car.

"We can't help the man who went over—whoever he was."

"There may be people needing you at the top. I'll call an ambulance on the radio."

It was nearly midnight when Mike stopped his car at the Gate House. Sandra, who had met him at New Salem Memorial after his visit to the tor, looked at the square granite dwelling, as though she were seeing it for the first time.

"Sure you don't want to come back to the hospital?" he said. "We can give you a bed until morning."

"I'll be all right here, Mike. I'm not afraid."

"You won't be here much longer," he said firmly. "I'm going to build our house in the Heights—on the far side of the lake. Will that suit you?"

"I'd love to be there, Mike. Are you sure you want me, after—?"

"That's all behind us now. We've agreed to say no more about it."

"You still haven't told me exactly what happened on the tor."

"There isn't much to tell, Sandra. If your brother were here, he'd have a quotation to sum up Paul's exit from the world. The only one I can think of is, *Nothing in his life became him like the leaving of it.*"

"I can't quite picture how he cleared the parking space."

"Paul was too good a driver not to make it. The kids who were there saw the whole thing. He missed a station wagon by inches, then exploded into the southern downgrade like a bullet. A car was coming up on the last hogback. The boy who was driving was hugging the inside—"

"The wrong side of the road?"

"Paul had to swing far out to avoid a crash. It was too much, even for a sports car. He jumped the guardrail. You saw how he exploded, on the first ledge."

Mike felt Sandra shiver, and held her closer. "You and Anna were together for quite a while before I came back," he said quietly. "I doubt if Paul was the type who'd make a will. He died after his mother—so Anna, as his wife, is now the Van Ryn heir. Did she tell you how she'd dispose of the land?"

"She's leasing all of Bearclaw Point to her father, for his new factory. Part of the money will finance new housing on Lower Street. The rest will start a fund for college scholarships, in that same tenant group."

"Of course that means Rynhook will go under the wreckers' hammers."

"I'm afraid so, Mike. At least it will wipe out the hepatitis threat."

"Anna couldn't have made a better choice."

Sandra stirred in the curve of his arm. "Isn't it time you asked how I happened to be at the Gate House tonight, instead of in New York?"

"You're here. Nothing else seems important right now."

"I still want you to know why. When I phoned you last night, I meant to go straight to Idlewild—and surprise Paul by meeting his plane."

"Must we talk about it? Last night seems a hundred years away."

"Let me finish, please. After I hung up, I realized I had time for a short detour—"

"What sort of detour?"

"To New Haven—and Jason's tryout."

"Then *he* persuaded you to keep clear?"

"I didn't even go backstage," said Sandra. "After I'd seen the play,

I was too shaken to speak to anyone. It's going to be a great success, Mike. For both Jason and its author."

"So the morning paper says. I'm still groping for the connection."

"Have you forgotten the title?"

"*The Demon Lover*, isn't it?"

"Surely you remember the Coleridge poem we studied in high school?"

Mike chuckled. "Jason's the walking Bartlett in our group. I didn't know you'd picked up the habit."

"*The Demon Lover* is the story of a Casanova who's all things to all women, and true only to himself. A man who lives for his appetites—and dies of them. The girl *he's* pursuing at the end isn't as lucky as I. She's still wandering in the chasm of her delusion as the curtain falls."

The silence between them was a perfect rapport. When he broke it, Mike did not speak above a whisper:

But O! The deep romantic chasm which slanted
Down the green hill athwart a cedarn cover!
A savage place! as holy and enchanted
As e'er beneath a waning moon was haunted
By woman wailing for her demon-lover!

When Sandra spoke, her whisper matched his own.

"Thanks for saying it, Mike. *I* still can't. Not without reminding myself of what a fool I was—and how badly I treated you."

"Was it Jason's performance that changed your mind?"

"Let's be honest, and admit the play gave me second thoughts—that I returned to the Gate House to think them out. When Paul arrived this evening, he was too busy trapping you and Anna to notice I was here. After he began shouting, I came to Rynhook to see for myself just how evil he could be. That's the end of my story."

Mike looked up at the dark bulk of the castle towering above them. Oddly enough, the light of the moon had softened its grim outlines, now that its days were numbered.

"It isn't quite ended, Sandra. What you've just told me has changed my plans completely."

"In what way?"

"Tomorrow, I'm sending your brother a receipt—instead of a bill. He owed me for an operation, until you saw his play last night and came back home. Besides, I can hardly bill a member of my own family."